# A WEDDING TO DIE FOR

"Ladies and gentlemen, I'd like you all to meet Svetlana Anatov, my future wife!"

The crowd cheered and confetti rained down from the second-floor windows of the hardware store. So did the music Charmaine had chosen for the occasion. Don't take my word for it, but I think it was Dean Martin. He crooned something about moon and eyes and pizza pies and though I knew for sure it wasn't Russian, Svetlana didn't seem to mind when he announced, "That's amore." In fact, she smiled to beat the band and kept right on smiling when across the street, six white doves flew from out of nowhere and looped in the air over the happy couple.

"Welcome, Svetlana!" Charmaine wiped a tear from her eyes. "We're all here for you, honey. We're ready and willing to help you plan the most wonderful and romantic wedding ever."

"Yeah, and when's that going to be?" one of the men shouted. "When's it going to be official, Al?"

Al blushed to the roots of his rusty-colored hair. "We've been so busy arranging everything else, getting Svetlana into the country, planning her trip here from New York, we really haven't discussed that. So, what do you say . . . darling?" He tried out the word, and when Svetlana smiled, Al threw back his shoulders and stood tall.

"Today is Thursday, yes?" she asked no one in particular. Her accent was thick but her English was good. "We get license tomorrow. A͟_____ Saturday!"

# Murder
## of a
# Mail-Order
# Bride

➤➤ *A Love Is Murder Mystery* ➤

## MIMI GRANGER

**BERKLEY PRIME CRIME**
New York

BERKLEY PRIME CRIME
Published by Berkley
An imprint of Penguin Random House LLC
penguinrandomhouse.com

ISBN: 9780593201589

First Edition: August 2022

Printed in the United States of America
1   3   5   7   9   10   8   6   4   2

Book design by George Towne

*In loving memory of dear Lucy Van Pelt,*
*the dog standing in for Violet on the covers*
*of the Love Is Murder books.*
*Lucy was abandoned at a shelter as a pup,*
*and she was trained and grew up in a prison.*
*She came to live with us when she was ten months old,*
*and she was sweet and easygoing.*
*She was loving, she was gentle, and she*
*shed more than any other animal on the planet.*
*I miss you, Lucy!*

# Chapter 1

S vetlana floated facedown in the water.

Her arms drifted out from her body and over her head. Her hands bobbed up and down on the current like she was waving a final goodbye.

Her long white gown was stained with the muck that gathered along the sides of the canal. A brown blotch traveled waist to hemline, a Rorschach stain that looked like a bat, its wings flapping when the water moved. There was a green blob of algae on her left sleeve. Her right shoe was missing. Her gossamer veil trailed in the water behind her, leaves and twigs already caught in the dainty lace.

Someone screamed.

It wasn't me. That would have been just about impossible, what with all the air being pushed from my lungs by the surprise. Not to mention the horror.

Besides, I was too busy to do any screaming. I kicked off my cute peep-toe sling-backs and scrambled down the em-

bankment. It was September, and the water in the Ohio and
Erie Canal had already lost the summer warmth that attracted
flocks of ducks and the gray herons that used the canal as
their own private fishing hole. When I took the plunge that
was both literal and figurative, the chilly brown water slapped
my knees and soaked my fuchsia chiffon dress. (For the record, I am so not a chiffon person, but let's face it, when a girl
has twenty-four hours to find a maid of honor dress and orders
from the bride that it must be pink, there aren't a lot of
choices.) A few more steps and I was soaked to the V-neck.
Skitters raced across my skin and all that chiffon, light and
swingy on dry land, clung to me like wet tissue paper.

Here in the national park, the depth of the water in the
canal was controlled by a system of locks and gates. That
meant it wasn't too deep. Thank goodness. I ignored the
shock of the water hitting my collarbone and the muck on
the canal floor squishing between my toes, and in spite of
the fact that I'm not very tall, I was able to wade toward
Svetlana. It wasn't until I was a couple feet from dry land
that I heard splashing next to me and realized Al Little, the
happy groom who had been a maybe-not-so-happy husband
for the last three hours, was at my side, paddling toward his
bride, the white carnation in his buttonhole already soaked
and drooping.

What with us floundering and the canal's current, the
usually calm water gushed and surged. Svetlana floated farther from our grasps.

Al was taller than me. His arms were longer. "Try to
grab hold of the hem of her gown," I yelled, my voice tight
with panic. He didn't answer. When I dared pull my gaze
from his bobbing bride to glance his way, I saw that Al's
expression was blank, his eyes glazed. Al Little, who everyone in Tinker's Creek, Ohio, considered a smart business-

man, an upstanding citizen, and a good friend, looked like a man who'd just woken and found out the nightmare he'd thought he was trapped in wasn't a dream.

"I've called the police!" someone yelled from up on the towpath alongside the canal.

"Joe's going to the car for a rope," another person called out.

"You need to stop her floating away!" I recognized that voice as belonging to self-righteous Meghan Watkins, our town librarian, and if I'd had the energy and wasn't afraid if I opened my mouth I'd swallow a boatload of gunk, I would have told her to keep her two cents to herself.

I didn't have that luxury.

I stood on tiptoe, swayed, and flapped my arms to keep from getting tugged over by the current, then flung out a hand to catch Svetlana's wedding gown, and when I had an inch of it pinched between my thumb and forefinger, I turned and looked over my shoulder at Al. "Here." Another tug and I was able to lug bride and gown closer to him. "Hang on. I'll go around to her head and stand there to keep her from floating away."

It wasn't the only thing I intended to do, but really, was there any point in telling Al I wanted to check to see if Svetlana was breathing?

I grabbed a handful of veil and pushed it out of my way and when I finally got to where Svetlana's honey-colored hair floated around her in sagging curls, I carefully turned her head to the side.

Her lips were blue.

She didn't have a pulse.

There was an ugly raw abrasion around her neck.

All discouraging, but that didn't mean I was going to give up. On dry land, we could at least start CPR.

"I'll push from here," I yelled to Al. "You tug her dress. Let's get her closer to the path."

It took a minute for the message to sink in for Al, and I suppose in the great scheme of things that worked out all right. It gave me a chance to realize there was something clutched in Svetlana's left hand. Her fingers were curled tight around whatever it was, and, one by one, I straightened them, then snatched at the fragment of soggy paper that floated out from her hand before it had a chance to either drift away or sink to the bottom of the canal.

That paper now tucked into my palm, I guided Svetlana's body while Al tugged her gown. We managed to get to the side of the canal, where sticks and bird feathers and a McDonald's coffee cup clung to the bank, but there was that two-foot embankment, remember, the one I'd scrambled down to get where I was. It was one thing for a barefoot woman in a fuchsia chiffon dress to slip slide her way down into the water. It was another altogether to try and hoist a body back up on dry land.

It felt like forever, but I have a feeling it was just a few minutes until the Tinker's Creek Fire Department showed up. One firefighter offered Al a hand. Another scrambled down the embankment, caught me in the crook of his arm, and climbed up the embankment with me dangling like a wet, fuchsia fish. A couple more firefighters in high boots that in no way would keep them dry, slipped into the water and took charge of Svetlana.

Side by side, murky water pouring from our clothing and with hands and arms and faces covered with goo, Al and I watched the firefighters lift Svetlana from the water, lay her on the towpath, and administer CPR.

"I have to go to her." Al's words were bitten in two by his chattering teeth. He stepped forward.

I slipped my arm through his to keep him in place. "She'll be all right," I told him, even though I knew it was a lie. "But we have to give them room. We have to let them work."

How had word gone around the wedding so fast? About the missing bride. About the maid of honor who'd gone looking for her and found the last thing she expected. How did so many people know there was trouble there at the canal?

I never did find out. I can only say that suddenly there were people all around us, their grim expressions in stark contrast to the happy smiles they'd worn only a short time before back at the pavilion decorated with streamers and balloons. A few of them sniffled. Others slapped hands against Al's shoulder, mumbling words that were supposed to help heal the hurt. Someone grabbed a blanket one of the firefighters offered and draped it over my shoulders. Someone else slipped off his suit coat and put it on Al. The guests, the best man, our mayor, Cal Patrick, who only a short time before had pronounced the couple man and wife . . . all of them gathered around us, offering their comfort, warming us, sharing in our shock.

I wasn't surprised when my aunt Charmaine broke through the crowd and made a beeline for me. It was a special occasion and she'd pulled out all the stops. She was dressed in a flowing blue caftan, a pirate's treasure chest worth of cheap but showy jewelry, and a pink feather boa. That was for solidarity, she said, to make me feel better about the fuchsia dress. Her too-blond hair, a carefully coifed beehive when we'd left the house for the wedding, hung around her shoulders. But then, she couldn't stop tugging at it.

She didn't care a fig about getting her clothes ruined, either. She zipped over and folded me into a hug.

"You're all right? You're okay? Oh, Lizzie, you're not—"

"I'm fine. See?" I backstepped out of her embrace, threw out my hands, and drip, drip, dripped over everything in sight. It was no wonder the tag on my dress said dry clean only. Streaks of fuchsia dye snaked down my legs. My arms were the same lurid shade of pink. "I'm just"—I tugged the blanket closer at the same time I shivered—"cold."

"We'll get you home." She flung an arm over my shoulders. "There's no reason Lizzie has to stay here, is there?" she asked no one in particular. "She needs to get home. She needs to warm up."

One of the firefighters poked a thumb over her shoulder. "She can wait in the ambulance," she said and I guess that meant no, I couldn't leave. After all, I was first on the scene. I had plenty of questions to answer.

"Ambulance. Ambulance." Mumbling, Charmaine shuffled me in the right direction. Because of the narrowness of the towpath here alongside the canal, the ambulance couldn't get near, but we saw its flashing lights around a corner and up a rise where I knew there was a public parking lot. We were halfway there when I stepped on a stone and winced.

"Your shoes!" Just like that, Charmaine was off to find them and I was left to watch the firefighters exchange looks and small bleak shakes of their heads over Svetlana's still body.

One of them went over to talk to Al, but I knew he had bad news to deliver and I couldn't watch. My heart breaking for Al, my body trembling, and my eyes on the path in the hopes of avoiding any more stones, I stumbled in the direction of the ambulance's flashing lights.

I was just about there when I slammed into what felt like a brick wall.

Startled, I let out a gasp and automatically stepped back.

At least until I realized the brick wall in question was actually park ranger Max Alverez.

I have to admit, my normal reaction in a situation like this would not be flattering. See, I may be the owner of the most successful romance bookstore in the Midwest. And I may know everything there is to know about romance in books. But when it comes to real life, romance and I are the equivalent of chiffon and scummy water. And when it comes to Max . . . well, could anyone blame me? When I thought about Max, romance was the first thing that popped into my mind.

Max was tall. Max was dark haired and dark eyed, athletic, and gorgeous. Since he'd arrived in Tinker's Creek, he'd made it clear he wanted to get to know me better and, believe me, if I wasn't such a nonstarter when it came to hearts and flowers, I would have liked nothing more. I couldn't take the chance. I had a bad history with cute guys. I didn't want to have to worry about saying dumb things and looking like a dork.

There was, however, a small silver lining to the very dark cloud of events happening around us. There was nothing normal about this situation, and even reluctant-to-commit-to-anything-more-than-small-talk me had bigger things to worry about than the cutest/nicest/sexiest guy I'd ever met. One look at the concern that flashed in Max's chocolate eyes and I burst into tears.

I guess Max was just as unconcerned about his trim park ranger uniform as Charmaine was about her caftan. He pulled me into a hug.

"Oh, Max!" I sniffled into the front of his olive jacket. "I was worried about tripping on my way up the aisle. I was worried about forgetting to adjust Svetlana's veil before she and Al exchanged vows. I was worried about dribbling something on my dress at dinner. I shouldn't have worried about any of those stupid things. I should have . . ." I burbled. "I should have . . ." I wailed. "Oh, Max!"

He rubbed my back and shushed me with soft words.

"You're freezing." Max's arms tightened around me.

They were good arms. Strong arms. But, then, I didn't expect anything else from a man who'd once played professional baseball.

When the murmur of voices from the wedding crowd grew louder, closer, Max hitched an arm around my shoulders and guided me into the parking lot and to his waiting cruiser.

He set my blanket on the seat, settled me in the passenger seat, and went to the trunk for two more blankets that he tucked around me, then turned on the car and cranked the heat full blast.

"I'll be right back," he said, and went to talk to the paramedics.

He was as good as his word, back in a few minutes, his expression grim. "There are bruises on her arms and shoulders," he said. "And I'm sure you saw the strangulation marks on her neck."

It could only mean one thing, but I hoped I was wrong. "Murder?"

He nodded.

"Then . . ." I pushed the blankets off me and held out my hand, offering the slip of wet paper in it to Max. "She was holding it," I said. "I don't know what it is."

He grabbed an evidence bag from the glove box and when he had the paper properly stored, he squinted through the plastic at it. "All I see is lines and shapes, no writing." He slanted me a look. "There was nothing else?"

I shook my head. "Just Svetlana. She was blue, Max."

His nod was barely perceptible. "You're going to be blue, too, if we don't get you home and out of those wet clothes." He put the car into gear and headed out of the parking lot. "I'll take you home. You start at the beginning," he said. "Tell me what happened."

# Chapter 2

*The Wednesday before*

Lizzie, I need you."

I was behind the front counter at the bookstore, re-arranging the books featured near the register and my back was to the store.

Maybe that's why my heart skipped a beat when I heard a male voice speak those words.

*Lizzie, I need you.*

My breaths sped up. My imagination flashed to a scene not unlike that on the cover of the newest Maureen Child contemporary romance I had in my hand. Me in slinky red. Max in a killer suit, his chocolaty gaze trained on me, pure desire, smokin' seduction.

My left arm itched. My mouth went dry. At the same time I wondered what I'd say in response to this blatant and outright declaration, I swallowed hard. Pasted on a smile. Twirled and—

"Al." I hoped I didn't sound too disappointed.

Al Little stood on the other side of the counter, and I slapped away the wild fantasies that made me imagine Max there instead, declaring his undying love. My stomach bunched, and I did my best to hide what I can only describe as supreme, stark, and out-and-out embarrassment.

The better to dash away the crazy notions that had played through my head, I set the book facedown on the counter and gave Al a smile.

"What was that you said?" I asked.

Al was a middle-aged guy, the owner of a hardware store that had been in his family for as long as anyone could remember. He was one of my favorite Tinker's Creek residents, a guy who was mild mannered, soft-spoken, and always willing to pitch in and help at town functions. Whether it was hanging banners over Main Street for parades or helping with cleanup after the crowds were gone, Al was always there. Today, like most days, he was dressed in brown pants, a white polo shirt, and a beige jacket with *Little's Hardware* embroidered in blue over his heart. He blinked at me from behind wire-rimmed glasses, inched closer, and lowered his voice.

"I said I need you."

The smile I tried for disappeared in a flash. "You? Need? Me?" As flattering as it might be, this declaration was out of the blue and so baffling, I ran a hand through my dark curly hair as if that would somehow help me make sense of the whole thing. "What are you talking about?"

"I'm talking about—" It struck him then. Exactly how that phrase sounded. What I might assume it meant. A rush of color stained Al's apple-round cheeks and he jumped back, distancing himself from what he'd said and whatever embarrassment it might have caused.

"Oh, gosh, Lizzie! I'm sorry. I don't want you to think I was—"

"No worries," I told him. No, I didn't bother to add that whatever embarrassment he might have caused didn't count anyway, since I was thinking about a certain park ranger who'd been haunting my dreams and fueling my fantasies since I met him. I laughed because, let's face it, it really was funny and it proved just how deranged my mind could get when I didn't keep it on track. "You just surprised me and—"

"Sorry. I should have said hello first so you knew I was here. I'm just so . . ." Al glanced around. We were at the front of the shop and it was early. Right now, there were no customers around. "I'm so excited, I can't keep still. That's why I said I need you, Lizzie. I didn't mean, I *need* you."

"I get it. I think. You need . . ." I checked, but Al wasn't holding a book. I didn't see him as a reader of romance, anyway. Al was one of the guys. He fished with his friends. He offered a hand whenever anyone in town needed something repaired. He occasionally taught a workshop over at the library on things like rewiring lamps or the right way to paint a room. He'd never made fun of romance novels or romance readers. Not to my face, anyway. Still, he didn't seem the type to dive into romance, and my nose wrinkled when I asked him, "You looking for a reading recommendation?"

"No, no. Nothing like that." He shuffled his work boots against the hardwood floor. "It's a little complicated."

"Explain it anyway."

He thought this through, nodded, cleared his throat. "Well, there's this woman—"

Note to self: do not ever forget that when it comes to even the slightest hint of town gossip, my aunt Charmaine has super spidey-senses. Al got just that far when she popped out of the back office, so eager not to miss another word she just about skipped to the front counter.

"What's this?" She stood right in front of Al so he couldn't escape the question. "Al Little, you old devil, you never told me you had anything going on in the affaires de coeur department."

Most people couldn't get away with that kind of blatant nosiness, but this was Charmaine Randall, and Charmaine had been a fixture in town—and resident queen of Tinker's Creek gossip—for as long as anyone could remember. Charmaine and Al were old friends. He knew better than to try and dodge. That was a hopeless cause.

"It's like this," he began.

"Yes? Yes?" Charmaine had been so eager not to miss a word, she'd come out of the office with the last of a raisin bagel spread with cream cheese in one hand, and she popped it into her mouth and chewed with relish. "What woman? Who is she? Because I'll tell you what, Al, if she's someone from town, I'm going to lose my title as Chief Know-It-All. I had no idea you were dating anyone."

He looked down at the floor. "I didn't say I was dating anyone."

"But you did say this has something to do with a woman." I steered the conversation away from the brink of drama where Charmaine would have dragged it and back in the right direction. "Is this something serious, Al? Would you like to sit down and talk about it?"

"Sit? Oh, I couldn't possibly sit. I haven't been able to sit for days. Not since things became official." As if to prove it, he did a little two-step dance toward the door and back to where he started. "I'm so excited, I feel like I'm tied into an electrical line."

"Then it's good news." I smiled because, really, whatever was going on, I was thrilled for Al. "Start at the beginning."

"Yes," Charmaine chimed in. "Tell us everything."

"Well." Al bit his lower lip. "You both know Dan Cameron, right?"

We did. Dan was a local building contractor, and though I couldn't say he was more than an acquaintance, I saw him around town now and again and we always exchanged pleasantries.

"And you know his wife, too, right?"

Charmaine and I exchanged quick glances. Everyone in Tinker's Creek knew Galina Cameron. She was young, pretty, and the most ornery woman ever put on earth.

I wasn't sure where Al was going with this, so I spoke carefully. "Sure we do, Al. Dan and Galina have been married for what, a couple of years now? She's Russian."

"A mail-order bride," Charmaine mumbled so that only I could hear it.

Al nodded. "Well, that's just it. See, I've been thinking about how Dan met Galina through one of those online services, how they got married, and how now they're living happily ever after."

Another exchange of looks with my aunt. Anyone who thought Dan and Galina were the ideal couple had never spent more than a couple minutes in the same room with the two of them. Galina complained about everything, from the house she and Dan lived in to the cars they drove to the size of the engagement ring he'd bought her, the way Dan laughed, and how he talked with his mouth full. Dan was no better. I'd seen him and his wife together at various town events and it was impossible to miss the looks he shot her way. He would rather have been anywhere else, with anyone else. That was clear.

"Uh, Al . . ." I let Charmaine take the lead here. She knew Al better than I did. "Dan and Galina aren't exactly—"

"I know, I know." He waved away the notion. "They may not seem like the ideal couple, but that's because they're still getting to know each other. I'm not kidding myself. I know they're not exactly a match made in heaven. But that doesn't mean other couples couldn't be, does it? That's what I was thinking. You know, about how Dan and Galina found each other online. I was thinking that maybe those online dating sites, maybe they're not so bad."

"I suppose it works for some people," I admitted at the same time I did not mention I was not one of them. Online dating? I'd tried it once. He was nice enough, but there was simply no chemistry, and if there had been, I had no doubt I would have made a mess of things anyway, tripping over my words, fumbling for something to talk about. "Is that why you said you needed me, Al? Are you looking for advice about online dating sites?"

"Oh, no. Not at all." He flushed. "I've found a site I really like and . . ." The tips of his ears got pink. "There's this woman, see?"

"Ah, back to the woman!" Charmaine's eyes gleamed.

"Yes." Al twisted his hands together. "We've been talking for quite a while now. All online, you know? We spend hours and hours chatting about this and that and the other thing. And we've gotten to know each other pretty well. That's why I need you, Lizzie. I need your advice."

"Because . . . ?"

"Because she's coming here. To Tinker's Creek!"

This was news, and I could just about see Charmaine shake with excitement in her tie-dyed canvas flats.

"That's really nice, Al." I couldn't help but share in his excitement. "So, when you say you need me, you mean you need me to help show this woman around. Maybe I could host a dinner with her and some of your friends. It's great that she's coming here so you can have the chance to get to know her better. You want her to have a good impression of Tinker's Creek so she'll want to come back."

"Actually, I was thinking of a little more than that. Not that all those things aren't terrific," Al added quickly. But, then, he was the type of guy who never wanted to offend anyone. "I figured with what you know about romance—"

"Romance novels," I pointed out. It is always good to make the distinction.

"Romance novels. Real-life romance. There's not much difference, is there?" he asked.

"There is, Al. If you're looking for novels with some wonderful romantic scenes—"

"I'm looking for advice. You know, about how to welcome Svetlana. About what to say. I'm not the flashy type, but I want to make an impression. Something tasteful. Refined, you know, but memorable."

All right, that didn't exactly sound challenging. And it didn't take an expert in romance—fictional or otherwise. Just a little common sense and some imagination.

"Roses?" I suggested, and Al reached for one of the flyers on the counter in front of me that advertised an upcoming book signing. I handed him a pen and he dutifully started taking notes in the margins.

"Ooooh!" Excited, Charmaine shuffled from foot to foot, all for the idea. "Ten or twelve dozen ought to do it! The long-stemmed variety. And red, I think."

I don't know why I bothered, but I shot a look at my aunt. "Al said tasteful and refined."

"And streamers." Charmaine threw out her hands, her fingers flapping like streamers fluttering to the ground. "When does she arrive? Do we have time to call Bess over at the mayor's office to get out the flags and bunting from

Fourth of July? We'll line Main Street. We'll decorate the gazebo at the center of the square."

Listening to it all, Al looked a little shell-shocked, and hoping to calm him, I locked my gaze with his. "Tasteful. Refined. I get it, Al. You're meeting Svetlana at the airport in Cleveland?"

"Well, I . . . uh . . ." He swallowed hard. "That's another thing I wanted to talk to you about. My old clunker of a pickup truck . . ." He knew the answer before he ever asked the question. "Do you think that's tasteful and refined?"

"How about a car service?" I suggested.

"Or a limo!" Charmaine trilled.

Al made note of this, too. "Oh yes, a limo would be very nice. The driver can collect Svetlana and I can be waiting outside the hardware store for her." He ran his tongue over his lips. "If you could be there with me, Lizzie? It's not that I'm not thrilled all this is going down. I am. I mean, I really am. But it never hurts to have a little moral support."

"Of course. We'll show Svetlana how welcoming Tinker's Creek can be. That way, she'll want to come back and visit again."

Al blinked and stared, stared and blinked, then finally shrugged. "Sorry," he said. "I guess I haven't explained myself very well. I'm not trying just to impress Svetlana so she comes back—I know she's staying. You see, ladies . . ." He looked from my aunt to me, so darned exhilarated, his nose twitched. "I've got myself a bride!"

# Chapter 3

I almost didn't recognize Al when I arrived at Little's Hardware. But, then, I'd never seen him in a suit before. It was gray. So was his tie. His face, though, was a little green.

"You know, I bet Svetlana's as nervous about meeting you as you are at finally seeing her in person." I wound an arm through his. It was that, or I was sure he was going to take off running down Main Street. "The limo should be here in just a couple of minutes."

"And isn't it exciting?" Charmaine burst out of the front door of the hardware store, a smile on her face as big as the bouquet of red roses she carried. She set the flowers down on the bench in front of the store window, stepped back, and curled a lip. "We should have ordered more," she told me. "You know, to make an impression."

"Al doesn't need flowers to make an impression." I brushed a hand over the lapel of his suit coat. "He's already friends with Svetlana. Right, Al?"

He swallowed hard. "Well . . . uh . . . yes. We've been messaging each other for a long time, but . . ." He ran a finger around the inside of the collar of his white shirt. "What if I'm not what she's expecting?"

"She wouldn't have accepted your proposal if you weren't." I backed up my assertion with a smile. "Deep breaths. You wait right here and keep an eye on the road. The limo should be here any minute."

I sidled over to where Charmaine waited. "What do you think?" I asked.

"He needs encouragement."

"That's what I was doing. Giving him encouragement. He's nervous."

"He needs his friends around him."

"We are his friends. We're here. He said he didn't want to make a big deal of Svetlana's arrival and—"

I saw them then. The sea of people who turned the corner from Church Street and headed in our direction. They waved banners and carried balloons. They called out greetings and when they arrived, the women kissed Al's cheeks and the men slapped him on the back and they all gathered around Al there on the front porch outside the hardware store.

I slanted my aunt a look.

"It's just a few extra people," she said. "I figured a special occasion deserved a little oomph."

"Al didn't want oomph."

"It can't hurt."

I spotted the limo. "We're about to find out."

The others saw the limo, too, and a cheer went up. A second later, the sleek car slowed and stopped.

Al gulped, and I went to his side and wound my arm through his.

We all held our breaths and watched a man in a dark suit pop out of the driver's door and head to the back of the limo. He swung the door open.

The first thing I saw of Svetlana was her shoes.

Three-inch heels. Black. Suede.

Slim legs.

A red dress. Belted. Three-quarter-length sleeves.

Finally, the whole of the woman.

Honey-colored hair that skimmed her shoulders.

A broad nose.

Red, red lips.

Crow's-feet at the corners of her eyes and a spiderweb network of wrinkles around her mouth that told me she was a smoker.

At my side, I felt Al tremble. "She's"—he sucked on his bottom lip—"not exactly what I was expecting," he whispered. "She looked younger online. Not that I mind!" Just like that, all the hesitancy flew out of him and he smiled first at me, then at the woman who was going to be his wife. Charmaine handed him the roses and Al stepped toward where his bride-to-be waited.

He made a showy bow and presented her with the flowers. "I've found the love of my life. Svetlana, welcome to Tinker's Creek—there's no way I could ever be happier than I am right now."

He had to stand on tiptoe to kiss her cheek. But, then, the heels on her shoes were pretty tall.

Svetlana grinned.

Al turned fifty shades of red.

When he took Svetlana's hand and turned to look around at his friends and neighbors, his smile went ear to ear.

"Ladies and gentlemen, I'd like you all to meet Svetlana Anatov, my future wife!"

The crowd cheered and confetti rained down from the second-floor windows of the hardware store. So did the music Charmaine had chosen for the occasion. Don't take my word for it, but I think it was Dean Martin. He crooned something about moon and eyes and pizza pies and though I knew for sure it wasn't Russian, Svetlana didn't seem to mind when he announced, "That's amore." In fact, she smiled to beat the band and kept right on smiling when across the street, six white doves flew from out of nowhere and looped in the air over the happy couple.

"Welcome, Svetlana!" Charmaine wiped a tear from her eyes. "We're all here for you, honey. We're ready and willing to help you plan the most wonderful and romantic wedding ever."

"Yeah, and when's that going to be?" one of the men shouted. "When's it going to be official, Al?"

Al blushed to the roots of his rusty-colored hair. "We've been so busy arranging everything else, getting Svetlana into the country, planning her trip here from New York, we really haven't discussed that. So, what do you say . . . darling?" He tried out the word, and when Svetlana smiled, Al threw back his shoulders and stood tall.

"Today is Thursday, yes?" she asked no one in particular. Her accent was thick, but her English was good. "We get license tomorrow. And we get married Saturday!"

# Chapter 4

I was whooped.

No, I wasn't the one officially in charge of a wedding that was scheduled to go down in less than forty-eight hours, but that didn't mean I was completely free from the magnetic pull of the drama that swirled around Al and Svetlana's plans. It was time-consuming.

Not to mention exhausting.

Svetlana, see, had taken one look at those white doves released when she arrived in town and decided Charmaine knew a thing or two when it came to spectacle, drama, and over-the-top. As it turned out, our bride-to-be loved spectacle, drama, and over-the-top.

For his part, Al had taken a gander at the tears of joy that welled in Svetlana's eyes when she heard the schmaltzy strains of Dean Martin and came to the conclusion right then and there that Charmaine knew everything there was to know about the right way to romance a woman.

The rest is history.

My aunt Charmaine—she of the overactive imagination, extravagant panache, and overblown notions of what is expected on an occasion of this importance—had been given Al's checkbook, carte blanche, and the green light to act as official wedding planner.

At least the venue was easy enough. Because Al loved the great outdoors, Svetlana insisted the ceremony and reception be held in the park, and Charmaine pulled some strings, turned on the charm, and secured a pavilion. No easy thing in September, when the weather's still good and people are itching to make the most of it.

But alas, it didn't end there. No sooner had Svetlana's feet touched Tinker's Creek ground than Charmaine offered to host her until the day of the wedding, so in addition to deciding on flowers, music, and the wedding dinner menu (thank goodness my best friend, Brynn Chisholm, was a caterer), we had the unexpected task of taking care of Svetlana's food preferences (did all Russians eat that much caviar?), her insistence that she could never fall asleep in anything smaller than a queen-sized bed (Charmaine took the guest room for three nights), and her penchant for trying out Charmaine's perfume, her makeup, and her body lotions so she could, in Svetlana's words, "look and feel like American!"

I, smart woman that I am, did my best to distance myself from the whole thing. I worked hard at Love Under the Covers, helping customers—or at least trying—while listening to an endless stream of questions from my aunt.

"What kind of flowers do you think we should order?" she asked in one breath and then answered herself with, "Roses, of course. Oh, and orchids. Lizzie, what do you think of orchids?"

The next minute, we were on to finding a DJ, making

sure Tinker's Creek's mayor, Cal Patrick, had the right legal chops to join the happy couple in holy matrimony, and spending hours with Brynn choosing a menu.

Thursday evening, Al announced that he was taking Svetlana out for a romantic dinner, and I wished him the best of luck. Thanks to the steam locomotive that chugged through the national park and the train station in Tinker's Creek that served it, our little town is a gathering place for people who are into old railroading. That day, the members of Steam Train Lovers of America had started to gather for their annual conference. The restaurants in our tiny town overflowed. The shops were wall-to-wall with buyers and browsers. All good news for me and the bookstore, of course, but I was a little worried that Al wouldn't be able to find reservations and relieved to hear he finally managed to secure a table at a nice place with good food and plenty of atmosphere.

Aside from the fact that I hoped the happy couple had a great time, I was glad Charmaine and I would have a few quiet hours without our guest. Charmaine said she was going to grab a quick dinner before she dove right back into planning for the big day. Me? Home from the bookstore, dead on my feet, and with visions of roses and orchids dancing in my head, I kicked off my shoes and promised Violet, my dog, I'd take her for a walk later. When I came up for air.

Violet, of course, did not voice an objection to this change in routine. Violet had once belonged to Brody Pierce, a local bison rancher who'd been murdered earlier in the year. She'd come to live with me by chance and since no one else had come to claim her, she had continued living with me, roommate, confidante, buddy. She was good-natured and always willing to go with the flow.

"Can you believe it?" I'd just finished telling Violet about the little girls Charmaine had recruited to strew rose petals in Svetlana's path as she entered the park pavilion to the strains of "Here Comes the Bride." "Charmaine is turning this into a circus. I don't know, pal . . ." I ruffled my fingers through Violet's luxurious white coat and came away with my hand covered with fur. "I'm thinking a wedding should be a little classier, you know?" Violet must have, she didn't disagree. "I only hope that someday—" Exhausted or not, I sat up like a shot, ice water suddenly filling my veins.

"If I ever get married, she'll do this to me, Violet. Can you imagine? Orchids and DJs and roses. Oh my!" I groaned. "She'll want to choose the music and the food, and the cake and—" My breath caught and my heartbeat cantered along a mile a minute. I forced myself to take a deep breath. Reminded myself that my own wedding was something I probably never had to worry about.

"Romance and me . . ." I rubbed my forehead along the top of Violet's head. She's a big dog, and I didn't have to lean down far. When I gave her a hug, my sigh rippled her fur. "Chances are I'll never have to worry about it," I told her. "Not with my track record when it comes to romance."

It was a sobering thought, and, eager to rid myself of it, I got up and got busy. I fed Violet, grabbed a container of leftover pasta for myself, and we finished our dinners, then went for a walk, dodging clusters of train lovers out enjoying the evening and getting their bearings. As soon as I got home, I put on my jammies, made a cup of herbal tea, and sat back to relax.

My head tipped back against the couch, my feet propped on the coffee table, Violet at my side, I slipped into a dream of me walking down the aisle wearing bridal white. Charmaine was right behind me, pushing my poor mom out of the way, fluttering and fussing, and tossing rose petals. Up ahead of me was a stained-glass window and light poured through it, obscuring the face of the man who waited at the altar for me. He had dark hair, I could see that much. He flashed me a dazzling smile. Could it be—

"Lizzie! Lizzie! Open the door."

"Max?" Shaking the cobwebs and the remnants of the dream out of my head, I sat up at the same time Violet went to the door and barked.

"Lizzie, hurry up!"

That wasn't Max's voice and truth be told, I was just as glad. The last thing I needed was to face gorgeous reality with the memory of my dream groom so fresh in my head.

I pushed myself off the couch and opened the door just as Charmaine was about to pound on it again.

"Oh, thank goodness!" She fell into the house and pressed her back to the wall, her face flushed, her breaths coming so hard and fast, I worried she might pass out.

I grabbed my aunt's arm and ushered her to the couch, but she refused to sit.

"No time for that," she told me. She pulled in a breath. "We've got trouble, Lizzie. Big trouble."

I can be excused for being just a tad cynical. This was, after all, Charmaine, and it had been a long day. "The roses don't come in the right shade of pink? The Sparkle Market is out of caviar?"

"Oh, no. Bigger than any of that. I just went upstairs to let Svetlana know I was making hot cocoa and ask her if she wanted a cup before she turned in. And Lizzie . . . Lizzie!" She grabbed my arm with both hands and held on tight. "Svetlana is gone!"

"No. No, no, no, no." I sounded convincing, all right,

and I hoped the way I pulled back my shoulders and lifted my chin showed Charmaine I meant business. "She's not missing. Svetlana is at dinner. That's all. She and Al—"

"She and Al finished dinner at least an hour ago. I heard his car when he dropped her off. I saw her come into the house. I watched her go upstairs."

"Well, then that's where she still has to be."

To prove this point, I marched to the door and let my aunt walk outside ahead of me. Charmaine's house faces Main Street. My house, once a carriage house, is at the back of the property. Her garden is between here and there and together we walked the stone path that led up front, past the last of the year's roses and the marigolds Charmaine never wanted to cut back and were as high as my knees, and the fountain in the center of the garden that would be turned off and wrapped in a tarp for the winter. For now, it still sent up a spray that sparkled even in the fading light and trickled back into the water below in a steady stream that sang a tinkling melody.

I didn't stop once I was inside Charmaine's house. I marched through the kitchen and to the bottom of the stairs.

"Svetlana!" I called up to her. "Are you there?"

No answer.

"I told you. I told you, Lizzie." At my side, Charmaine twisted her hands together. "She isn't here."

"Then she's got to be outside." I thought of our walk from my house to Charmaine's. There was no sign of Svetlana in the garden. "Or what about . . ." What about what, I didn't know, I only knew that I thought about Tinker's Creek and how every last person in town was looking forward to the nuptials on Saturday. I thought about Brynn, home that evening, baking the layers of the fancy cake

Svetlana had requested, and about how Cal Patrick was tickled pink to be asked to officiate the ceremony.

And I thought about Al.

Of course I thought about Al.

How excited he was. How in love he was.

"You don't suppose she could have gotten cold feet and left town?" I asked my aunt, and maybe because I didn't want to hear it, I didn't wait for her to answer. I took the steps two at a time and raced into Charmaine's bedroom.

There were three suitcases, still closed, up against the closet door. Another one stood open on a chair near Charmaine's desk. "That's good," I told myself, as if the suitcases and the clothes still in them somehow proved our Russian bride hadn't taken a powder. "And look!" I hurried to the desk and scooped up the passport, birth certificate, and ID that were there, lined up and ready, no doubt, for when Al and Svetlana went to the courthouse the next day for the marriage license.

"She wouldn't have left without all these things," I told my aunt, who stood in the bedroom doorway. This was good news, so I smiled. But Charmaine did not smile back.

Instead, she threw back her head and wailed, "Then where is she?"

"Soaking in a hot bath." To check this out, I peeked into the bathroom. No sign of Svetlana there. "Well, all right, she's not in the house. But if that's the case, if you heard her come in after dinner . . ." I pinned Charmaine with a look. "Why didn't you hear her go out again?"

She pressed her lips together. "Glory and I were on the phone." Glory Rhinehold is Charmaine's best friend. "You know, talking details. Going over wedding plans and the playlist we're going to give to the DJ. We're starting out with 'That's Amore.' Won't that be sweet? 'When the moon hits your eye,'" she launched into the song, but by the time she got to "pizza pie," her shoulders sagged and her bottom lip puckered. "I guess I was so busy talking to Glory, I wasn't paying attention to anything else. I didn't know I had to pay attention." Charmaine threw her hands in the air. "I never expected Svetlana to take off."

"She hasn't taken off." I wished I felt as sure as I sounded. "She'll be back. We'll just wait and maybe if we take a look around . . ." I glanced around the bedroom, hoping it contained some clue as to where our missing bride had gone. One of the pillows on the bed was sitting crooked and I went to straighten it, then noticed there was a book tucked underneath it.

*Outlander.*

I fished it out and the book automatically flipped open to a dog-ear folded all the way down to a line in the middle of the page, no doubt pointing to the exact sentence where my aunt had left off reading.

I waved the book at Charmaine. "You forgot your book when you moved out of your room."

"Not mine," she said. "I read that years ago. Must be Svetlana's."

Telling myself that she'd want it when she returned— that she would return—I tucked the book back where it came from and did a quick turn around the room. There was a pile of papers on the nightstand next to the bed, and I picked it up, looked them over.

"These are printouts of the chats Svetlana and Al had online," I told my aunt. "She brought them along."

"Well, isn't that the most romantic thing!" Charmaine pressed a hand to her heart and hurried forward to lean over my shoulder for a better look. She snatched the papers from me and shuffled through them. "Look, she's even underlined special sections. Here they're talking about their birthdays and how they celebrate—Svetlana in Russia and Al here in Tinker's Creek. And look, here, they're telling each other all about their years in school. It really is sweet." She pressed the papers to her heaving bosom. "And that girl told me I had to be in charge of the wedding because she didn't understand romance. This shows just how wrong she is. I bet she'll keep this record of their relationship for years and years. Can't you just imagine it, Svetlana and Al reading these over every year on their anniversary, thinking about how they met and how happy they are."

"We can only hope." I retrieved the papers and put them back where I found them. "Before any of that can happen, we need to find Svetlana. Maybe . . ." I whisked aside the curtains and looked out at Main Street. "Maybe she went for a walk. Or—"

The way my words dissolved made Charmaine step closer and look where I was looking.

"My car," she said, her head tipped as if she was trying to make sense of what she saw. Or didn't see.

Charmaine leaned closer to the window. "My car! It's gone!"

"We can't panic!" I said this at the same time I spun for the door, all set to race down the steps and head outside. I stopped myself. Took a breath. Got a grip. "We have to approach this calmly. Logically."

"Okay. All right." Charmaine gulped and pointed. "You go first. Be logical."

"Well, all right. I will." Like a kid called on to recite in class, I clutched my hands at my waist and did my best to put myself in Svetlana's place. "If I was getting married in just a couple of days and if I just had an enjoyable, romantic dinner with the man I was going to marry . . . If I wanted to tell him everything he meant to me and how I loved him, I dunno, maybe I'd hop in the car and show up on his doorstep."

"Yes, yes." Willing herself to believe it, Charmaine nodded. "That's plenty romantic. Do you think she threw herself into his arms?"

"That I do not know. I do know . . ." Before I left the house, I'd tucked my phone in the waistband of my pink pajamas and I pulled it out. "There's only one way to find out." I went through my contacts, found Al's number, and hit dial.

"What are you going to say?" Charmaine asked, but by that time, it was too late for me to realize I had no idea. Al answered.

"Hey, Lizzie. What's up?"

"Not a . . ." I couldn't worry Al. Not before I knew there was really something to worry about. Not two days before his wedding. I packed a smile into my words. "Not a thing, Al. Just wondered how your dinner went with Svetlana."

"She's a doll. It was wonderful."

"And now you two are—"

"The two of us aren't doing anything. I'm going over the monthly receipts for the hardware store. I took her back to Charmaine's," Al told me. "More than an hour ago. If you happen to just pop in at your aunt's and see Svetlana, tell her I love her."

"Will do, Al." I disconnected the call and gave my aunt a look. "They're not together."

"That means—"

"It's time to panic!" I raced down the steps and headed outside, though what I hoped to do when I got there was anybody's guess. While I was trying to figure it out, I peered up and down Main Street, a woman in pink pajamas dotted with bright red hearts and wearing her fuzzy bunny slippers, looking bewildered and worried and ignoring the calls and waves of the railroad aficionados who tramped by across the street.

Then I saw it.

A familiar flash of purple up the road.

Charmaine's vintage Volkswagen Beetle.

"It's her. She's back!" I swear, I didn't even realize how anxious I'd been until the words whooshed out of me on the end of a sigh of relief. I slipped my arm through Charmaine's, and together we watched Svetlana pull into the driveway.

I waited until she was out from behind the wheel before I hurried over.

"We were worried," I said. "Where were you? And why did you take the car?"

Svetlana was dressed in a green sweatshirt and jeans that had mud caked around their hems.

"You . . ." She pointed a finger at me. "Worry on me?" She poked the front of her sweatshirt with that same finger. "I am fine, yes?"

"Of course you are. But we didn't know—"

"Have to get to know town." Svetlana swept by. "Now we have, what you call, night hat?"

My aunt smiled. She was relieved, too. "Nightcap?"

"Yes, yes." Svetlana went inside and my aunt gave me the thumbs-up. There was no crisis. All was well. Svetlana was right where she was supposed to be.

I reminded myself of exactly that as I turned to head back home. It was then that I realized there was something wedged behind the front license plate of Charmaine's car.

I bent for a better look.

A plant. Something with dark green oval leaves and little red berries pocked with silvery dots.

Automatically, I looked back to the house, all set to ask Svetlana where the heck she'd been and why the heck she'd been driving through vegetation in my aunt's precious car.

But I was too late. The door was closed. Charmaine and Svetlana were inside.

Rather than let Charmaine see it and worry how else Svetlana might have mistreated the car she affectionately called Arlo, I tugged the plant free and took it along with me. I hadn't gone more than a dozen steps, around to the other side of the car, when I stopped cold.

The passenger door was scraped.

I wavered between screaming, moaning, and marching to the house to drag Svetlana out by the scruff of her neck and demand an explanation.

In the end, I left her—and Charmaine—in peace. There was no use adding to Charmaine's stress level and, unlike our wayward bride, that scrape wasn't going anywhere.

# Chapter 5

*Friday evening*

I worked like a dog (apologies to Violet) that Friday. Since Charmaine was hosting the prewedding dinner and reception that evening and needed to get herself, her garden, and the bathtub-sized punch bowl of Moscow mules (get it?) ready, I'd given her the day off. That meant I had to handle the crowds at Love Under the Covers by myself. Between my wonderful regular customers and the train-loving folks who streamed in, wearing their distinctive red steam locomotive pins, checking out the town, and buying books (hoorah!), I barely had a moment to myself. When the store closed at six, I wanted nothing more than to collapse, but instead, raced home and changed into black pants and a long-sleeved wrap-front shirt the color of the apricot dahlias in Charmaine's garden. Not too casual. Not too formal. I slipped into nice comfy shoes, too, so I could help Charmaine with hosting and Brynn with serving the simple dinner of chicken kebabs, salad, and grilled vegetables.

Before I walked out the door, I apologized to Violet for leaving her home. "You never know who likes dogs and who doesn't," I explained without bothering to add that most people didn't like tons of fur shed all over them. There was no use making Violet self-conscious.

As ready as I'd ever be, I started out across the garden, stopping on my way by to give the fountain a little nudge. It usually flowed into the basin in a steady, calming stream, but that night of all nights, it had decided to burp and plop. I got it flowing again the way it was supposed to, and reminded myself to check it now and again as the night went on. Charmaine had worked hard on this little shindig, and I wanted everything to be perfect.

And it was.

Well, at least at the start.

Though the music was packed with lush strings, smooth rhythms, and plenty of schmaltzy lyrics, Charmaine made sure as it oozed from the house that it wasn't too loud and set the right romantic mood. Brynn had gotten tables from a rental place and they were set up around the garden, decked out in linen cloths. Each one had a candle flickering in the center, scenting the air with the soft perfume of late summer. Everyone in town would be at the wedding ceremony the next day, but for this special do, we'd kept the guest list small. There would be thirty of us total, and just as I grabbed a tray of cheese, crackers, and olives from Brynn and set it down on the serving table, our guests started to arrive.

Cal Patrick was there, of course, and I was sure he'd spend the evening glad-handing and politicking like always. Loyal bookstore customers and Al's longtime friends, Tasha Grimes and Callie Porter, had been invited, too, and I guess now that Brody Pierce was gone and they didn't have to compete with each other for his affections, they were actually friends. They walked in together, grabbed glasses of punch from a serving tray, and sat side by side at one of the tables. Al's fishing buddies. Al's poker crew. A few of Al's hardware suppliers and a dozen or so of his best customers.

Glory was there, too, of course. She was a tiny woman with shimmering silver hair, and she fluttered around the garden in a mint-green outfit, greeting guests and handing out drinks, helping Charmaine all she could.

If only . . .

"Hey, wipe that look off your face."

When Brynn poked me, I jumped and immediately went on the defensive. "What look?"

Brynn is a little taller than me, a little rounder. She was dressed in black pants and a black shirt and had a white apron looped around her neck. "You're wishing Max could be here tonight."

"How did you—?" I didn't bother to wait for Brynn's answer. She was my best friend. Of course she knew what I was thinking. I pasted on what I hoped looked like a confident smile. "He's been busy working at the bison education center, and getting it set up and ready for visitors means lots of extra hours. And he's going to have to be there most of tomorrow, too. He said he'd try to stop by the wedding for a few minutes."

"Uh-huh. And when his replacement shows up to take over that education center, that boy is going to be off to parts unknown on his next assignment for the national park system. I'm telling you, Lizzie, you need to make your move and make it fast."

"And what move is that, exactly? Should I throw myself at the man?"

Even though she was grinning, she pretended to have to consider this. "There could be worse places to land."

"There couldn't be anything worse than proving to him what a dork I am." My shoulders drooped.

"Hey, cheer up!" Brynn gave my arm a pat. "You two got along great when you were working on solving Brody's murder. You weren't the least bit dorky then. With any luck, maybe another body will turn up."

The very thought sent chills cascading through me, but I didn't have a chance to tell Brynn to take back her words. At that moment, the music swelled, then stopped. The next thing we heard was a drum roll and the crash of cymbals.

Al walked out of the house with Svetlana at his side.

Our crowd of partygoers cheered and Brynn went over to hand the guests of honor their Moscow mules in special glasses engraved with *Mr.* and *Mrs.*

"Thank you, all!" Al flushed a color much like the red tie he wore with a charcoal suit. He lifted his glass and looked around the crowd. "My nearest and dearest. I'm so glad you could all be here tonight. I want to offer a special thank-you to Charmaine for welcoming us to her lovely home and taking care of all the details." There was a round of applause. "And to Lizzie, of course, and Brynn, who pulled all this together so quickly and who's going to make sure we're all well fed tomorrow, too. And of course . . ." Beaming, he turned to Svetlana. "I want to offer my thanks to the wonderful woman who has agreed to be my partner in life." He lifted his glass to her and the limes that floated in his drink sparkled in the evening light. "Svetlana, here's to us, and to years of happiness."

More applause, especially when the two kissed.

"Now let's hear from Svetlana," someone called out and

on cue, the bride blushed. She, too, raised her glass and looked all around.

"To my new home. My new life. My new husband. Al Little, you have made me—"

What, what anybody's guess. That's because Svetlana didn't have a chance to finish. Two latecomers walked into the garden and when they did, Svetlana stopped cold. Her jaw went slack. Her eyes went wide. She took one look at Dan and Galina Cameron, and the glass she was holding slipped from her hand and crashed to the pavement.

"Oh!" Svetlana's face was pale. She stepped back and away from the cocktail puddle at the same time Al grabbed a napkin from a nearby table and dabbed at the spots of liquid that dotted her pink dress. "I—I—" She looked at the pieces of glass shimmering around her feet, but I didn't give her a chance to even think about cleaning them up.

I hurried forward, knelt on the pavers, and gathered the bits and pieces, tucking them into the napkin Brynn tossed me.

This, of course, meant I had an unusual viewpoint to watch the rest of what happened.

From my place on the ground, I looked from Dan to Galina. He was tall and dark haired, with the slim body of a runner and a square jaw. She was a short woman, athletic and tanned. Word around town was that she played tennis at least four times a week. Galina had bleached hair that hung as straight as a board around her shoulders and the boniest knees I'd ever seen.

But, then, from my vantage point, pretty much all I could see of her were those knees and the hem of her black dress that fluttered around them.

Still on the ground, I watched Dan tip his head. "Galina and I, we're the ones who should be offering our apologies,

Svetlana, we obviously surprised you. There's no way you could have possibly been expecting us."

Al hurried forward to clap Dan on the back. Truth be told, I couldn't actually see this manly gesture of comradery, but I heard the good-natured slap. "Of course we were expecting you! I knew you'd be here any moment. Svetlana was so busy concentrating on her toast, she was just startled to see you, that's all. Ladies and gentlemen . . ." I think Al must have kept his hand on Dan's shoulder because as if they'd choreographed the move, I saw four shoes pivot when Al and Dan turned to face our guests. "Most of you know Dan and his lovely wife, Galina. I'm happy to tell you that I talked to Dan earlier today and he's agreed to be my best man."

More applause and whoops of approval.

"And what about a maid of honor?" Glory wanted to know.

By this point, I'd gathered up all the bits and pieces of glass. Still, I didn't stand up. This seemed like a particularly important conversation. I didn't want to pop up (literally) in the middle of it and steal Svetlana's thunder. I stayed on my knees, that napkin full of glass shards carefully balanced in my hand.

"Maid? Of?" Svetlana's voice was quizzical.

"Like a best friend," Al told her. "A woman who will help you tomorrow. You know, make sure you look perfect before you walk down the aisle. Hold your flowers while we exchange vows. Like the best man, she'll act as a witness and sign our marriage certificate. You know, so everything's official."

"Maid of honor." Svetlana nodded. "Yes, yes. I need. Maid of honor, she dresses like bride?"

Charmaine knew that when it came to fashion, there was

no use depending on Al for answers. When she stepped forward, I saw her long aqua skirt sway around her ankles and brush her sequin-studded sandals. "Well, no matter who it is, she won't be anywhere near as beautiful as the bride tomorrow," she told Svetlana. "But, yes, the maid of honor wears something special. A gown or a pretty dress."

"Pink," Svetlana touched a hand to the skirt of her own dress. "Maid of honor will wear pink."

This was all, of course, mildly interesting, but I had other things to worry about, like getting to my feet and disposing of the broken glass. I finally made the move to do that just when Svetlana threw out her arm and swung a finger toward the pavers. At me.

"You," she pronounced.

"Me?" I pulled myself to my feet and when Brynn held out a hand, I gave her the napkin-wrapped pieces of glass and brushed my hands together. "Me, what?"

I'd like to say Svetlana's smile was friendly. It actually might have looked that way to everyone else. But the way she stood there, the way she grinned, the evening sunlight glinted against her perfect, even teeth and I was reminded of a lion eyeing a particularly juicy gazelle. Why did I think naming me maid of honor was Svetlana's way of getting even with me for questioning her about using Charmaine's car the night before? About scaring us to death when we thought she took a powder?

Not that she let on. Svetlana pulled back her shoulders and set her chin. "You maid of honor," she declared.

And even if I had the words to object, no one would have heard me. The decision was made, and our guests cheered and got down to partying.

There was no use second-guessing the decision or trying to weasel my way out of what everyone else seemed to think was a perfect choice. Svetlana and Al walked away. Charmaine cranked the tunes. Brynn stationed herself behind the serving table.

I followed her. "Pink? The only pink things I own are my tennis shoes and a pair of pajamas."

"I don't think that's what the bride has in mind," she told me.

"Yeah. But—"

"Not to worry." Brynn patted my arm. "The wedding isn't until three tomorrow. You'll have all morning to go out and find a dress."

"A pink dress."

She slid me a smile. "If you promise to make it a quick shopping trip, I'll come with you."

I showed my appreciation with a hug. As I was looking over Brynn's shoulder, I noticed Galina walk up to Svetlana. Galina and Svetlana, they were both Russians. Both had met their significant others online. I tried to watch the way they greeted each other, a hint of what women who shared this strange sisterhood might say.

Galina spoke too quietly for me to catch a word, but that doesn't mean I missed the look on Svetlana's face. Her mouth pulled tight. Her eyes narrowed. She reared back and said something to Galina from between clenched teeth.

After that, everything happened fast. I mean, what with Galina throwing her Moscow mule in Svetlana's face. I watched vodka arc through the air and limes scatter. Svetlana blubbered and burbled and Galina turned on her heel and marched out of the garden before any of our stunned guests could make a move.

"What on earth . . . ?" I pulled away from Brynn and was all set to go to Svetlana's rescue, but Al got there first. He wiped Svetlana's face and escorted her to the nearest chair, pulling it away from the table, settling her, kissing the top of her head before he went over to where Dan had watched the whole thing, his eyes wide and his mouth hanging open.

"I can't imagine . . ." Dan's apology floated over to me. A word here. A word there. "I don't know . . . I can't even think what I'll say, but . . . You'll let me apologize to Svetlana, won't you?"

Al, always gracious, stepped back, and Dan hurried to where Svetlana sat and knelt next to her chair, their heads together, their voices low.

"Oh, this is awful! It's terrible!" Charmaine came running, shaking her head, wringing her hands. "I feel so bad for Svetlana. I'm going to take her in the house and get her cleaned up. She might want to change her dress. Then . . ." She looked my way. "Dinner?"

To me, it sounded like the perfect plan. I made an announcement and invited everyone to enjoy the appetizers and one by one, our guests shook away their stunned surprise. With any luck, they'd be so busy oohing and aahing over Brynn's terrific cooking, they'd forget the ugly incident between Svetlana and Galina completely.

I, however, did not.

At my first opportunity, I sidled up to Dan. "What was that all about?" I asked him.

"That?" He took a drink and pretended to have to think about it. "Oh, you mean Svetlana. And Galina—"

"Throwing her drink at the guest of honor. Yeah. That's the *that* I'm talking about."

"It's the craziest thing!" He emphasized his point by pulling a shrimp from a cocktail toothpick with his front teeth and chomping it down. "Galina's and Svetlana's families, they actually knew each other back in Russia."

"And obviously didn't like each other."

He made a face. "Something about some long-ago family feud. I apologized to Svetlana. And I'll make sure Galina does, too. You know how she can be." Because he knew I did, he coughed away his discomfort. "She's a passionate creature. She was taken unawares, that's all. She never expected to run into Svetlana. Not here in Tinker's Creek."

And if the look on Svetlana's face when she saw Dan and Galina walk into the party meant anything, Svetlana never expected to run into Galina, either.

There was no use belaboring the point. I went on to chat with our other guests and saw Svetlana arrive back at the party, her makeup retouched, her lipstick reapplied, and wearing the same red dress she wore when she arrived in town.

There was no sign of Galina, and I breathed a sigh of relief, gave the fountain a little thump when it started acting up again, and invited our guests to the buffet table.

They were all done eating and the high school kids we'd hired for the evening to help with cleanup had just about finished with all the tables when Charmaine came over. "Everyone is enjoying themselves now."

I looked around at the smiling faces, the groups of people chatting and laughing. "Maybe they'll forget all about it."

"You don't think . . ." The sun had set, and the only light in the garden was from the candles on the tables and the strings of twinkle lights Charmaine had strung from here to there to everywhere. Still, her face looked pale. "What's going to happen if Galina comes to the wedding?"

It wasn't something I wanted to think about.

Instead, I helped Brynn serve coffee and dessert (individual ramekins of crème brûlée), and when we were done, I stretched.

"Tomorrow's got to be better," I told Brynn.

"Yeah." She sipped her coffee, glanced around. "If there's a bride at the wedding."

"What? You don't mean—"

As if it was some secret, as if no one else had noticed, she stepped closer, leaned nearer. "I don't see Svetlana anywhere."

I didn't, either, and consoled myself with the fact that she'd just stepped into the house. Except when she didn't come back after five minutes, I couldn't help but think of what happened the night before. I slipped out of the garden and went to the front of the house.

Thank goodness, Charmaine's car was right where it was supposed to be.

And Svetlana was standing not six feet from it, her finger stabbing the air. I'd like to say she was talking to one of the train lovers (I could see the steam locomotive pin the lady was wearing), but I have to admit, it looked more like a tirade than a talking-to.

Svetlana stomped her foot.

The train lady tossed her head, turned on her heel, and walked away.

It wasn't until Svetlana turned, too, and nearly ran into me that she realized I was there.

"What happened?" I asked.

Her top lip curled, she sniffed. "Woman." She looked over her shoulder in the direction the woman had walked. "She comes to me. Asks me questions. Where to find this in town. Where to find that."

"And that turned into an argument?"

"I tell her I am new here. She does not listen." Shaking her head, Svetlana headed back around the house to the party. "She does not listen at all."

Me?

I stood there wondering what Tinker's Creek, Charmaine Randall, Lizzie Hale, and most importantly, Al Little had gotten themselves into and consoling myself with the facts.

The next day was the wedding.

Things had to get better.

Right?

# Chapter 6

*Saturday afternoon*

I'm not sure hiring Declan Marvin, a sophomore at Tinker's Creek High, to DJ the wedding was the best idea Charmaine ever had. Declan, a tall, skinny kid with bad skin who billed himself as Declanx, liked to whoop into his microphone between and sometimes during songs and had a fondness for Justin Bieber that bordered on enough already, even before the party officially began. Then again, he was the only DJ available on such short notice.

Fuchsia chiffon fluttering around me, I zipped over to the far side of the park pavilion festooned in white and pink streamers, pink balloons, and a garden's worth of pink freesia so I could remind Declanx that in just a few minutes, he'd need to cut the rock and start the more dignified music we'd chosen for the ceremony. Then I checked the time on my phone.

Again.

It was ten minutes after Svetlana was set to arrive and there was still no sign of her.

"You should have insisted on staying with her." Charmaine slipped an arm through mine and—don't ask me how she did it—offered the comment out of one corner of her mouth at the same time she nodded and smiled at Tasha Grimes and Callie Porter, who were headed toward the appetizer table. "You would have kept things moving along. You could have helped her into the limo. You could have helped her out of the limo. You could have done all the things a maid of honor is supposed to do. Including making sure the bride showed up on time."

As far as I was concerned, wearing the fuchsia concoction of a dress was already going above and beyond. I didn't need to remind Charmaine of that, so instead I told her, "You heard her this morning at breakfast." In case she didn't remember, I repeated Svetlana's words in an exaggerated Russian accent. "'Bride must arrive alone. Bride must be center of attention.'"

Charmaine pursed her lips. "Well, she better get a move on. Poor Al is just about to burst with anticipation."

I looked where she was looking, at Al in his rented tux, pacing the front of the pavilion with Dan Cameron and Cal Patrick at his side, and I don't think it was a figment of my imagination that a cloud really did pick this particular moment to blot out the September sunshine.

I shivered. But, then, my maid of honor dress was sleeveless. "Dan's here. Galina didn't have the nerve to show up with him, did she?" I asked my aunt.

As if she were praying, she squeezed her eyes shut. "No sign of her." Double-checking, she opened one eye and, seeing that the coast was clear, she breathed a sigh of relief and jiggled her shoulders. She was standing close. Her pink feather boa tickled my arm. "We can only hope that after what happened last night, Galina has the sense not to come and ruin the festivities."

"And that the bride shows up before I have to listen to any more Justin Bieber."

As if in answer to my own prayer, the white limo Charmaine had hired for the occasion slipped into the parking lot and stopped near the pavilion. Svetlana may have wanted to make her grand entrance alone, but I knew my duties. I sliced a finger across my neck to signal Declanx to cut the music, then hurried outside and stationed myself near the limo's trunk. Out of the way so I didn't block any of our guests' view of the bride.

A hum of anticipation rippled through the crowd and when a soft and dreamy harp rendition of "When I Fall in Love" oozed from Declanx's speakers, our guests automatically moved to stand between the picnic tables Brynn and I had covered with white linen cloths, creating an aisle for Svetlana's grand entrance.

It wasn't my wedding, and I had no reason to be nervous (well, except for tripping when I walked down the aisle, dropping my flowers, and twisting an ankle in the shoes I bought to match my la-la dress). Still, I couldn't help but hold my breath and pray for smooth sailing as I watched the limo driver walk to the back car door.

Hours of planning. Plenty of stress. Lots of worry about who would do what and how it would all fall together.

It all came down to this.

The chauffeur opened the door and Svetlana didn't so much step out of the limo as she oozed out of it, one over-the-top fashion faux pas after another.

Frills. Lace. Beads. Poofs of tulle. A satin skirt so wide, it made Svetlana look like a shiny marshmallow. A satin purse to match. A gauzy veil the size of a banquet table-cloth. When the clouds slipped away, the crystal tiara she wore over that veil sparkled in the sunlight.

This wasn't the moment to question Svetlana's taste in wedding wear. I rushed to adjust her ten-foot train and carefully fluffed her veil around the hair softly curled over her shoulders so that the lace would float behind her as she walked, a gossamer cloud.

Except—

Just about to give her the thumbs-up, I squinted at the veil and at the something that caught the sunlight and glinted back at me. "Don't move," I told Svetlana. "Not yet. There's something caught in your veil and I want to get it out and not rip the lace."

Carefully, I plucked at the lace and finally freed what looked like a piece of wire coated with green plastic. I showed it to the bride, who squinted and curled her lip at the offending object, then I palmed it. "Must have been in the car," I told her. "You're all set now."

"Perfect?" she wanted to know.

"Perfect," I told her.

"So I start?"

"The little girls with the rose petals go first. Then me." I wondered if weddings were different in Russia. "When I'm all the way up front, that's when Declanx—er, Declan—will change the music to 'Here Comes the Bride.' Charmaine will give you the high sign."

"High sign. Yes." Svetlana pulled back her shoulders. "You go. Now." She gave me a poke. "It is time for me to be bride."

I hurried to the pavilion, grabbed the bouquet of white and pink carnations Charmaine had been hanging on to for me, and waited while our flower girls went down the aisle

to a general chorus of *oohs, aahs,* and *aren't they adorable.*
Then it was my turn. Noteworthy point: I didn't trip or twist
my ankle. In fact, I smiled at all the guests—the wonderful
folks of Tinker's Creek—and when I got to where Al
waited, I gave him a peck on the cheek and moved to stand
next to Dan Cameron.

The harp music ended and for a couple earsplitting seconds, the music swelled to ear-damaging intensity as Taylor
Swift's "Shake It Off" blasted through the pavilion. A red-
faced Declanx finally managed to hit the right computer
keys, Taylor went away, and the familiar strains of "Here
Comes the Bride" filled the air.

And after all that planning and all that worry? Just a few
minutes later, it was all over except for the partying. The
vows were exchanged, our guests cheered, Cal gave a
champagne toast.

And thank goodness, no one threw a drink at anyone
else.

I breathed a sigh of relief and while the guests lined up
to give Al and Svetlana their best wishes, I ducked outside
where a long line of grills and serving tables were set up.

"Of course I don't need any help." In answer to my question, Brynn rolled her eyes. "You've got celebrating to do."
She put a hand on my shoulder to turn me back into the pavilion. "I hired help for this afternoon. Everything's under
control. Go!" A little shove propelled me toward the dance
floor. "Eat appetizers. Drink bubbly. Have a good time."

I did my best. I knew just about everyone there, and introduced myself to those I didn't, including Dan Cameron's
grandfather Otis. Otis was something of a legend in Tinker's Creek, a small elderly man in a rumpled gray suit who
had a man standing at his elbow, a well-muscled guy in
understated khakis and a golf shirt. A caregiver, I imag-

ined, because I knew Otis was blind. He was also enough of a recluse that I'd never run into him in town. If the rumors were true, he was as rich as Christian Grey. He was not especially pleasant or at all impressed by the festivities, and I didn't stay to chat. Instead, I mingled and, yes, I admit it, every once in a while, I looked over at the parking lot and thought about how Max said he'd try to stop at the wedding when his work was wrapped up for the day and I wondered if he'd show.

Before dinner was served, I was asked to give a toast. Usual maid of honor stuff, I suppose, and probably not hard when the maid of honor actually knows the bride. I kept it short and sweet. "Here's to Al and Svetlana." I raised my glass. "Proof that you don't find romance just between the covers of a book!"

After that, we breezed through dinner (grilled salmon piccata), and then Declanx cranked the tunes and the real party started.

"It's going great!" Charmaine had just finished setting the dance floor on fire with the macarena. Her cheeks were red and her forehead glimmered with sweat. "We did it, Lizzie!"

"You did it." I gave her a quick hug. "Without you, none of this would have happened."

"Ooh, now they're playing 'The Chicken Dance'!" She grabbed Glory and sailed back onto the dance floor, and I took the opportunity to step out of the pavilion for a little peace and quiet and a breath of fresh air.

What did I say about peace and quiet?

I'd just rounded the far side of the pavilion, where I'd planned to relax and watch the canal roll by in the distance, when I heard Al's voice, sharp with disbelief.

"What are you talking about?"

I couldn't help myself. I sidled along the back of the pavilion and peeked around the corner to see what was up.

There was Al, toe to toe with Svetlana. His eyes bulged. His cheeks were dusky. Her hands were curled into fists. Her head was high. The look she shot his way was pure malice.

"You hear me," she growled. "You know what I talk about. Marriage is official. Sucker!" She tossed her head, and all those crystals on her tiara sparked like swords. "Your fortune now mine!"

She spun on her high satin heels and went back into the pavilion just as Al sputtered out, "But, darling—"

Dang! I wish I could have heard more. But Al went chasing after Svetlana and just as I turned around to go inside and see what was going to happen next, I nearly smacked right into Phillip Wilmington. Phillip was another Tinker's Creek neighbor I didn't know well, a retired geology professor who was always pleasant and usually so preoccupied with thinking about rocks, he never had time for small talk.

"Sorry, Lizzie!" Automatically, he grabbed my arm to keep me from toppling over, then dropped it just as quickly. "Just stepping out here for a breath of fresh air."

"Exactly what I was doing," I told him. "Until I stumbled on those two."

"Those? Two?" Phillip was a tall man with a shock of iron-gray hair and a long, thin face that was more interesting than it was handsome. I'd usually seen him only when he was setting out for the park on some geology quest or other, dressed in jeans and heavy work boots, a satchel of tools slung over one arm. That afternoon, though, he was wearing a snappy navy suit, a white shirt, a deep aquamarine tie that perfectly matched his eyes. When he looked over my shoulder, a gold hoop winked at me from his left earlobe. "Was there someone else out here?"

I wasn't much of a gossiper, especially when the scuttle-butt was about the newly hitched. Whatever had happened between Al and Svetlana, I didn't feel it was right to betray their secret.

"Thought I heard someone." I shrugged it off. "But I guess I was wrong."

"And I—" Phillip tilted his head, listening, and his eyes lit. "I hear Billy Joel. Come on!" He grabbed my hand. "Let's dance."

We did, to that song and a couple more, and I decided right then and there that geology is obviously a better way to keep in shape than running a bookstore. Phillip was still good to go, but winded and hot, I begged off the next dance and headed to the sidelines for a bottle of water just as Charmaine zipped by.

"Cake," she mumbled. "Cake, cake, cake."

"Uh, yeah." I looked over at the table where the cake sat, a confection of white icing adorned with pink flowers. "The cake is right there."

"Yes. And it's time to cut it."

I figured I could help, so I tapped a spoon to my water glass. When the voices around me shushed, I announced, "Time to cut the cake," and people started to gather around.

Charmaine made a face. "I wish you hadn't done that. It might be time to cut the cake, but Svetlana's not here."

I thought back to the quarrel I'd overheard and wondered if Al and Svetlana had slipped away to talk out their differences and make up.

But Al was on the sidelines. He looked harried, sure, but we had our groom.

We had our cake.

But the bride? The bride was MIA.

# Chapter 7

*Saturday, late afternoon*

A nd that's when I went looking for her."

"And that's when you found her."

I nodded and, shivering, burrowed further into the once-dry blankets Max had tucked around me when I got into his patrol car. I shook my head, doing my best to pull myself away from the memories of the past days and the horrible last hour. It was the first I realized Max and I were parked outside my house.

"You've told me everything?" he wanted to know.

Actually, I hadn't. I mean, I'd told him everything that mattered. About how Svetlana came to town, about how she'd disappeared that first evening, about how she'd argued with Galina on Friday and with Al at the wedding.

I did leave out all the stuff about how I'd been watching for Max. And how every time I thought about him, my blood heated and my insides melted, and my fantasies kicked into high gear.

That, after all, had no relevance. Not to the murder, at least.

Or to my life, either, I reminded myself. Max was working as interim director of the bison education center outside of town and I'd heard his replacement had been chosen. He'd be off to work in a new national park very soon, and I didn't like the idea of being the brokenhearted woman he left behind.

"You need to get inside." Luckily, he didn't know what I was thinking, but he looked where I was looking, at my mustard-yellow carriage house with its creamy trim, at the single light I'd snapped on when I left because I told Violet I wasn't sure when I'd be home and I didn't want her to wait in the dark. "You need a hot shower and a change of clothes."

I did. Too bad I couldn't make my legs move. Instead, I tunneled further into the blankets, my teeth chattering. "Too cold to move."

"Which pretty much proves my point." He got out of the car, came over to the passenger door to open it, and bent to look me in the eye. "That's why you need to get inside and get changed. If you're legs are feeling weak, I can always carry you."

I was waterlogged.

And still in shock.

It was the only thing that explained why I almost said "Go right ahead."

Fortunately, I came to my senses. I peeled away the blankets and swung my feet out of the patrol car. "I can walk," I told Max, then promptly stepped on a stone and winced.

He put an arm around my shoulders and braced me against his side and I found myself wishing the front door was farther away. Max was warm. Max was steady. Max was exactly who I needed to lean on at a time like this.

I unlocked the door and Violet rushed to greet us.

"Go on." Max gave me a nudge toward the stairs that led to the loft. "Get showered and changed. I'll take Miss Violet for a walk and get her fed."

There was no way I was going to argue.

Thirty minutes later, the fuchsia dress was in the garbage, the pink stains were (mostly) off my arms and legs, and I was as warm and comfortable as a woman who'd just found a dead body was likely to get. As tempting as it was, I'd nixed the idea of slipping into my jammies. Too personal. Too intimate. When I went back down to the living room, I was wearing jeans and an oversized flannel shirt. The bunny slippers? Hey, a girl has to allow herself a certain amount of comfort.

Max and Violet were nowhere to be found.

"In here!" He called from the dining room and I followed his voice to find Max setting out plates and silverware. "I hope you don't mind, I rummaged through your kitchen. Thought you could use something warm to eat."

Mind? Having dinner made and served by a handsome man?

Some of the stress eased from my shoulders. Some of the knots in my stomach loosened. I pulled out a chair and sat down while Max dished up scrambled eggs and toast.

He took the chair across from mine. "Not exactly gourmet."

I breathed deep. "Perfect."

"Dig in before it gets cold."

I did, and sighed with satisfaction. "Where did you learn to cook?"

"Well, my mom's a great cook. But you know how moms are." He rolled his eyes. "She never let me help in the kitchen much. But, hey, when I was living on my own when I played in the minors—"

It was my turn to roll my eyes. Had Max forgotten that I was something of a whiz kid when it came to baseball trivia? "You didn't have much of a minor-league career. What, twenty-four games before you got called up to the big leagues?"

"Twenty-three." He grinned. "That's why I never had time to learn to cook much of anything other than scrambled eggs."

"Well, they're mighty good scrambled eggs." I scraped the last of them off my plate with a corner of toast, swallowed it all down, and pushed back my chair.

"Oh no!" He was up in a flash. "I'm cleaning up. You're sitting and relaxing." He disappeared into the kitchen with the dishes and came back with a bottle of wine. "I figured it was too late for coffee. Wine doesn't exactly go with scrambled eggs."

"Today it does." When he poured, I gladly accepted a glass, and though I would have liked to sip and enjoy, I couldn't get rid of the picture that floated through my mind. "It was awful, Max. Poor Svetlana."

"Yeah." He rubbed a hand over his chin. "On her wedding day. Doesn't get much sadder than that."

"Well, at least we have some things to go on. I mean, the way Galina and Svetlana went at it at dinner last night. And the fact that Svetlana and Al were arguing at the wedding. Al didn't do it," I was quick to add. "He's too nice a guy. But there's that lady with the steam train lovers group, too. I never really believed she was just asking Svetlana for directions last night. It looked like they were talking about more than that, you know?"

"I know"—he set down his wineglass so that he could brace his arms on the table and give me a steady look—"that I have a murder to solve. Me. And I know that civilians—"

"I helped when Brody was killed."

"You did. But—"

"But you never would have caught the killer if it wasn't for me."

"And you were lucky you didn't get yourself killed, too."

"That won't happen. Not this time."

"No, it won't. Because you're going to steer clear of this investigation." He leaned forward just enough to emphasize his point. "Got that?"

"Al's a friend."

"I know that."

"And his heart is broken."

"You told me they were fighting."

"Which doesn't mean he killed her. He jumped into the canal with me, Max. Al tried to save Svetlana. That means it has to be one of those other people I mentioned. We could talk to—"

Since Violet was too much of a lady to ever growl, I knew the rumbled warning came from Max's throat.

I sat back. Tucked my hands under the table. Crossed my fingers.

"I won't interfere," I said.

"Which is not the same as saying you won't investigate."

"I won't do that, either. But if I hear anything useful—"

"I'll know it before you do. Your job is to sell books. My job is to catch the bad guys." One corner of his mouth pulled into a smile. "And make the scrambled eggs."

"And pour the wine." Since my glass was empty, I slid it across the table toward him.

Before he had a chance to lift the bottle, though, his phone rang.

And Charmaine pounded on my front door.

"Lizzie, you've got to come. Quick!" She had a hold of

my arm even before I had the door all the way open. "Al will listen to you. He likes you. He respects you. And—"

Max sidled between the two of us and hurried outside. "Got to go," he said, holding up his phone as if that explained everything. "I need to get back to the park."

"Yes, the park." Just before Charmaine dragged me outside and closed the door behind me, I grabbed a pair of sneakers. "We've all got to get to the park. It's Al. He's over at Brandywine Falls. And he says he's going to jump!"

# Chapter 8

L ike most visitors to the national park, I'd played tourist at Brandywine Falls. It's a spectacular sight: torrents of water flowing across dramatic rock formations, cascading over the precipice, plummeting more than sixty feet into the gorge below. It's ear blasting. It's gorgeous. It's the most popular destination in the thirty-three-thousand-acre park.

Which explains why most days it was hard to find a spot in the small parking lot closest to the trail that leads to the falls.

And, of course, that day—that fateful Saturday—was nothing like most days.

Just as Charmaine had heard through the grapevine about what was happening at the falls, everyone else in Tinker's Creek had also gotten the message. The lot was packed to the gills, with town residents parking two deep in the places where they had no business, jostling for a spot between lanes, leaving barely enough room to get by. Luckily, Arlo is compact, and Charmaine has little regard for No Parking signs. She wedged the car between Al's pickup truck and the restrooms, and together we joined the crowds streaming around Max's patrol car, parked and with its roll bar flashing, and toward the boardwalk that led to the falls.

"I just can't believe it. It doesn't seem possible." Charmaine walked as fast as a woman in sparkly sandals can, wringing her hands and sniffing back tears. "It was supposed to be such a happy day. And now this!"

"Hardly surprising." I hadn't realized town librarian Meghan Watkins was walking along beside us until I heard her and saw her slide us a look. "Word is Svetlana was murdered. If Al knows the cops are about to close in on him—"

"That's crazy and you know it. Al loved Svetlana," I told her and, yes, a nicer person than me would have let it rest there. But it had been a long day. And I was out of patience. And my arms were still a little pink. I can hardly be blamed for adding a little jab. "And even if the cops think he did it, you should have a little more sympathy, Meghan. It wasn't that long ago that the cops considered you a murder suspect."

She tugged her navy blue cardigan tighter around her shoulders. "That was a mistake and you know it."

"Well, if they think Al could have killed anyone, that's a mistake, too," I snapped.

"Except why else would he be threatening to jump?" Tasha and Callie zipped by on my left and Tasha threw the comment over her shoulder. "If you ask me, that makes Al look plenty guilty."

Meghan tossed her head. "And if you ask me—"

"No one did, Meghan." I grabbed hold of Charmaine's arm and hurried her along so that we didn't need to continue the conversation.

We didn't get far. All those cars up in the parking lot?

They'd been packed with people, and now those people jammed the wooden boardwalk that led through the trees and on toward the viewing decks around the falls. From here, we could already hear the water crashing in the gorge below us, and up ahead I caught the sounds of my cousin Josh's voice. Josh was Charmaine's son and a Tinker's Creek cop, and we rounded a corner to see him holding out his arm, stopping people in their tracks so they couldn't get any closer to the falls—and to watching what was going on.

"You stay here," I told Charmaine and ducked out of the queue to sidle up to my cousin.

"What do you know?" I asked Josh.

He shook his head. "Not a heck of a lot. Some hiker spotted Al where he shouldn't be. He called the rangers' office."

"And the office called Max." I stood on tiptoe to try and catch a glimpse of Max, but Josh was smart. The way he had the crowd controlled, we couldn't see much of anything. "What's Max going to do?" I asked my cousin.

"Nothing he should be doing, I can tell you that." One corner of Josh's mouth pulled tight, and when the surge of townsfolk tried to get past him for a better look, he tugged me out of the way, closer to the gigantic sandstone boulders on our right, and raised his voice to tell them in no uncertain terms that nobody was going anywhere. I lost sight of Charmaine in the crowd. "There are more rangers on the way. A few of our guys are here to handle traffic. We've even called for backup from a couple of the closest fire departments. I told Max to wait, but . . ."

In spite of the mist that flew off the falls and hung in the air, my mouth went dry. "But?"

"Maybe you can talk him down," Josh suggested. "While you're at it, maybe you can talk both of them down."

I didn't wait for details.

And I didn't even try to be polite.

I elbowed my way around the crowd and onto the empty boardwalk ahead.

Gigantic boulders rimed with moss to my right.

Gorge and thundering water to my left.

I saw Max the moment I rounded the next corner.

When he'd arrived at the canal in answer to the emergency call about Svetlana, he'd just come from the bison education center and had been dressed in his formal ranger uniform: forest green pants and jacket, gray shirt, and that Smokey Bear hat that should have been downright cute and was instead as sexy as sin on Max. His hat and jacket were off now. Max had pulled on a pair of knee-high rubber boots.

He was inside the strictly off-limits fifty-foot enclosure at the top of the falls.

So was Al.

Twenty feet from Max.

Closer to the thundering falls.

From where I stood, there was no way I could hear the words Max said, but I caught the rumble of his voice, a mellow contrast to the boom of the falls. As if he was doing nothing more remarkable than chatting with a friend, his shoulders were loose. His expression was calm. He finished tying a rope around a sturdy hemlock, looped the other end of it, and cinched it around his waist.

"No!" There was no way Max could hear me, not with all the noise of the falls, but that didn't stop me from crying out and waving my arms. I raced to the top observation deck and closed in on the barrier constructed to keep people from getting too close to the water. I ignored the signs posted nearby. No Trespassing. Danger. Blah, blah, blah. I climbed the barrier and landed on the other side.

"Get out of here, Lizzie." Max must have had eyes in the back of his head. How else could he have known I was standing behind him when he never took his eyes off Al?

I didn't have his nerve. Rather than watch Al, rather than wonder what he was going to do and when he might do it, I kept my gaze on the rushing water. "I'll get out when you get out," I told Max.

"I'll get out when Al comes with me." His voice still calm, Max held out a hand in Al's direction. "What do you say, Al? Now that both Lizzie and I are asking, you've got to come over here, right?"

Al ran his tongue over his lips. He was on the very edge of the raging creek that plunged over the precipice, his shoes and the cuffs of his pants already soaked. He took one tiny step away from us, one step closer to the edge.

My breath caught over a hiccup of fear. "You can't do this, Al," I called out.

He looked down at the water before he looked at me. "Why not?"

"Because it's not what Svetlana would have wanted."

I didn't hear him gulp, but I saw his neck tighten, watched as he got buffeted by a gush of water. He swayed and rocked to brace his footing.

I held my breath.

Like a circus performer on a tightrope, Al stuck his arms out to his sides, steadying himself. "You have no idea, Lizzie." His voice was high and choked with emotion, and even from where I stood I knew the water that shone on his cheeks wasn't from the spray of the falls. "You have no idea what Svetlana wanted. I guess . . ." When he looked away from us and down at the water and kept his gaze there, Max took the opportunity to sidle closer.

Al's shoulders drooped. "I guess I didn't really know what Svetlana wanted, either."

I knew I had to keep Al distracted so Max could inch closer. There was no better way than to keep him talking. "Is that what you were arguing about at the wedding?" I asked him. "She said something about your fortune. But when she did, you looked confused."

"Fortune!" Al puffed out a breath of disbelief. "You know better than that, Lizzie. Everyone in town knows better than that. I don't have a fortune. I never have."

"Then she must have been kidding." The way I remembered the spark in Svetlana's eyes when she spit the words at Al told me otherwise, but, hey, desperate times, desperate measures and all that. If ever there was a time to lie in the name of boosting Al's spirits, this was it.

Hope wavered on the edges of Al's expression. "Kidding? You think so?"

"I think . . ." I gulped down my fear and in spite of the look Max shot me, I took another step closer to Al. "I haven't had a chance to tell you a story, Al. About what Svetlana showed me the evening she came to Tinker's Creek." Okay, sure, I was twisting the truth. Just a little. But it was for a good cause. "Did you know, Al, she printed out each and every conversation you two had online together? She had the pages right there by her bed, right where she could read what you said to her." I exaggerated my sigh. "Nobody knows more about romance than me, Al." There I was, twisting the truth again. "And I'll tell you what, that's one of the most romantic things I've ever seen."

"You . . . you think so?" Al squeezed his eyes shut.

Max slid closer to him.

"I think there's no way a woman does something like

that unless she's very much in love," I said and I bought Max a little more time by adding, "That's why I think she must have been joking. Back at the wedding. When she talked about your fortune, I think she was teasing you, Al. And that tells me she loved you, too. That she felt comfortable enough with you to play a little game."

He ran his tongue over his lips. "But if anyone else heard what she said—"

"No one but me did. I swear." Like I was taking an oath, I held up a hand. "I was the only one out there and I haven't told a soul."

Al hung his head. "I'd hate for everyone in town to think my happily ever after didn't last long enough for us to cut the cake."

"But it would have." Yeah, call me a hopeless romantic, but from the day Al told me about Svetlana, I'd hoped for nothing but the best for the happy couple. Automatically, I took another step forward and, realizing it brought me closer to the raging water, I froze. "I know you two would have been happy, Al. I had a chance to get to know Svetlana over the last couple of days, and you know what? Every single time she talked about you, her face just glowed. Her eyes sparkled. She had to be teasing when she talked about your fortune, Al, because that woman was head over heels in love with you."

"I didn't kill her." Al lifted his chin, his voice suddenly as steely as the set of his shoulders. "Now everyone thinks I did."

I'm not sure how I managed a what-are-you-talking-about flip of one hand. I mean, what with my knees quivering and my insides shimmying. "There's not a person in Tinker's Creek who thinks that. And you know what? They're going to prove it, Al. The cops and the park rangers and—"

"And you, Lizzie? You figured out what happened when Brody was killed. Will you help me now?"

"Will you step away from the water?" I asked him.

Like he was waking from a bad dream, Al shook his head and glanced down at his feet, and I swear it was the first he came to his senses and saw exactly where he was. And exactly how much danger he was in. Al's face turned pasty. His mouth dropped open. His hands shook and his knees buckled and—

I never saw him move. But I guess a lifetime athlete has lightning-quick reflexes and the moves of a superhero. The next thing I knew, Max swooped forward and curled an arm around Al's waist. Linked together, they swayed toward the falls and Al went limp. Max never hesitated. His arm tight around Al, he pulled him away from the falls, farther from certain death.

Max slowly and carefully walked Al back to the barrier and handed him over to the firefighters waiting there. He didn't crack a smile.

"Are you crazy?" His question ricocheted against the boulders, ping-ponged through the gorge.

I didn't feel steady enough to answer it until I met him at the barrier and, with the help of one of the firefighters, climbed over it and to the safety of the other side.

"Al didn't do anything crazy," I told Max. "That's all that matters."

"It sure isn't." His glare was epic. "It was bad enough I was worried about Al. I didn't want to have to rescue both of you."

"As it turns out, you didn't need to, did you?" I didn't realize my posture mirrored Max's.

My chin was high.

Just like his.

My shoulders were rock steady.

Just like his.

Behind us, the paramedics checked out Al, offering their reassurance, and my voice knocked against theirs.

Just like Max's did.

I pulled in a breath that felt like fire in my lungs and forced myself to straighten my arms and hold them tight against my sides. "You think I was careless." It wasn't a question, so I didn't wait for an answer. "You're just as bad. You could have waited for the firefighters to get here. You didn't need to risk your own life."

"That's my job."

"And I'm glad I was able to help."

"Oh no!" My blood pressure might not have shot up to the puffy clouds over our heads if he hadn't wagged a finger at me. "You didn't help. You hindered. There's no excuse for that." And with that, he stomped away.

Good thing that waterfall is so freakin' loud. Otherwise, all those firefighters, the cops, the rangers, and Al's buddy Dan Cameron, who was waiting there, would have heard my screech.

When I pounded away from the falls and on toward the boardwalk, Al grabbed my arm.

"Will you really help me, Lizzie?" he asked.

It took a second for me to figure out what he was talking about. But then my blood buzzed. My gaze was focused on Max—tall, muscular, gorgeous, and annoying—as he walked away.

"Huh?" seemed the only appropriate response.

"Find out who killed Svetlana." Al pressed my hand in both of his. "Please. I have to know what really happened. I have to show the world that I never would have hurt her." His eyes were swollen and rimmed with red. "I loved her,

Lizzie. You know I did. I need your help to prove that to the world."

"Yes. Of course." Like I could have said anything else, what with him standing there pleading with me and the paramedics waiting to lead him away?

Al offered me the smallest of smiles. "I'm sorry I caused all this trouble. I never really would have . . ." He looked toward the falls and gulped. "I think maybe I just need some time to rest. Some time to think. I need to come to terms with what happened to Svetlana today."

"Of course you do," I told him. "And if I can help, let me know. My shop is closed on Mondays, if you need me to open the hardware store for you—"

"Would you?" The creases of worry disappeared from Al's face. The weight lifted off his shoulders. He patted down the pockets of his beige jacket. "I'll give you my keys and—" He stopped, considered, checked his pockets again. "I've always got the keys to the store in my pocket. Maybe I dropped them. No matter. Check behind the store, Lizzie, under that big rock near the back door. There's an extra key hidden there. If you could just make sure everything's okay—"

"I will, Al. I promise."

"And I . . ." Dan stepped forward. "I'll take Al home," he told me. "Don't worry. Galina and I, we'll take care of him."

Watching them walk away, knowing at least that Al had a good friend to help him when he needed it most, I let go a long breath and felt the adrenaline drain from my body. My legs were heavy. My feet dragged. I hauled myself back to the boardwalk.

The excitement was over and when I rounded the corner to where Josh had corralled the crowd, I saw that most everyone was gone. I was glad. I didn't need to give anyone the play-by-play of what happened there by the falls. There would be plenty of time for that when, one by one, townspeople showed up at my shop as I knew they would, intent on getting the details of what they hadn't been able to see for themselves. Until then, peace and quiet sounded like the best plan to me.

I was grateful there was only a single person left on the observation deck. Her back was turned to me, and I didn't recognize the maroon leather jacket, the tall black boots, the skintight jeans. I did sneer, though, when I saw her exhale a cloud of cigarette smoke and saw her flick a butt down into the gorge.

"That's probably not safe," I said. "Fire hazard and all, you know."

The woman turned. Galina Cameron. Her ho-hum look told me she didn't really care. "He is coming?" she asked me.

I looked back over my shoulder. "Dan? I think he's waiting until the paramedics check on Al. I'm sure he's anxious to get him to the car. He said he was taking Al home so you two could keep an eye on him."

She pressed her lips together. I couldn't tell if that meant she was thinking about the arrangement. Or if she'd already decided she didn't like it.

She didn't give me a chance to ask. Tugging on a maroon leather glove, she turned on her boot heels and I watched her walk away.

I can't say how long I stood there, I only knew that by the time I heard a voice behind me, Galina was nowhere to be seen.

"That's enough excitement for one day, don't you think?"

Startled, I spun to find Phillip Wilmington, out of his

suit now, back in the jeans and the sturdy boots I was used to seeing him in as he tromped through the park, studying the geology of the place. "Happened to be hiking," he said, tipping his head back toward the falls. "After the ugliness back at the wedding, needed to get out and get some fresh air. Good thing I did. Guess I was just in time."

I looked from the edge of the falls—blessedly empty now—to Phillip. "You're the one who called?"

"I would have handled things myself but . . ." He jiggled his shoulders. "Once upon a time, I made my living doing things like scaling mountains. These days I know better than to be rash. And I've never been enough of a fool to go up against a waterfall."

"Yeah." The very thought of all that could have happened—to Al, to Max—made me shiver. "At least we had a happy ending here."

"Not so much back at the canal." He shook his head. "No one can blame Al for being crazy out of his head. A wedding. A death. It's too much for any man, and—"

Spotting something on the deck, Phillip bent and picked it up. A maroon glove.

He backed away a step. "Galina's. I'll see if I can catch up with her and return it."

I didn't follow him. Not right away. Instead, I braced my hands against the wooden railing, drew in a breath, thanked my lucky stars (and Al's!) that things turned out all right. As for Max . . .

A spurt of annoyance shot up my spine and sent my heartbeat racing. First he warns me away from investigating Svetlana's murder? Then he actually has the nerve not to thank me for helping save Al's life?

"Men!" I slapped the railing and headed for the parking lot.

I was still on the boardwalk when I saw Max coming the other way.

Good.

I stopped, pulled my arms to my sides, raised my chin.

He'd finally come to his senses.

He was ready to apologize.

He stopped three feet from me, his suit jacket back on, that Smokey Bear hat of his cocked at just enough of an angle to shade his eyes. He had a single sheet of paper in one hand and it flapped in the evening breeze. "I figured you might still be hanging around."

"I'm not exactly hanging around. I wanted to make sure Al was going to be all right. The paramedics checked him out, and now he's going home with Dan Cameron."

A muscle twitched at the corner of Max's mouth. "I heard."

"And . . . ?"

He leaned forward just a fraction of an inch. "And what?"

"And isn't there something you want to say to me about that?"

"About Al going home with Dan Cameron?"

I thought a guy who was poised enough to face the media in a major-league clubhouse would be a little smoother when it came to admitting how out-of-bounds he'd been when it came to criticizing what I'd done.

I bit my lower lip and gave him another chance and when he didn't say what he should have said, I reminded him, "I'm talking about Al being alive and well and going home with Dan Cameron."

As if he'd just remembered it, he held up the paper. "Al being alive and well. Yeah, that's exactly what I'm talking about, too, and why I came back to find you." With a flourish, he handed me the paper.

I took a quick glance and my mouth dropped open. "What's— What's this?" I sputtered.

Damn the man, he had the nerve to grin and look me in the eye. "It's a ticket," he said. "For trespassing."

# Chapter 9

*Sunday*

It was official.

I was a felon.

And just for the record, I wasn't at all happy about it.

Even after I wrote a sizable check to pay the fine on my trespassing ticket and took Violet for a walk to the drop box outside the post office so I could mail it and (technically, anyway) put the incident behind me, I couldn't slough off my anger. Or my resentment.

This was how Max wanted to handle things?

Like he was the big bad cop in charge and I was nothing more than a meddling civilian?

All righty then. He set the ground rules. As I told Violet, that left me with no choice. With or without Max, I was determined to find out what happened to Svetlana.

For one thing, I had to prove to Max that I was smart and capable and perfectly able to work my way through the mystery.

But more important, I had to keep my promise to Al.

"It's the least I can do for him, don't you think?" We were back home now, and Violet and I had just finished lunch. Mine was half a chicken salad sandwich. Hers, a couple of pumpkin treats. Organic, of course. I wanted to get in a talk with her before she settled down for her afternoon nap. "After all, an engagement, a wedding, a murder . . . all in the space of just a few days. The poor guy. It's no wonder he was so distraught, he actually talked about jumping at Brandywine." The memory caused a shiver to shoot up my spine. "When Al asked for my help, of course I had to say yes."

Over in her favorite corner, a cozy spot between the couch and the fireplace, Violet turned around once, twice, three times before she settled down, stretched out her long legs, and yawned.

"I've been thinking about it," I told her at the same time I leaned way back so I could see Charmaine's house out of one of my living room windows. "I need to do a little reconnoitering. With any luck, the cops have come and gone. You don't mind if I duck out for a bit, do you?"

Of course she didn't. Aside from the fur—and there was plenty of it, in heaps, everywhere—Violet was the ideal roommate. She knew I had a bookstore to run and lately that I had to deal with murder as well as romance, and she didn't mind. As if to prove it, she closed her eyes and her breaths eased into a steady, relaxed rhythm. It was my cue to slip out of the house.

It was sunny that day, but cool, and as much as I would have liked to linger and enjoy the crayon colors of Charmaine's dahlias, I didn't have the luxury. In fact, I stopped only long enough to give the fountain a little slap when I saw that it was acting up again, spurting and spitting instead of flowing. That taken care of, I knocked on Charmaine's back door.

It was after noon, but when she answered, she was still in her teal terry cloth robe. Her hair was tucked under a purple and blue velvet turban and her eyes were rimmed with red.

"Since when do you knock?" she wanted to know. "You never have to knock. You're family."

"I didn't want to disturb you."

"I'm not doing anything but . . ." She stepped back to let me into the kitchen and waved a hand toward the table, where she'd set out a French press coffeemaker, a cup, a jar of Nutella, and a spoon. A big spoon. "Just sitting here thinking." Charmaine sniffled. "You know, about everything that happened yesterday. About poor Svetlana, and how Al is so unhappy, and . . ." Her shoulders rose and fell. "You want coffee?"

"I want to take a look through Svetlana's room." I started for the stairway. "The cops have already come and gone?"

"Oh yes." Seeing the possibility for a little excitement, Charmaine scampered behind me, and together we went up the stairs. "They were here for a couple hours after we got back from Brandywine Falls yesterday. Max was in charge. I thought maybe you'd stop by to talk to him."

I wasn't proud of my life of crime, such as it was. I hadn't mentioned the ticket to Charmaine. Or how I was so mad at Max that the night before I'd dreamed about stomping on his Smokey Bear hat. If I tried to explain, my temper was sure to hit the roof. Again. Instead, I kept to the matter at hand.

"What did the cops take away with them?" I asked her.

This, she had to consider. Or maybe she was just trying to figure out why I'd dodged her comments about Max. From the landing at the top of the stairs, she eyed me and apparently something in the set of my chin warned her to watch what she said. For once, Charmaine actually listened to her common sense.

"Like I said, they were up here for a while, but when they left, they weren't carrying much. Her passport, I think. Her birth certificate. Things like that. Max . . ." She paused, waiting to gauge my reaction, and when I didn't do anything at all, she cleared her throat and went on. "He said until he knows if he needs anything else, I'm not supposed to go back into my bedroom."

Yeah, I could see that. We'd made our way down the hallway Charmaine had decorated with everything from Erté posters (quintessentially Art Deco) to framed photos of her friends. Her bedroom was on our left, and there was yellow tape strung across the doorway.

I guess all the anger that had been building inside me since my not-so-pleasant encounter with Max the evening before had really gotten my blood pumping. I didn't hesitate, just limboed my way through the crisscross of tape, twisting, turning, and ducking until I landed on the other side. As if it had actually been some major accomplishment to make it from there to here, I brushed myself off and grinned at Charmaine, standing in the hallway. "Max told you not to go in here. Good thing he didn't say anything about me. You stay right where you are. I'll take a look around."

At first glance, the room didn't look much different than it had on Thursday night when Charmaine and I realized Svetlana was missing and came upstairs to look for her.

The transcripts of her conversations with Al were still out on the nightstand, though they were cocked at a different angle than when I set them down. No doubt, Max had

taken a look. Had he decided what Charmaine and I both
knew? That Svetlana was a romantic at heart? That she
treasured every word Al had ever said to her?

Svetlana's copy of *Outlander* was still under her pillow, too.

Her suitcases were open on the floor. A couple of them
were empty and I figured those must have been the ones she
used to transport the overblown wedding gown.

"What are you looking for?" Charmaine wanted to know.

I had to admit I had no idea.

Until I had a chance to figure it out, I kept my hands
behind my back, my fingers linked, and while I was at it, I
peered into the nearest suitcase.

Three pairs of shoes, underwear, stockings, black pants.
It was impossible to see anything else.

At the same time I grumbled, Charmaine zipped down
the hallway and I heard her rummaging around in the bathroom cupboard. When she came back, she tossed me a pair
of blue latex gloves.

I slipped them on and smiled her way. There were ad-
vantages to having an aunt who thought like a criminal!

Feeling a little more comfortable and a little less likely
to be caught by a certain law enforcement officer who obviously didn't have a kindly bone in his body when it came to
searching for the truth and saving lives, I dug through the
rest of the contents of Svetlana's suitcases. When I was
done, I shook my head. "Nothing," I told Charmaine.
"Nothing interesting, anyway. And if there was anything,
I'm sure the cops took it."

I found the same nothing on the desk.

And more of the same nothing in the dresser drawers,
where Svetlana had stashed some of her clothes.

I drifted into the attached bathroom, where I found

makeup scattered across the countertop that surrounded the sink—Ulta concealer and L'Oréal mascara, Lancôme lipstick (Rouge Ruby) and Estée Lauder foundation, brushes and sponges and false eyelashes so bushy and long, I half-expected them to crawl away.

There was an open cosmetic case nearby and I looked inside. One, two, three more tubes of lipstick. That made sense. But the rest of the stuff in there . . .

Curious about what I thought I saw, I swept aside the makeup so I had room to dump the contents of the bag onto the countertop.

A small magnet.

A piece of glass.

A bit of unglazed tile.

"Why would Svetlana carry around a magnet?" I called to my aunt.

"Well . . ." From where I was in the bathroom, I couldn't see Charmaine, but I could imagine she looked like she always did when she was thinking hard. Her head tipped. Her bottom lip sucked in. I heard the beat of her fingers tapping the doorframe to a tempo designed to get her brain in gear.

"Maybe Svetlana was trying magic," Charmaine finally said. "Some Wiccans use magnets in love spells."

I did not ask her how she knew this. I didn't want to know.

Instead I stuck to logic. "Why would Svetlana need a love spell? Al was already in love with her. And she was in love with him. If she wasn't, she wouldn't have come all the way from Russia to marry him. And how about . . ." Again, I looked at the little pile. "A piece of glass? Got any ideas how that would work into a magic spell?"

Charmaine didn't.

I wrinkled my nose. "These aren't beauty accessories, that's for sure." My own brain kicked into gear and I thought about how Max and his cohorts had searched the room. Like anyone could blame me for feeling just the littlest bit self-satisfied? "I bet anything Max and the other cops didn't know what to make of this stuff. They saw it in the cosmetic bag and assumed these were things women just naturally carry around with them. Leave it to a man not to know the difference between what matters and what doesn't."

"Do you think it matters?" Charmaine wanted to know.

This, I couldn't say. But I was plenty curious. I pocketed the magnet, the glass, and the tile and left the bathroom. I was standing exactly at the window where Charmaine and I were that previous Thursday evening when we realized Charmaine's car was missing when something outside caught my eye.

Or I should say, someone.

The same woman I'd seen Svetlana arguing with in front of the house on Friday evening.

As quickly as I could, I squeezed through the web of yellow tape, raced downstairs, and was out on the sidewalk before the lady wearing the I Love Steam Trains button had a chance to move.

I pulled in a steadying breath before I asked, "Can I help you?"

She looked from me to the house. "Do you live here?"

"Do you have a reason for hanging around here?"

She laughed, a tight, uncomfortable sound. "Really, I'm just in town with the train enthusiasts and—"

"And for the second time in just a couple of days, you just so happen to be standing out here in front of my aunt's house."

Her smile was stiff. "It's a nice house."

"It's mustard yellow with purple trim." This, I shouldn't have had to point out. Much like Charmaine herself, her choice of house colors was anything but subtle. "What do you really want?"

The woman was middle-aged, middle-sized. She had brown hair that was short and choppy, sallow skin, a bit of an overbite, and she wore glasses. Red frames. Round as saucers. When her gaze flickered from the house to me, the lenses flashed. "The other day, I was talking to a woman here."

I remembered the way Svetlana stood toe to toe with this lady, her finger stabbing the air. "To me, it didn't exactly look like talking. And the woman's name was Svetlana."

"Yeah, sure. Svetlana." Like it was a mouthful of borscht and she wasn't sure how she felt about beets, the woman rolled the name over her tongue. "We were chatting, me and Svetlana, and she asked me to stop by today."

"She told me you were just asking for directions."

"Sure. Of course." The woman shifted from foot to foot. "That's how it started. With me asking for directions. I'm here with the train group, see." She touched a finger to the button pinned to her yellow shirt. "I was out exploring the town and I walked by and we just started talking. You know, about this and that. I told her how excited I was about the train convention and she invited me here today. She said from the backyard she could hear the sound of the steam train whistle and it was so cool, and she thought since I'm a train lover, I'd like to hear it, too, and—"

"So you weren't asking for directions?"

"Directions? Sure." She ran her tongue over her lips. "Because I wanted to find the diner and that Svetlana, she told me where it was."

"I thought you were talking about train whistles."

"That, too."

I crossed my arms over my chest and stepped back, my weight against one foot. I tilted my head, too, the better to give her a penetrating look. "So you were talking about train whistles."

She nodded.

"And you were asking for directions and Svetlana helped you out."

Another nod.

"Except I doubt she knew where the diner was. Svetlana never set foot in Tinker's Creek until Thursday."

The woman's smile came and went. "She didn't mention that."

"She says she did."

"That's not how I remember it." She backstepped away from me. "I really should get going. There's a lecture this afternoon. About . . ." She shrugged. "Well, you know, train stuff. I'd hate to miss it."

"And I'd hate for you to leave here and not know what's going on."

Okay, so it wasn't technically true. I didn't really hate for her to leave. But I hated for her to leave before I found out anything that might be useful. Like if she knew anything about what had happened in the park the day before. To that end, I watched her carefully when I said, "You heard the news, right, Miss . . . ?"

"Kowalski," she answered automatically. "Annalise Kowalski. And news . . . ?" She scraped her hands against the legs of her brown pants. "What news are you talking about?"

"The news about Svetlana, of course," I said.

Her eyes went wide. "That's not . . . it isn't . . ." She

gulped. "I heard people talking this morning at breakfast. They said there was a murder in the park yesterday. You don't mean to tell me Svetlana had something to do with that?"

"In fact, she had plenty to do with it. Svetlana Anatov was the victim."

Annalise let out a groan. "No! That's not possible. We were just standing here the other day talking and—"

"I'm sorry, but it's true. Tell me what you were really talking about. And why hearing about the death of someone you said you don't know has got you so upset."

Annalise flinched. She shook her head and flapped her arms. Then just like a bird, she took off down Main Street, a mile a minute.

"That," I said, "was peculiar." I hadn't completely lost it. I wasn't talking to myself. Charmaine's face was pressed to the dining room window and she'd raised the sash enough that she hadn't missed a word.

"I'll say." She left the dining room, came outside, and plopped down on the front step. I smelled Nutella on her breath. "She couldn't have known Svetlana. She was new in town. She was new in the country. You know I'm an empath." She smoothed a hand over her robe. "Highly sensitive. Able to sense what other people are thinking and feeling. But really, Lizzie, it's not as common as you might think. Maybe one or two percent of the world's entire population? I find it hard to believe another empath just so happens to show up in town when there's a murder and feels so overwhelmed by the news, she can't deal with it."

"Yeah." Annalise was long gone, but I looked down the street in the direction where she'd disappeared. "That's not the only thing I'm finding really hard to believe."

"Oh." Intrigued, Charmaine got to her feet. "Do tell."

"You heard it. Now think about it."

She did, her eyes squeezed shut, her lips pursed. After a minute or two, she let out a huff and gave up. "If you're talking about how Annalise claims she was asking for directions, I guess it's possible."

"But the train isn't," I told her.

The fog of confusion that wreathed Charmaine's expression told me she still didn't get it.

"Annalise claims Svetlana invited her here today to listen to the sound of the steam train whistle from our garden, right?"

Charmaine nodded.

"But Svetlana had only been in town since Thursday."

Another nod.

"And this time of year—"

Charmaine's mouth fell open. "The train only runs on Saturdays and Sundays!"

"Which means there's no way Svetlana could have known you can hear the train whistle from here."

Charmaine made a face. "And that tells us . . ."

"That Annalise is lying, of course. The only question now, is why."

# Chapter 10

Love Under the Covers is my happy place and, boy, did I need it!

My mind still spinning over the puzzling second sudden appearance of Annalise Kowalski, her stories, and her lies, I left Charmaine to her Nutella and hopped on over to the shop. It was Sunday, and the shop wasn't open. That meant I had the whole, wonderful place to myself. The moment I was inside, the door closed behind me to hold back the world, the worries, and the aggravations of the last twenty-four hours, I breathed deep and instantly felt my blood pressure throttle back.

Books!

Like readers everywhere, I found so much comfort, so much joy, in books.

The shop was always closed on Sundays and Mondays, and I usually used those two days to catch up on all the work I didn't have time to get done the other five days of the week, things like ordering and shipping, planning events for readers and writers, diving into my TBR pile, so gloriously huge it promised me hour after happy hour of reading.

But that week, of course, the store had also been closed on Saturday. I was, after all, the maid of honor in the ill-fated wedding and I couldn't very well work the shop, too. Besides, everyone in town was at the wedding. Aside from the train lovers who packed our little corner of the world, there wasn't anyone left around to buy books.

An extra day of being closed meant I had plenty of catching up to do, and hoping to keep my brain busy and my thoughts on anything but murder, I got to work.

I unpacked six boxes of books and put the newest releases out on the table just inside the front door. So many delicious books, and they didn't all fit so I spent the next half hour going room to room, distributing books, enjoying the silence and the endless possibilities of the fictional worlds that buzzed around me.

The contemporary room had once been the dining room of the house and was now painted a modern, steely gray. I shelved the books that belonged there, then ducked into the historical room. With its Oriental rug, its fireplace, and its soothing sage green walls, it had always been a favorite of mine. As long as I was in there, I flopped down in the wing chair nearest the window, rested my head, and closed my eyes.

I breathed deep.

Squirmed.

I told myself to empty my mind and relax my spirit.

Wiggled.

I knew if I could just clear my head, the answers to the questions that had been plaguing me might pop into my brain.

It was no use.

As much as I tried, relaxation was not in the cards.

Not when my brain wouldn't let go of the facts and figments that floated through it.

Magnets and pieces of glass.

Makeup and *Outlander*.

A dead bride with a scrap of paper in her hand, a groom who'd wanted to end it all.

And a killer.

Somewhere out there. Maybe close by.

A shiver scraped up my back and I sat up and shook it away. While I was at it, I grabbed the books I'd brought into the room with me, arranged the batch alphabetically (Jane Austen, Alyssa Cole, Lorraine Heath, Eloisa James) and shelved them where they belonged.

I'd just finished when I heard a familiar voice from outside the store and saw Dan Cameron. He'd been walking but stopped just where the sidewalk met our brick-walled patio, his phone to his ear.

He was one of the people I wanted to talk to, so I raced to the door and went outside.

As soon as he ended his call, I closed in on Dan.

"Hey, Lizzie!" Dan stuck his phone in the pocket of the blue blazer he wore with gray pants and gave me a wave. "No terrible aftereffects from all the excitement yesterday, I hope."

"I'm fine," I assured him. "But I wanted to ask you about Al. Is he . . ." I leaned forward so I could look up and down the sidewalk, but there was no one else around. "Did he come into town with you?"

Dan shook his head. "Al's doc stopped over to see him last night, gave him some pills to help him relax. I made sure he took one this morning after breakfast. When I left the house, he was snoring on the couch in the sunroom."

"Probably the best thing for him."

"That, and some home cooking." Dan was carrying a reusable grocery bag and he held it up. "I'm going to make chili for dinner. Figure it's comfort food, you know? Thought Al could use it. Between that and him getting all the rest he needs . . . well, I'm not sure I can say he'll be all right. I mean, how can he be after everything that happened? But I know he'll feel stronger and better."

"I told Al I'd work the hardware store for him tomorrow," I said, just in case Al hadn't mentioned it. "So let him sleep in and relax all he wants."

Dan smiled. "You're a good friend. And what you did yesterday—"

Like I could help it? Still stinging from Max's ham-handed handling of the situation, I lifted my chin and my shoulders shot back. "Are you going to lecture me, too?"

Dan was honestly surprised. "Lecture you? About how you helped save a friend's life?"

He was so genuine, and (unlike a certain someone else) so obviously grateful that I'd done what I could, I was instantly embarrassed. "Sorry." I backed away, both from Dan and from my momentary anger. "Yesterday was a long day. I'm a little touchy."

Dan nodded. "I get it. I've been feeling the same way. Helpless."

"At least you're making chili."

He grinned. "And you're going to open the hardware store tomorrow." Dan stepped closer and lowered his voice. "Al told me you promised to help find out what happened to Svetlana."

There was nobody around, but I spoke quietly, too. "I'd like to keep that on the down low."

"I get it." As if it somehow proved he was genuine, Dan

gave me the thumbs-up. "I just wish there was more I could do to help."

"Maybe there is." Rather than stand there on the sidewalk, I waved Dan toward one of the tables set up on our patio and once he took a chair, I sat down opposite him. "I'm trying to make sense of everything that happened and it's hard to do that without an understanding of the whole picture. You can help."

He flattened his hands against the tabletop. "Anything."

"Tell me about online dating—how exactly do you meet and arrange to marry a woman through the Internet?"

Dan's laugh had an uncomfortable edge. "You mean—"

"How does it work? What's the procedure for setting up the marriage? How did Al and Svetlana end up finding each other online, anyway?"

"Wish I could say. I mean, I know how it worked for me and Galina." I wasn't imagining it, when he spoke his wife's name, his voice did turn a little sour. "But that was a few years ago. We met through a company called Cupid's Choice."

"And Al used the same service?"

Dan shook his head. "I'm pretty sure Cupid's Choice went out of business soon after I dealt with them. No, Al used another site." Thinking, he tapped his fingers against the table. "Bride of Your Dreams! I think that's what Al said it was called. He never even told me he was looking for someone, not until things were settled and Svetlana was already on her way here."

"Were you surprised?"

Dan shot me a look. "Come on, Lizzie. You and everyone else in Tinker's Creek knows Galina and I aren't exactly the happiest couple on the planet. Was I surprised that Al wanted to get married? After the way he saw how things turned out for me? Sure. Because it seemed to me if Al was paying attention, he would have known his marriage might have ended up like mine."

I winced. Partly because I hated to hear him admit his unhappiness. Partly because I felt embarrassed about probing. "You and Galina, though, you're still married."

"Yeah." His smile was tight behind clenched teeth.

And I knew better than to push any further. At least about Dan and Galina's relationship.

"They seemed compatible enough," I said. "Svetlana and Al."

"You think so?"

I shrugged. "I guess so. I hope so. It all seems pretty baffling to me. Maybe Galina can explain. You know, about what makes a woman on the other side of the world start looking for love here. How she knows things will work out. How she chooses the company she's going to work with."

"Galina won't be any help." Dan scraped back his chair and stood. "Like I said, different company, different people. She certainly doesn't know anything about Svetlana."

I thought back to the ugly incident in Charmaine's garden. Splattered Moscow mules. A soaked bride-to-be.

"Then why were they fighting the other night?" I asked Dan.

He barked out a laugh. "Russians! Passionate people!"

Which didn't seem like an answer to me.

Still, it was obviously all I was going to get out of Dan. He grabbed his grocery bag and left. He was barely out of sight when I noticed Galina on the other side of the street watching him. She caught my eye, signaled that she'd be right over. Before she stepped onto the patio, she checked to her right and her left. When there was no sign of Dan, Galina came closer.

"What he tell you?"

"Dan?" Yeah, like we could have been talking about anyone else. "What do you mean? What did he tell me about what?"

She was wearing the same maroon leather jacket she'd worn at the falls the evening before, the same knee-high leather boots. She rolled her eyes. "About Svetlana, of course. What else we would be talking about?"

What, indeed. "Actually, I asked Dan about Al. I wondered how he was doing."

"He is better off single."

"That's cold."

A small smile lifted her top lip. "You say this because you are single."

"Al didn't want to be single."

"No." Galina glided a hand over the nearest table. Apparently Phillip Wilmington had found her as he left the falls the evening before and returned her lost glove. She was wearing both. "But Al, he maybe did not choose so wisely."

"You mean Svetlana. You knew her in Russia?"

"What, you think all Russians know each other? It is a big country, Lizzie." I guess I was a dolt for having to be told this because she shook her head and her bleached hair shivered around her shoulders.

Dolt or not, I wasn't about to give up. "If you didn't know her, why did you throw a drink in Svetlana's face? Dan said it was because your families knew each other. He said something about an old family feud."

Her eyebrows tilted.

"It isn't true?"

Galina chewed the red lipstick off her lower lip. "It is hard to admit, yes? When you are not so happy? When the dream you had for a life of love, of loyalty . . ." She cleared her throat and lowered her head, the picture of misery. "I think maybe you do not realize what Dan is really like. I think maybe no one in this town really does."

"So, tell me. What's he really like?"

Her head shot up, her eyes were narrowed. "Like a man who would have an affair, yes? With a new woman in town."

"Dan and Svetlana?" There was no way I could keep the skepticism from crackling through my voice. It pinged against the brick patio. Ponged across the bookshop. Crashed back over me and I didn't even care. "Svetlana just got here! They didn't know each other. You can't possibly think they were—"

"No, no, no." She waved one leather-encased hand to emphasize her point. "You are right, they did not know each other. They did not have time to get together. Not yet."

I swallowed down my disbelief. "Are you saying Dan and Svetlana would have—"

"Oh yes." Her nod was solemn. "I have seen it many times before. I know the signs. The little looks. The smiles. The nods. I saw this, yes? At your aunt's house. At the dinner. I saw him look at Svetlana. I know . . ." She tapped a finger to her forehead. "I know what Dan is thinking."

"And you warned Svetlana off."

"This is what I tried, yes. This Svetlana, she tells me to mind my own business."

"And you told her Dan was your business."

Galina's eyes lit with what was almost appreciation. "You have been here, too, yes? You understand what it is like to have a partner who is unfaithful."

"No, not really," I had to admit. "But I can imagine how worried you must have been. And I can see why Svetlana reacted badly. She was probably shocked at what you were suggesting."

"You think? Yes, maybe. Maybe I should have given her what you call the doubt of benefit. But I have seen this so many times before. It starts so innocently. Oh yes, I knew what was going to happen. I told Svetlana it was a not very good idea."

It seemed a little out there to me, this idea of Dan and Svetlana hitting it off instantly. Especially at the dinner the night before Svetlana's wedding.

"Thursday night. Svetlana disappeared for a while. I've been trying to figure out where she could have gone since she didn't know anyone in town. But if she was meeting Dan—"

"He was out." Galina nodded. "Yes, that evening, Dan went out. He did not say where he was going."

"And at the wedding?" As soon as the words were past my lips, I flinched. "Sorry. You weren't at the wedding. You have no idea what happened at the wedding."

"I know Dan, he come home early."

"We all came home early. After I found Svetlana's body, the party broke up. Everyone left."

"No. No. Before that, I think." Galina thought it through. "I was on tennis court because I was not at wedding. And I hear Dan's car. I call to him, but he says nothing. He goes in house. A little while later, I hear him leave again."

Back to the wedding? He must have. Dan was on the towpath, ready to comfort Al when the two of us were pulled from the canal.

As if she was trying to make sense of something, Galina tilted her head and mumbled, "It cannot mean anything."

"You've just remembered something," I ventured.

She shook herself back to the present. "It is nothing, I do not think."

"I might be able to help you decide."

"It is just that Dan . . ." Once more she thought things through. "I cannot be sure. I do not know. But, Lizzie, he wore a suit to the wedding, yes?"

I pictured Dan at the front of the pavilion with Al while we waited for Svetlana to arrive. "Navy blue," I told her.

"Yes." She nodded. "But later, when he comes home from wedding, when he tells me what happened to Svetlana, he is wearing a dark gray suit."

"He changed clothes?"

"It cannot mean anything." Galina got rid of the thought with a shake of her shoulders. "Maybe he spill something on himself. Maybe he dance too fast with some Tinker's Creek floozy and he rip his pants."

"Maybe," I agreed. Not about the floozy part. Not only wasn't I exactly sure what qualified someone to be a floozy, I wasn't sure we had any of them in Tinker's Creek. "But maybe—"

"Do not say it." She held up a hand to stop me mid-sentence. "Do not think it. It wasn't because suit got wet and muddy because Dan was in park doing . . ." Galina pressed her hands to her eyes. "No. Do not think such a thing, Lizzie. Dan is not a good husband. This is true, and it makes me sad. But he is not murderer. No. Don't even think it. He is not murderer."

She was still shaking her head and muttering when she walked away.

And I was left feeling more confused than ever.

Rather than stand outside and wonder about it all, I went into the shop and got back to work. Halloween was coming, and I wanted to feature our selection of paranormal romances for the holiday. What better way to lay aside the problems of real life than with a good dose of fantasy? I went to the solarium at the back of the shop. I love our funky paranormal paradise. Exotic plants. Stained glass witch balls hanging from the ceiling. Charmaine's collection of vintage Halloween memorabilia. We could have a Halloween tea, I decided right then and there. Cookies with black sprinkles. Orange punch. And—

When I heard the front door bang shut, I jumped.

"We're closed!" I called out.

There was no answer, and at the same time my imagination rocketed into overdrive and ricocheted in all the wrong directions, I gave myself a figurative slap for not locking the door behind me.

"We're not open!"

Great. We had a murderer on the loose, I was here alone, I should have been doing my best to sound tough, and my voice wobbled. Kind of like my knees suddenly did.

I gave myself a figurative kick in the pants. Rather than stand there, shaking in my shoes, I made a move for the doorway, adding as much gumption to my voice as was possible for a woman who'd found a body twenty-four hours earlier.

"You're going to have to come back another time! And—"

When I stepped to my right and slammed into Max, I let out a yelp.

"Sorry." He grabbed my shoulders to keep me from going down. "I didn't mean to startle you."

Automatically, I backed away from him and eyed him up and down. Just in case he'd brought another ticket with him. "I wasn't startled," I insisted. "And what are you doing here?"

"Well, that's the thing." I'd seen Max look embarrassed

only once, and that was when he was forced to give a talk about park animals to a group of local school kids. Now it was only the two of us, and still he shifted from foot to foot and looked down at the floor. The tips of his ears were red.

He wasn't working. He was dressed in jeans and a green golf shirt that said St. Louis across the front and had a red cardinal perched on a bat embroidered on the sleeve, a memento of his days in the majors. He backed away and scrubbed a hand across his chin.

"I just thought we should set some things right between us."

I crossed my arms over my chest. "You mean like you being a knucklehead and costing me a bundle?"

"Not about that. I was doing my job. There are laws, and people need to obey them. Especially when they involve safety."

"Then what?"

He grinned. Grimaced. Wrinkled his nose. Shrugged. "I didn't want anything to happen to you."

"That makes two of us."

"No. I mean, the reason I reacted the way I did . . ." He pulled in a breath and let it out slowly. "When you popped over that barrier at the falls, I just . . . I was ready to grab you and haul you off to jail right then and there. I would have, too, if I wasn't so worried about Al. You made me that mad."

"All right. I get it." Oh, how I hated to admit he was right. "I should have stayed back and let you professionals do what you do best. It was stupid."

"It was stupid." He dared to flash me a smile. "But that's not why I was mad. I mean, it was. I mean . . ." He scraped a hand through his dark hair. "After it was all over, I was still steaming. And it took me until this morning to realize it wasn't just because you're a criminal."

I offered him a sour "Thanks."

"But don't you get it?" Before I even realized he was going to do it, he grabbed my hand and led me back into the paranormal room. We sat side by side on the couch. "I was mad because if something happened to you . . . Lizzie, I don't want to miss out on all the things I think we could have together."

My heart bumped. My blood thumped. I gave my left arm a thorough scratching and did my best to deflect the warmth in his chocolate eyes.

Play it cool, Lizzie, I reminded myself.

Make a joke of it.

Remember your track record, and don't forget that this tall hunk of gorgeousness is going to be heading out of town sooner rather than later.

The last thing he needed to take along with him was memories of fumbling, bumbling Lizzie Hale, loser at romance.

I managed a laugh. "You're talking going to high school baseball games and munching popcorn in the bleachers, right?"

"That." How he managed a smile that was shy and as hot as lava at the same time was a mystery to me. "And I dunno. We'll see where those ball games take us. Maybe other things, too."

I scratched a little more.

"That's why I did it."

"Did . . . ?"

"That's why I lost it yesterday. I mean aside from the fact that you were clearly breaking the law and that I, as a sworn officer of the law, had to do something about it. But, Lizzie . . ." He scooped up both my hands in his. "When I saw you out there, acting like a total idiot—"

My shoulders shot back, but I couldn't stay angry. Not when he smiled at me.

"I couldn't let anything happen to you. It made me realize I had to tell you. And, hey, I brought a peace offering!"

The way he said it told me something was up. "Info about the case?"

"Nobody else knows yet."

I sat up. "You're sharing?"

"I'd like some input. Besides . . . well, I know what it's like around here. Word's bound to travel fast and I didn't want you to hear this from anyone else." He gave me a sidelong look. "Tell me what you noticed about Svetlana."

I knew this wasn't a game. When it came to an investigation, Max was all business. I was glad. Thinking about the case meant I didn't have to think about what Max had said, what he implied, what he promised. I told myself not to forget it, closed my eyes, and thought about Svetlana. "She had lousy taste in wedding gowns," I said.

"So I hear. But what else?"

I thought back over the last days. "She liked reading romances. I'll give her that. She had a copy of *Outlander* under her pillow."

"And?"

"And that means I suppose eventually, Svetlana and I would have had plenty to talk about. If she liked the same sorts of books I like and if I could get by her lousy English and her heavy accent and—"

An idea tickled my brain, and I think Max knew it. He leaned forward.

"Max, Svetlana's English wasn't all that good. How was she able to make her way through *Outlander*? And speaking of that . . ." This time, the thought that struck landed with a thump, and I popped out of my seat.

"The makeup!"

The way Max screwed up one corner of his mouth, I could tell he didn't follow.

"It was from Ulta, Max. And Estée Lauder and L'Oréal, and Lancôme. And I guess there's probably a way for someone in Russia to buy American products, but it doesn't seem all that likely, does it? And even if those companies had some sort of Russian subsidiaries or whatever, you'd think the labels would be in Russian. The labels on Svetlana's stuff, they were all in English."

"Makes perfect sense," he said.

To which the only logical reply seemed to be "Huh?"

"Here's what had me stumped from the beginning," he confessed. "How could Svetlana possibly have any enemies? She was a total stranger here in Tinker's Creek."

"Maybe not a total stranger. Galina says she's sure Dan had an eye on Svetlana."

"Really?" Max was surprised. "You think—"

"Galina wasn't at the wedding. She says she was home, nowhere near the park. And I don't think she would have killed Svetlana because Dan was attracted to her. I think if that was the case, she would have murdered Dan."

He ran a finger around the inside of his shirt collar. "I'll keep that in mind."

He would have seen my self-satisfied smile if he wasn't so busy thinking.

"Anyway, you can see where my thought processes were going," he said. "Why kill a stranger? Who could possibly gain from that? And then . . ." He gave me one of those aha looks I always imagine detectives in books use on a room full of unwitting suspects. "We ran Svetlana's fingerprints."

A sizzle tingled up my spine and I held my breath, waiting for what I was sure was going to be earthshaking news.

I wasn't wrong.

"The woman we knew as Svetlana Anatov," Max told me, "is actually Sharona Schwartz from Newark, New Jersey. She's the owner of the business where Al found his soul mate, Bride of Your Dreams."

# Chapter 11

*Sunday evening*

W here's the real Svetlana?"

We'd both sat quietly for so long, lost in thought, considering Max's astonishing news, that when I asked the question, he actually winced.

"That's the question I've been asking myself," Max said. "I've checked with Customs and Border Protection. She landed in New York, all right."

"So her passport, her birth certificate . . . all those things Svetlana—er, Sharona—had, those are genuine?"

"Looks like it."

"Which means somewhere along the line, Sharona met up with the real Svetlana, got all her papers, and . . ." I gulped. "Oh, Max, do you think she might be dead?"

His shrug was hardly encouraging. "Wish I knew. I've put out an APB. That's all-points bulletin," he added and I forgave him. He had no idea how much romantic suspense I'd read over the years. "If she's out there somewhere, she might be in trouble. She's a foreigner with no passport and maybe no identification."

"If she's out there." The words settled on my shoulders, as cold as the touch of death, and I shook them away at the same time Max stood.

"Come on," he said. "I want to show you something."

He took my hand and led me up to the front counter. When he'd come in, Max had left a laptop there, and now he flipped it open, keyed in what he needed, and side by side we waited to see what would pop up on the screen.

"The website for Bride of Your Dreams!" I tilted the laptop screen for a better look and checked out the home page, a riot of pink swirls, white roses, and enough hearts to make even the most love-crazy Cupid proud.

Interesting, yes?

But there was more.

I leaned closer and squinted. The block of text at the top of the page was written in a font that swirled and whirled so much it made my eyes ache:

*You know you're ready.*

*You feel the longing as your heart aches with solitude.*

*Alone. Dreaming of that certain someone. That special someone. Her face haunts your fantasies. The thought of her tender smile lights your life. You wake at night, reaching out into the darkness for her.*

*And find nothing. Nothing but emptiness.*

*Until now.*

"Wow." There was no way I could unsee the words, but I stepped back and away from the counter, hoping some breathing space would help me forget. "And people think romance novels are filled with purple prose!"

He gave the web page a dodgy look. "That's what I thought. And then when I looked over the website this morning, I wondered. You know, about this whole bit about finding romance. I knew you'd be the one to help me figure it out."

"When you looked at the website this morning?" Pretending to have to think about this, I gave Max a sidelong glance. "Does that mean you've been looking for a bride?"

It wasn't my imagination. He did move a hairsbreadth closer. "Maybe."

That'll teach me.

One little question.

One little hint at flirting.

And my insides turned to mush.

When it came to Max and romance, we might be talking intriguing. And we were definitely talking hot.

But there was no way we were talking permanent.

Not when it came to the two of us.

I told myself not to forget it and concentrated on the web page open in front of me. It was better than watching that spark that flickered in his dark eyes. Safer. Saner. To that end, I looked over the menu bar at the top of the page.

Eastern Europe
Asia
South America

"Russian?" I asked him.

The way he pursed his lips told me he was teasing. "You mean for me? I don't think so. A Russian woman might not understand Texas."

"And you've got Texas in your blood."

"Everyone born there has Texas in their blood."

I made sure to keep my voice level even as I changed the subject just a little bit. "You going back?"

"You mean with the Park Service?" As if he had to think about it, he hesitated. "Haven't gotten the word yet. For now, though"—he clicked on the Eastern Europe heading—"I'm here, and I've got a murder to work on. Take a look at this."

The new page that opened featured a bride-of-the-month photo of a long-legged woman with very red hair wearing a very low-cut blouse. She was lying on a plush purple couch, her head thrown back, one arm folded behind her head, the other reaching out, beckoning.

"Wowza." This was in no way an exclamation of admiration or approval. It was more like a polite version of *yikes*. "Do all the women on the website pose like that?"

"Apparently that's just for the special woman of the month." Max zipped past that page and on to the next. There, neatly in rows of three, were headshots of women.

Lots and lots of women.

"It goes on for pages," he told me. "And see, if you're interested in chatting with the woman, you click the photo and you're sent to a page where you sign up to be a Bride of Your Dreams member."

"And let me guess, you're charged a bundle for that privilege."

"Yeah. But you've got access to a whole lot of young ladies." To prove it, he scrolled through page after page that showed pictures of women (most of them young) dolled up and smiling, doing their best to look sexy and wholesome and eager and modest all at the same time.

"All these wannabe brides, but just for the record, that's not what I was looking for. Here." Max got to the bottom of the page where "Engaged!" was written in bold pink letters, clicked, and we were instantly on another page. This one showed a dozen or so women, the words "Soon to Be Married!" displayed (in pink, of course) in the corner of each pic.

"It's Svetlana! Or I guess I should say it's Sharona." I pointed to the one and only face that looked familiar. "But why would she put her own picture on the website? I mean, if she's not the person she said she was? If she's really the owner of the bride-finding business?" My brain spun, and I shook my head trying to clear it. "It doesn't make sense."

"It doesn't," Max agreed. "That means you need to look again. Closer this time."

I did.

The woman in the picture had the same long honey-colored hair as the bride we'd known as Svetlana, but her face was smoother, younger looking. There were no crow's-feet at the corners of her eyes.

"Airbrushed?" I asked Max.

"It's certainly possible. I imagine most of these pictures are. But while it's easy to hide things like wrinkles, other features are tougher to disguise."

He was right. This woman's nose was longer and slimmer than the nose of our murder victim. It could only mean one thing and, realizing it, my heart bumped. "That's the real Svetlana!"

Max nodded. "Exactly what I'm thinking. And on first glance, Sharona, she looked a whole lot like Svetlana, don't you think?"

I did. "No matter what color Sharona's hair really was, that would be easy enough to change. And the face . . . well, Al said it. That very first day!" Annoyed that I hadn't paid more attention, that I'd sloughed the whole thing off as just one of those things, I slapped a hand to my thigh. "The minute our Svetlana got out of the limo, Al mumbled something about how she looked younger online."

"Hey, it's not your fault. There was no way you could have been suspicious."

"But should we be worried?" It was another baffling question and because I didn't have an answer and I didn't like that at all, I grumbled a curse. "Does this mean something happened to the real Svetlana? And does it have anything to do with Sharona's murder? Why was she pretending to be Svetlana, anyway? If she wasn't who she pretended to be—"

"It means someone might have known she was a phony. Maybe someone even knew who she really was." Max snapped his laptop shut and scooped it off the counter. "Want to find out?"

"Are you inviting me to be part of the investigation?"

"Don't get too carried away, Sherlock." He chuckled. "I just think it's time I had a little one-on-one with Al, and I figured he might be more comfortable talking when there's a familiar face in the room."

"So that's all I am now? Just a familiar face?"

It was hard to be angry with a guy whose smile sent a sizzle up my spine. "It's a very nice face."

"And . . . ?"

"There's a really good brain at work behind it."

"Better," I told him. Right before I got my keys, locked up the shop, and we headed out.


Dan and Galina Cameron lived outside Tinker's Creek at what folks called the Compound.

Dan's grandfather Otis owned the three-acre property, and when Dan graduated from college and joined the family business, Otis built him a house near his own.

Generous, some people said.

Others insisted Otis was a micromanager and a meddler who held the family purse strings in tight fingers. Dan's father, the story went, had never gotten along with Otis and had gone his own way, moving out west and dying there. When Dan came back to Tinker's Creek as a young man, Otis made sure he stayed. Town gossip said any time Dan talked about moving on, Otis dangled fat pay raises in front of him and kept an eye on every move his grandson made.

Whether all that was true or not, I had to admit that the house was lovely: a brick colonial with overflowing flower boxes on every window, a wide bed of perennials up front, and a door that was more beveled, leaded glass than wood.

It was opened by Galina, who greeted us.

If a grunt followed by a "What you want?" can be considered a greeting.

Max explained and she obviously recognized him as being an official, even out of his ranger uniform. She didn't argue, just stepped back to point him through the wide foyer with its polished hardwood floor and a stairway that curved up to the second floor. Before I could follow, she stepped in front of me.

"You did not tell him, did you?" Her voice nearly a whisper, she watched Max walk through the kitchen, where I saw black stainless appliances gleam in the afternoon sunlight.

"What I say about Dan? How I say he came home from wedding and change his clothes? I tell you, Lizzie, this does not mean anything. It was just us talking, that is all. Like girlfriends, yes?"

I'd never thought of Galina as a girlfriend, but as a matter of fact, I hadn't had a chance to tell Max what Galina said to me earlier that day. I didn't have to lie.

"Dan is lousy husband," Galina reminded me, "but he is not murderer."

I told her I'd keep that in mind and followed Max, and together we found Al in a room with a slate floor and three walls of floor-to-ceiling windows. The view was nothing short of spectacular—a slice of garden, a bit of tennis court, a glimpse of an in-ground pool, water shimmering in the sunlight. Al, it seemed, saw none of it. He sat on a wicker couch, a lightweight red plaid blanket over his shoulders, staring straight ahead, his eyes blank.

When I said hello, he jumped.

"We won't bother you for long." Max sat on the chair opposite the couch and I took the chair next to his. "There are some facts we need to get in line."

"Yes." Al's chin dipped. There was a steaming mug on the table next to him and he lifted it and cupped it in trembling hands. Al's face was pale and there were dark smudges under his eyes. He'd always been so happy-go-lucky, seeing him like this broke my heart.

Al's gaze, so filled with pain, traveled from me to Max. "I'm sorry," he said.

Max raised his eyebrows.

"Yesterday." Al hung his head. "I was overly dramatic. Not to mention irresponsible. I endangered more than just my own life, and I offer my apologies to both of you. I just didn't . . ." When he shrugged, the blanket slipped from his shoulders. "I wasn't thinking clearly."

"You'll have to face a judge," Max told him.

He nodded. "Yes. And I'll pay whatever fine I'm required to. Or do community service. Or—"

"The judge will probably take into account that you were under emotional distress."

I'd never been given that option, and the look I shot at Max told him so.

His one-shoulder shrug told me maybe I shouldn't have jumped the gun and paid my trespassing fine so quickly.

Al's head came up. "You think so? That a judge would take the circumstances into consideration? It's not that I don't think I should be penalized for what I did. It was stupid. But I'd hate to have any sort of . . ." He scraped his tongue over his lips. "A record. That wouldn't be good for business."

"We'll see what we can work out. But for now, that's not what we're here to talk about, Mr. Little."

"Al. Please." He sipped from his mug. "You two, you want tea? Dan's been great about taking care of me, I'm sure he'll make you some."

"No need." Max sat back. "Tell us how you got to know Svetlana Anatov."

Noticing right away he didn't give away the revelation of our mail-order bride's real identity, I took my cue from Max and kept my mouth shut about the bombshell discovery.

Al set down the mug and leaned forward, his elbows on his knees, his fingers twisted together. "I'd been doing a lot of thinking. About how I wasn't getting any younger. About how I work so hard, it's really tough for me to get out and meet women. Naturally, that made me think about Dan and how he'd found Galina."

"I'd think knowing about Dan and Galina would have made you run for the hills." Since Al and I were friends, I knew I could get away with the honest assessment.

Al gave me what was almost a smile. "Believe me, I know what you mean. But at first when the idea hit, I didn't take it seriously. I was just messing around. But then I tripped over that website."

"Bride of Your Dreams."

Al nodded, confirming Max's information. "I just started paging through, looking around, thinking that, sure, maybe Dan and Galina weren't exactly the happiest couple in the world, but they worked with some other company, one that maybe wasn't as careful about making the right matches. There are a lot of people this works out for, you know? Online dating, I mean. I thought, why not? I just kept on looking at all those faces, all those women. And that's when I saw her."

Al's eyes glowed. "I know it sounds crazy. Well, maybe not in those romance novels you read, Lizzie," he added. "But the moment I laid eyes on her—"

"Svetlana," I said.

"Uh, no." Al sat back. "I mean, not at first. That's the crazy thing about the way this all worked out. At first, I was totally smitten by another woman, one named Anastasia."

It wasn't what I expected to hear and I guess Max was confused, too. He'd brought his laptop into the house and he opened the web page we'd looked at earlier. "Is she still here? On the site?"

Al got up so he could stand at Max's shoulder. He had Max scroll through three pages. "That's her. See?" He pointed to the screen and the black-haired, dark-eyed woman whose picture was on it. Anastasia was a tiny thing. Fine-boned. Elfin features. She had a delicate mouth with Cupid's bow lips, a mole on her chin, a little crescent-shaped scar in one corner of her left eye that instead of marring her looks, somehow made her more delicate and fascinating.

She didn't look a thing like Sharona Schwartz.

Max saw it, too. That would explain the look he sent my way.

I studied Anastasia's face for a while longer before I shifted my gaze to Al. "If you were instantly attracted to this woman," I asked him, "how did you—"

"End up with Svetlana? Like I said, that's the crazy thing." He sat back down on the couch and grabbed his mug of tea. "It just goes to prove that working with really professional people and a really first-class organization can make all the difference in the world. Anastasia and I chatted online for a couple weeks. And I thought we were really hitting it off. But then I heard from that wonderful woman, Ms. Schwartz, the one who owns Bride of Your Dreams."

I was almost afraid to ask. "Heard what?"

"Well, it's a little hard to admit." Al grimaced. "But Ms. Schwartz, she said Anastasia told her . . ." He cleared his throat. "Anastasia confessed that she wasn't at all interested in me, that she'd just been playing along, learning the ropes of online dating. I was her guinea pig."

My heart squeezed with sympathy. "That's awful."

"It felt awful at the time, but then . . ." Al sat up and smiled. "That's when Ms. Schwartz suggested I start chatting with Svetlana."

"It was her idea?" Rather than an accusation, Max made the question seem like the most natural thing in the world. "Ms. Schwartz steered you to Svetlana?"

Al's chuckle was uncomfortable. "I wouldn't exactly say she steered. It was more like Ms. Schwartz did her homework. She read through dozens of applications. She did some background checks. She determined that Svetlana and I were right for each other, and, you know, she was one hundred percent dead-on. Oh!" Al's expression fell. "Dead. Not a good word to use, not when my Svetlana—"

"Well, that's the thing, Al." Max scooted forward in his seat. "That's what we're here to tell you. The woman you knew as Svetlana Anatov was actually Sharona Schwartz."

Al's mouth dropped open. His hands shook so badly, I got up and took the cup away from him and set it on the table. Fighting for words, his jaw flapped.

I hated to see him so suffer.

I put a comforting hand on Al's shoulder. "You didn't know."

"I didn't . . ." He shook his head, passed his hands over his eyes. "How could I? I never met Ms. Schwartz in person, but I'd seen Svetlana's picture. I recognized her the moment she got out of the limo."

"Do you think the fact that Ms. Schwartz was impersonating Svetlana had anything to do with the altercation you two had at the wedding?" Max asked.

"Alter—" Al gulped down the rest of the word. "I wouldn't call it that. I was . . ." He lifted his shoulders. "Confused. And Svetlana—er, Ms. Schwartz—she was going on and on about some fortune I was supposed to have. About how now that we were married, it was all hers. I tried to tell her I didn't know what she was talking about, but she wouldn't listen and—" What little color was left in Al's face drained away completely. "Is that what it was all about? This Schwartz woman took Svetlana's place and married me because she thought I had money?"

"That's what we need to find out," Max told him. "Because when we do, we might be closer to finding out who killed Ms. Schwartz."

"And Svetlana?" Panic choked Al's voice. "What about her? Where's Svetlana?"

I hated that we didn't have an answer for him.

# Chapter 12

Al's hide-a-key for the hardware store was right where he said I'd find it, under a rock near the back door.

I only wish it was as easy to find the answers to all the questions that baffled me.

"Sharona purposely pushed Al into a relationship with Svetlana," I told Violet. She'd come to the hardware store to keep me company and I filled her in on everything that was happening. "It's pretty obvious that means she knew she was going to impersonate Svetlana right from the get-go. But why?"

Instead of answering, Violet trotted into the hardware store as soon as I had the door unlocked. She'd been there before, once when I shopped for shelving to add space in the former kitchen of Love Under the Covers, where I now housed the Inspirationals, and a second time when I needed some paint to touch up a nicked wall (Charmaine, champagne bottle, popping cork. Don't ask!). Violet was a smart

girl. She knew Al kept treats for special canine visitors below the front counter and she headed right there.

I flicked on the lights and followed. Little's Hardware
had been owned by Al's family for generations. The building was old. The floors creaked in a way that spoke of time
passing and years gone by, and I couldn't help but picture
all the people who'd come and gone through the place.
Men, for the most part, I imagined, and in the very early
days, most of them were workers on the nearby canal. Al's
great-great-great-grandfather Junius, whose portrait hung
in a place of honor behind the cash register, would have
supplied them with the pickaxes and the hammers, the
shovels and the hoes they needed to open up the wilderness.

Junius was a middle-aged man with a gray beard that
hung to the center of his chest, crazy-wild eyebrows, and
small, dark eyes. From the pinched expression on his face,
I always thought his shirt collar might have been too tight.
Or maybe he was just uncomfortable having some frontier
artist immortalize him. That artist had caught the essence
of the man. Upright. Hardworking. Tough. People who
carved out lives in the back of beyond that was Ohio in
those days had to be.

From where I stood, I could see exactly what Junius
could see from his place on the wall. How different did the
building look? Would he recognize the place? I wondered,
too, if like me, he'd savor the scent of raw lumber, the
tangy, chemical smell of spilled paint near the mixing machine. I imagined that light had poured into the store back
in the day just as it did now when it glinted against a peg-
board full of tools and the glass display cases where Al
kept small things like tape measures and flashlights. It illuminated the dust motes floating in the morning air like
glitter all around me.

Because I didn't want to disappoint her, I gave Violet a treat, and while she crunched, I checked the cash register and made sure there was enough change for the day. Speaking of money . . .

"For some reason, she thought he had money," I told Violet, and then because I didn't want to confuse her, I added, "Sharona. She told Al his fortune was going to be hers once they were married. But fortune?" Violet didn't need the demonstration, I mean, she could see it all for herself, but I threw out my arms and spun around, randomly pointing out the this and that of the store. "It's a great store. A rock in our community. And Al's great, too. But there's no way small mom-and-pop stores like these can compete these days. Not with the big boxes. Al loves what he does. He loves this store. But he's not loaded, that's for sure."

That might not be technically true in Violet's eyes. To her, any man with a stash of Milk-Bones might as well have been a king.

While she (literally) chewed over the thought, I kept on thinking, too.

"It explains the printouts of their conversations," I told Violet, just as I'd mentioned to Max the night before between the pizza we ordered for dinner and the slices of wedding cake Brynn stopped by to give me because, she said, it was better to hand them out all around town than throw them away. "I bet those conversations were the real deal. You know, between Al and the real Svetlana. But when Sharona took her place . . ." My sigh rippled the still morning air. "Sharona had to do her homework. That's why she underlined things like the names of schools and birth dates and such. And here I thought she was being romantic! That'll teach me, huh? Just more proof that this girl . . ."

Violet knew who I was talking about, but I pointed my thumb at my blue shirt, anyway. "I guess I really don't know what romance is all about. They weren't loving memories. They were crib sheets! Poor Al. And to think Sharona pushed him toward Svetlana just because there was a resemblance between Svetlana and Sharona. And now . . ." As underhanded as I knew she was, I couldn't help but feel sorry for Sharona. What a terrible way to die!

"We need to figure out what's what, pal." I rubbed a hand over Violet's shaggy head, then scraped my fur-covered hand on my jeans. "There's something nasty going on, and I don't like it."

Violet's bark told me she didn't, either.

Or maybe she was just alerting me to the arrival of the first customer of the day.

Mondays, it turns out, are brisk at a hardware store. Violet and I had little time to chat the rest of the morning. People were in and out, and as familiar with the store as I was, it didn't mean it was easy keeping things going smoothly. I had to search for paint stir sticks. I had to rummage through boxes for a couple of odd-sized ratchet wrenches. I had to fetch and carry for Ms. Tindrall, the lady who lived in the house behind the post office who the local kids said was a witch. She bought four gallons of paint. Purple and orange. Maybe the kids were onto something.

For the record, running a bookshop is totally different, because books, see, give me energy. They feed my soul and lift my spirits. Hardware, not so much. By lunchtime, I was tired. I brewed coffee in Al's small but neat office and grabbed the ham sandwich I'd thrown together before I left the house.

When Violet watched me take a bite and licked her lips, I caved and offered another Milk-Bone.

She gladly accepted.

"Whew!" I plunked down on the high stool behind the front counter and took a deep breath. "Who would have thought a hardware store was this much work?"

Here's the thing about small business owners, though—tired or not, we're always conscious of how much needs to be done and of how, ultimately, that work falls on our shoulders. I grabbed a paper towel from a nearby roll and wiped down the counter. There was a booklet open on it, a publication of the local chamber of commerce touting local businesses (like mine, hooray!), restaurants, and of course all the natural wonders of the park, and I knocked against it and sent it flying off the counter.

I didn't grumble, at least not too much, just bent to retrieve it, and gasped.

*Helltown.*

I read the headline on the page open in front of me, and dropped the booklet like it was on fire.

Okay. All right. I admit it. My stomach tied in knots. I gulped, then instantly felt like a fool.

"It's nothing," I told Violet because she had an uncanny way of picking up on my moods and I didn't want her to worry. "I mean, nothing to be afraid of. It's just that . . ."

Like it or not, I couldn't help but think about all the summers I'd spent there in Tinker's Creek visiting Charmaine and Josh. It was a close-knit community and once the other kids got to know me, they welcomed me back every year like one of their own. We rode our bikes together. Watched movies. Hung out at the local ice cream place and the library and at Katie Barber's house, where her mother let us experiment with all the makeup she didn't want anymore.

And we explored Helltown.

All these years later, and I still shuddered thinking about it.

I knew I was overreacting. There was absolutely, positively nothing to be afraid of. Right? I mean, Helltown was nothing but a figment of local imaginations, what had formerly been the small community of Boston, a once-thriving place thanks to woolen mills, the canal, and ultimately the railroad. Those days passed, and Boston fell into sleepy obsolescence. At least until the national park stepped in and bought up local properties and the residents were moved out. Houses and churches stood empty for years.

And legends grew up around the place.

A haunted, abandoned school bus.

A giant python that slithered through the woods.

A crybaby bridge, where instead of hearing ghostly baby cries, those who were brave enough to park later found tiny handprints in the dust on their cars.

Mutants created by a chemical spill at an old dump.

Now, just like then, I told myself it was all folklore. All just fiction. But, let's face it, I'm a reader. Fiction had a way of taking hold of me.

I'm not proud to admit it, but back in the day, there were plenty of nights after we'd explored the crumbling cemetery in Helltown that I went back to Charmaine's and hid my head under the blankets!

"Silly," I told Violet and reminded myself. Especially since these days, the park had completely cleaned up the area. The old buildings had been demolished. The decrepit roads were replaced with rolling meadows. I'd heard the haunted school bus had long since been hauled away.

"It's all just stories anyway," I assured Violet at the same time I gave my shoulders a shake. "Nobody really believes that kind of nonsense."

And I didn't have the luxury of thinking about it.

Another rush of customers arrived. Thank goodness Ned Baker took pity on me and didn't insist I replace the screen in his patio door right then and there. He left the frame, and I told him I was sure Al would get right to it as soon as he came back to work. Ned, like librarian Meghan Watkins, had been a suspect in the all-too-recent murder of bison rancher Brody Pierce, and I'm not bragging when I say I helped get him off the hook. He didn't push the patio screen project.

Brynn and her son, Micah, walked in just as Ned left.

"Just picked up the kiddo from school." Brynn got in a quick ruffle through Micah's shaggy blond hair before he raced over to greet Violet. "We can take Miss Furry for a walk if you like."

"That would be great." I got Violet's purple leash and clipped it to her collar. "And it's already late. Would you mind dropping her at home?"

Of course Brynn didn't mind.

With the dog gone, I swept up what Violet fur I could, took care of a few more customers, and poured another cup of coffee. I was halfway through drinking it when Phillip Wilmington walked in.

Just like on Saturday when I ran into him at the falls, he was dressed for a trek in the park. Heavy boots, sturdy jeans, a satchel slung over one arm.

"Any word?" he wanted to know.

I knew he wasn't talking hardware.

I shook my head. "Nothing helpful."

He raised his eyebrows. "Except that Svetlana wasn't Svetlana. Everybody's talking about that."

I wasn't surprised. In a town like Tinker's Creek, all news travels fast. And news this provocative? I wondered how many theories were already being talked about at Ken's Diner and the library and the gas station down the road.

I also wondered what a guy as smart as Phillip might make of it all. "What do you think?" I asked him.

"Curious."

Well, yeah, I knew that. Except I don't think Phillip was talking about what I was talking about or even listening to me. He'd picked up that chamber of commerce booklet from where I'd set it on the counter and he flipped it open, smoothed out a page, and looked it over. Did I see what I thought I saw? I didn't have a chance to find out. Not right there and then. When he realized I was watching him, Phillip turned the page and smiled over at me.

"What's that you were saying?"

It was my turn to lose focus. Because the page Phillip turned to featured a picture of the newly restored prairie in what had been the vast wasteland that was once Helltown. It was pretty, all right, especially taken from an angle when the sunlight backlit a host of native plants. One of them was familiar looking, and lucky for me, there was an insert photo, a close-up.

Dark green oval leaves. Little red berries pocked with silvery dots.

I thought back to the Thursday evening before. To our missing bride-to-be. And to the vegetation caught behind the license plate of Charmaine's purloined purple car.

"What is that stuff?" I asked, pointing.

His lips pursed, Phillip peered at the picture. "Doesn't say. And really"—he shook his shoulders in a way that made the tools in his satchel rattle—"I know zero about flora. If it was a picture of rocks—"

I laughed. "I get it. I just wondered if that stuff grows all over the park."

"Says here"—he pointed to the caption beneath the picture—"that it's part of that new prairie planting, but of course, that doesn't mean it couldn't be found in other places. That ranger of yours, he might know."

"He's not exactly my ranger," I was quick to point out. "And Max is the first to admit he doesn't know much about plants."

"More the tough cop!" The way he said it told me Phillip didn't hold this against Max. "You taking up an interest in botany?"

"More like an interest in who's been where and why."

In an effort to egg me on, he raised his eyebrows, but I guess he realized I wasn't ready to share. A good sport, Phillip gave up and said, "I'm here to pick up a special order."

"Order? Sure!" I sprang to attention. "What am I looking for?"

"Small box, I'd say. Al said he'd write my name on it."

"And the special orders"—I scooted out from behind the front counter—"are kept in Al's office. Let me go have a look."

It didn't take long. There was a shelf above Al's desk where he'd methodically stacked customer orders. All the boxes were marked, all were in alphabetical order by name. The box marked "Wilmington" was on my right at the bottom of a pile of three, and I guess I didn't realize how much taller Al was than me. To reach it, I had to stand on tiptoe, lean over the desk, and stretch.

I caught the bottom of the box on top of the pile with one finger and nudged it closer. A little more. A little nearer. If I could move that box and the one below it, I could more easily grab the one I needed. Except the top box felt awkward, heavy, and I prodded it a little more and—

It happened so fast, at first I couldn't say what happened at all. Something rolled off the top of the box and came at me. Automatically, I squealed and jumped back, just as it slammed onto the desk.

"What? What happened?" Phillip came running and stuck his head into the office. "Lizzie, what's wrong?"

I pressed one hand to my heart and pointed with the other at the rod that had rolled off the top box and nearly clunked me. It was maybe a half an inch around and five inches long and looked to be made of lead. If the divot it left in the desk meant anything, it was plenty heavy, too.

"Didn't see it," I said, my voice still breathy with surprise. "Need to pay better attention."

"I'll say." Phillip hefted the lead rod, then skewed a look from me to the shelf. "If you were just a little taller, that thing would have hit you smack in the middle of the forehead."

"Guess I'm glad to be short, then!" I forced a laugh at the same time I thanked my lucky stars. For once, five foot two was a blessing.

When Phillip handed me the rod, I took it from him and tried not to think about how much damage it might have done. I set it aside along with my momentary surprise and felt my blood pressure throttle back. Before I could make another attempt at getting Phillip's order, he reached over and easily pulled the box off the shelf, and together we headed back to the front of the store.

According to the note Al had taped to the package, the order was already paid for, but Phillip opened the box, anyway. He'd dealt with that particular supplier before, he told me, and they weren't always careful when they packed orders.

The box contained a rubber mat. Green. Maybe ten

inches wide. There were grooves it, some straight across, others V-shaped.

Since I know nothing about what makes rock hounds' hearts go pitty-pat, I couldn't appreciate the whatever it was, but Phillip nodded his approval.

"Perfect," he purred, and tucked the mat back in the box. "Thanks for your help, Lizzie." He slipped the satchel from his shoulder and stored the box inside. "And be careful, will you? You don't need any other crazy accidents happening."

"No worries," I assured him. "Next time, I'll look before I reach."

With Phillip gone, I was able to take a couple minutes to remind myself not to forget it. I could have been hurt—or worse—when that lead rod came crashing down, and I would have to mention it to Al. I wasn't about to accuse him of carelessness, but he did need to know why there was a new and deep indentation in his desktop.

I wrote him a note he'd find the next morning when he came into the store, and then I got down to real business.

Phillip was gone—I checked out the front window just to make sure—and I scurried over to check out that chamber of commerce booklet he'd looked over while he was there, to see if my imagination was playing tricks on me. Had I really seen what I thought I saw when he skimmed a hand over that page in the booklet?

Oh yes.

When Phillip smoothed out a page of the booklet, he wasn't just being fastidious. My bet was he was trying to hide the fact that the page had been dog-eared, folded all the way down to a line in the middle of the page that showed just where someone had stopped reading.

And here's the thing.

I've seen a lot of books in my day.

I've seen a lot of things used as bookmarks. Things like tissues and ribbons and cash register receipts and movie tickets.

But I'd mostly ever seen what I'd come to think of as a typical dog-ear. One corner turned down. Left or right, top or bottom, it didn't seem to matter.

I'd only ever seen such dog-ear overkill once before.

It was in a copy of *Outlander* left under the pillow in Charmaine's bedroom by a woman who would be dead just a couple of days later.

And I knew what it meant.

Sharona had been in the hardware store. She'd looked over the booklet and paid special attention to the article about Helltown.

Why would a total stranger care about a crazy legend?

Yeah, that was the big question.

I gulped. I shivered. But I knew what I had to do.

I had to go to Helltown.

# Chapter 13

*Monday evening*

There's a certain splendor in September twilight, and that Monday evening was the perfect example. The sky was pink and edged with a color that reminded me of tangerines. The puffy clouds that floated directly above my head were outlined in sharp, metallic gray. Bugs buzzed by, taking in the last of the day, getting in their bedtime snacks. They zipped and zinged in my ear, and when one got a little too close, I swiped a hand in front of my face to shoo it away.

Here, we weren't far from the Cuyahoga River, and when I pulled in a breath, I could smell the damp. The last of the sunlight warmed my cheeks and I couldn't help but think that back in town I would have gone on record as saying this was the most ideal evening ever.

Too bad we weren't back in town.

I was warm and comfy, dressed for the adventure in jeans, a long-sleeved T-shirt, and the boots I'd once bought when my parents convinced me to join them at the Grand Canyon (where they mostly hiked and I mostly sat back and read). Still, I poked my hands into the pockets of my denim jacket. I shivered.

"Not scared, are you?"

When I turned to Brynn, I saw her tiny smile. Yes, she was teasing. No, I wasn't about to admit how close to home the comment fell.

"Hey"—she clapped a hand to my shoulder—"you're the one who talked me into this. You wanted to explore Helltown this evening."

I did.

I had to.

"It was the way that corner of the chamber of commerce booklet was turned down," I explained to her, just as I had when I showed up on her doorstep soon after I closed the hardware store and told her what I was up to. "It was just like Sharona turned down the page in *Outlander*. I'll bet anything she was at the hardware store and that wouldn't be so odd, would it? Of course she'd want to see where Al worked. I bet she read the article about Helltown and something, something made her want to come here. We know for sure that plant was stuck under Charmaine's license plate, the same plant shown in the picture. That proves that Sharona was here. Somewhere." I looked out at the rolling meadow in front of us. At this time of year, it was dotted with purple joe-pye weed and delicate white wood asters, the tall grass winding through it all just starting to tinge with gold.

"But what was she doing out in the middle of nowhere on her first night in town?" I asked, even though I knew Brynn didn't have an answer. "Why here? And why—"

Something rustled in the tall grass not six feet in front

of me, and I didn't so much scream as I did squeak. It was only natural to be startled, right?

Hoping for reassurance, I asked Brynn, "You don't suppose that giant python is slithering around here somewhere, do you?"

"Definitely not." I'd heard her sound that sure of herself before. Like when she was talking about the ingredients for her famous quiche. Or discussing the benefits of buttercream frosting over plain ol' vanilla.

I breathed a sigh of relief.

At least until she added, "I hear it hangs around a certain romance bookshop in town."

"All right. I get it." The well-tramped path through the meadow was up ahead, and I started walking that way. "I'm a total wimp."

"You always were." Brynn fell into step behind me. "Why do you think we took you to the old cemetery so many times when we were kids? You always were one to get sucked into a story, and we knew it. We were messing with you!"

I stopped, stunned, and whirled to face her. "That's awful!"

"Oh, come on! It was all in good fun. Remember the night we left the cemetery on our bikes and went to explore that rickety old school bus?"

Remember it? That had been the stuff of my nightmares for years after, and because I didn't want Brynn to know it, I turned around and kept walking.

"And how about the time we found a way into that old, empty church?" She scooted closer so she could lean over my shoulder and lower her voice. Spooky, Brynn was not. But she tried her best. "The way I remember it, you were the first one to crawl through the window."

"Only because the rest of you made me do it."

"Actually, the boys were convinced you'd run for the hills."

This was a revelation, and thinking about it, I stopped and Brynn came to stand at my side.

She shrugged. "The boys, they figured you'd chicken out. That you'd back off. And, you know, I wouldn't have blamed you if you did. Why do you think I always hung back when we went near the church? That place scared me to death."

I remembered the building well, and the night I was dared to take a closer look. The weathered paint outside, the way the rotted wood floor inside sagged beneath my Nikes. The smell of mold and mildew. The rustles from dark corners. Animals we'd disturbed? Or something more sinister?

"You showed them what you were made of that night." Brynn smiled. "And from that day on, you earned the respect of every kid in town. I guess we should have expected that when you came back to live here, you'd shake things up."

"All I really ever wanted to do was introduce readers to the wonders of romance novels."

"And solve murders."

I gave my head a shake. "No, that's not something I ever planned to do. But . . ." My sigh rippled the still evening air. "A promise is a promise, and I promised Al. Except the whole thing is so confusing, it's making my brain hurt. A bride who wasn't the bride we thought she was. A murder that shouldn't have happened because no one knew the victim. The sooner we get to the bottom of things—"

"We?"

"You don't think I talked Charmaine into watching Micah and dragging you along just for the fun of it, do you? I don't care how much they've changed and renovated and planted. Sure it's pretty, but major transformation or not, there was no way I was coming back out here alone."

From somewhere behind us, a bird called out. Just like she had so many times when we'd explored Helltown as kids, Brynn had been playing it cool. But at the lonely, eerie sound, I saw the way one corner of her mouth pulled tight. I noticed her glance from side to side, checking out the shadows. "Maybe we should have come during the day."

"I have to sell books during the day."

"And I—" The tall joe-pye weed to our right swayed and Brynn's eyes got wide. She stepped closer to me.

"I thought I was the only one who had bad memories of this place," I told her.

She tried for a cocky laugh that didn't quite make it. "Remember when we saw that person slinking through the woods? What were we that summer? Twelve, maybe? We never did find out who it was. We were sure it was one of the mutants."

Another adventure I'd rather forget. "My guess is that Sharona wasn't out here looking for mutants." I was more comfortable thinking about the mystery than I was remembering that night we'd all raced home at warp speed, totally terrified, so I concentrated on the problem before me—and told myself to ignore the legends. "What could she have been looking for?"

"Meeting someone?"

"Galina thinks it could have been Dan, but I'm not buying it. Not on Sharona's first night in town. Unless . . ." An idea flickered. "What if they knew each other? I mean, sometime before Sharona showed up here? What if he knew she was coming to Tinker's Creek, that she knew he lived here, and they arranged to meet?"

"Here?" Brynn looked all around. "Why not at the diner or the coffee shop?"

"Because they didn't want anyone to see them together?"

"I guess." Brynn lifted a shoulder. "Honestly, Lizzie, I don't know how you do it, think through all these details and all these possibilities. None of it makes much sense to me."

"It's a puzzle, and I need to put the pieces together." To that end, we kept on walking. In another few minutes, we were on the far side of the meadow, and here we saw there was an access road that looped around the meadow and led from the parking lot where I'd left my car.

"For maintenance, I bet," Brynn decided, and I supposed she was right. At the end of the access road, there was room to park one vehicle and I got off the path and went to check out the spot.

"You can get to the river from here," I called back to Brynn and when she joined me, I pointed through the trees and to the strip of water that lay beyond them where the last of the light gleamed and flickered.

"The rangers probably stop in and check on things once in a while," she commented.

But I was hardly listening.

I caught sight of something at the edge of the parking space fringed with undergrowth.

"It's the same plant!" I told Brynn. "Look at the leaves and the little berries. This is the same plant, the one there's a picture of in the chamber of commerce booklet. The one that was stuck behind Arlo's license plate."

"What does that tell us?"

I gave her a sour look. "I have no idea. But . . ." I looked all around and, though I was plenty pleased, I can't say I was all that surprised to see that the tree over on our left had a streak of purple paint on it. Yeah, like someone had parked too close and carelessly scraped a car door.

"She was here!" I closed in on the tree, pointed, and nearly jumped up and down with excitement. "This proves it, Brynn. Sharona was here on Thursday night. She parked right here, and then she . . ." I looked into the meadow and toward the trees and in the direction of the river. I even studied the ground at my feet.

I threw my hands in the air and screeched. "But why? Why? Why? Why?"

Best friend that she is, Brynn wound an arm through mine. "You'll figure it out."

"Maybe we can retrace her steps." I pulled away from Brynn and hurried to the spot where I imagine Sharona would have stepped out of the car. "Nothing back there," I said, looking toward the meadow. "And all this is under-brush here." I pointed to my left. "I don't think she would have gone that way." I glanced to my right. "Maybe something down by the river?"

"Maybe," Brynn agreed. "But it's getting dark and by the time you get there, it will be harder than ever to see where you're going. Not to mention how you're going to find your way back."

I lifted my chin and narrowed my eyes and I swear, I even sounded as cocky (it was all for show now as it had been then) as I had that night long ago outside the old church. "Are you calling me chicken?"

She laughed. "I've learned my lesson in that department. Nothing scares Lizzie Hale."

If only she knew that at that moment, a shiver scraped my back. "Plenty scares me. This place, for one thing."

"Then how about you come back in full daylight?"

"If I wait until school lets out tomorrow, you could leave Micah at the shop with Charmaine and come with."

Brynn made a face. "No can do. Catering a luncheon for the book group over at the library tomorrow and I know there will be plenty of cleanup." An owl hooted from the stand of trees between us and the water and, even though she was doing her best to play it cool, I saw the way Brynn skimmed a tongue over her lips. "I don't think you should come back here alone."

"I thought you said there's nothing to be worried about. Helltown is gone. Nothing but a memory."

"Yeah. Gone. Except it still feels weird around here, doesn't it?" Together, we started back in the direction of the car. "Maybe it's just because it's getting dark. Or maybe it's the quiet. Or—"

A noise over on our right caught my attention and I put a hand on Brynn's arm to stop her. "Except, listen!" I whispered. "It's not all that quiet."

As if to prove it, I heard the noise again, and Brynn did, too, this time. That would explain why her mouth dropped open.

From somewhere over on our right in the dense foliage pockmarked with those round olive-colored leaves and the spotted berries, we heard a twig snap.

"Animal," Brynn mumbled.

"Wind," I suggested, and I was fully prepared to convince myself it was true.

At least until we heard another twig crack. Definitely a footfall.

It wasn't like we had a plan. We didn't need one.

Brynn looked at me.

I looked at Brynn.

We took off running.

And here's the thing, even with my blood pumping and my breaths straining, I could still hear those noises from the brush. Whoever—whatever—was on the other side of all that greenery, it kept pace with us.

I ran a little faster and I would have kept going if not for the fact that somewhere near the center of the meadow, Brynn stopped to bend over and put her hands on her knees. "Can't . . . do it." She pulled in breath after staggered breath. "Go, Lizzie." She gave me a push. "I can't . . . run . . . anymore. Let the mutants get me."

She was kidding the way people do when they don't want to admit they're terrified.

"No mutants," I insisted even as I angled a look through the trees hoping to see a racoon or a fox or, heck, at this point, even one of the bears that was occasionally seen in the park, looking back at us.

Nobody.

Nothing.

Just the crack of a branch, the slow sway of the bushes in that direction, as if someone—something—was passing through.

I didn't hesitate. I grabbed Brynn's arm and dragged her along with me. Oblivious now to the colors of the fall flowers and the play of light and shadow, we twisted and turned through the meadow. In a couple minutes, my car was finally in view.

"Almost there," I promised Brynn, my breaths heavy and stuttering. "Just around one more corner and—"

The figure that stood on the path between us and the parking lot was black and bulky. The shadow blended into the quickly darkening world, tall and misshapen, a lump like a horrible growth protruding from its back.

I threw out an arm to keep Brynn from going any farther just as it twitched and stepped closer.

I tensed. Held my breath. Curled one hand into a fist, though how exactly that was going to help in the face of something so large and so deformed, I didn't know. All I knew was that I was ready, arm cocked, feet planted.

I guess that would explain why I felt like such a fool when I heard, "Lizzie! Brynn! What are you two doing out here at this hour?"

I can't say I'm much of an expert, but I didn't figure it for a mutant greeting.

My suspicions were confirmed when the shape stepped closer and out of the shadows, that shape on his back coming into focus, a satchel, not some hideous growth.

"Phillip!" I pressed a hand to my heart. "I could ask you the same thing."

"Just making the most of an evening as fine as this." He slid the satchel from his shoulder and set it on the ground, then stretched his neck. "One of these days, the weather's going to go from glorious to lousy and I'm going to regret not getting out here and exploring a little more."

"Find anything?" I asked him.

His shrug pretty much said it all. "Some interesting rock formations down by the river, but this is national park land, you know. I can't take samples. But . . ." He pulled his phone from his pocket. "I can take plenty of pictures. I'll enlarge them on my computer for a better look when I get home. You two . . ." His gaze traveled from me to Brynn and back again. "You're not staying out here much longer, are you? Once in a while coyotes come through. And there's the python to worry about, too."

I managed a smile. Always easier to do in a group. Close to the safety of the car. "Not too worried about the python.

And just wondering . . ." Phillip already knew I was looking into the murder so I didn't need to explain. "You're probably around here a lot. Have you seen anyone else around? Recently?"

He pursed his lips, thinking. "You mean like tourists?"

"I mean like the woman we thought was Svetlana Anatov."

"Oh, Lizzie." Phillip bent to retrieve his bag and slung it over his shoulder and, sure, the light wasn't the best and my imagination was still bouncing all over the place thanks to the legends of Helltown and the scares of the last few minutes, but I swear when he smiled, his eyes were cold and his teeth looked razor-sharp. "You should know better than to ask me that. If I'd seen a murder victim somewhere where I didn't think she belonged, I would have definitely reported it to the authorities. Now, ladies . . ." He backed away. "I'll bid you a good evening. I want to get back to my car before it's pitch-dark."

We watched him go, and kept on watching him until he disappeared into the quickly gathering shadows.

"Let's get out of here," Brynn said.

It was the best idea she'd had since forever.

It wasn't until we were back at the car that I felt some of the tension loosen in my stomach. I popped the locks but stood for a moment, glancing back at the meadow, telling myself there was nothing to worry about.

"I'm coming back," I told Brynn and myself.

She opened the passenger door. "Of course you are."

"And I'm going to figure out what Sharona was doing here."

"Naturally, you will."

"And then I'm going to—"

What, I can't say exactly, but then Brynn and I both

heard the sound of leaves rustling, of twigs breaking. Brynn and I both saw a hulking shape slip through the meadow, low to the ground.

"Mutant?" she squeaked.

We didn't wait around to find out.

# Chapter 14

W as disappointed you weren't open yesterday."

The woman who stood on the other side of the front counter of Love Under the Covers from me was short and squat and wore a name tag that said she was Dottie. She had a mouth that reminded me of a rectangle, hair that was mostly red but dark at the roots, and a way of squinching up her eyes when she talked that made me automatically check over my right shoulder because it looked like she was sure there was something there that I wasn't aware of.

There wasn't.

"Always closed on Monday." I smiled and gladly accepted the stack of books Dottie handed over the counter to me.

Dorothy Garlock, Samantha Hunter, Donna Cummings, Meg Maguire.

All from our Previously Read display (the books were

donated and when I sold them, all the money went to the local food bank). Older titles, but I knew they all had one thing in common.

"You like trains."

She stepped back, smiled. "You know your books!"

"I know these all have a connection with trains or subways. Great choices, by the way." I slipped the books into a bag and took Dottie's money. "And let me guess, you're with the train group that's in town."

She raised her chin at the same time she touched a finger to her name tag. "President."

"Nice!" I handed her the change. "It can't be easy arranging a full week of programming and outings to keep train people interested."

"They're a good group—they pretty much take care of themselves. There's a railway preservation society in Cleveland and tomorrow we're headed up there for a private tour. One of our members arranged that. Tonight, we're doing a murder mystery dinner on the train in the park." She wrinkled her nose. "Considering talk going around town is all about that bride who was murdered, that's probably in bad taste. But we paid to use the script and our volunteers went above and beyond as far as costumes and props. Seems a shame to abandon it all."

"I totally agree." I slid the bag of books across the front counter, but I didn't take my hand from it. "Do you know all the people who are here with the group?" I asked her.

She didn't have to think about it. "Pretty much. I've been national president for six years now, and I'm from upstate New York. We've got an active chapter there."

"How about Annalise Kowalski?"

"Hmmm, that one." This time, she did have to think. I had a feeling she knew exactly who I was talking about, she just wasn't sure what to say. "Never met her before she showed up here."

"But she's a train lover. Just like you."

"Can't imagine she'd be here if she wasn't. Lucky to get in. We had a cancellation. Old Henry Seabrook. Great fellow. From out in Kansas somewhere. Exploring an old train yard out there, tripped, and broke his leg."

"Last minute?"

"Annalise?" Dottie nodded. "Sure. As it happens, heard from Henry and that was the very day Annalise called to see if we had any spots open. Told her how lucky she was."

"Bet she agreed."

"Oh yes, absolutely. Only . . ." Dottie gave it a moment's thought. "She doesn't seem as keen on trains as I thought she would be. I mean, not like the rest of us. It's all we talk about. Annalise, she kind of just sits on the sidelines taking it all in. She's not even coming to Cleveland with us tomorrow." She shrugged, setting aside the mystery of it all. "Maybe she's new to the train game. Just getting her feet wet, so to speak. Just absorbing it all."

"And getting to know Tinker's Creek?"

"You mean . . . ?"

"I've seen her around a couple times. I talked to her the other day. I just wondered if Annalise ever said anything about knowing anyone here."

Dottie pursed her lips. "Not to me. Though I did hear her talking to one of our other members. She might have been asking about an address."

"On Main Street?"

"Sorry, can't help you there." Dottie took the bag off the counter and tucked it under her arm. "Off to a board meeting. Thanks for your help!"

"No, thank you for yours," I mumbled after she was gone. Not that she'd told me an awful lot.

Except that Annalise Kowalski decided to come to Tinker's Creek at the very last minute.

And that she came with the train group but she didn't know anything about trains.

And that she might—just might—have been looking for Svetlana (or was it Sharona?) at Charmaine's house from the very beginning.

Interesting, yes?

Even if I had no idea what any of it meant.

I was still considering it all when Max walked in.

Uniform.

Official.

I greeted him with a smile. "Good morning, Ranger."

"You up for a ride-along?"

"You still trying to make up to me for acting like a Neanderthal?"

He tipped his Smokey Bear hat. "Just doing my job, ma'am. Keeping the public safe and making sure lawbreakers are held accountable."

It would have been too easy to be annoyed at him. Well, except for that hint of a smile that brought out the dimple in his right cheek. I did my best to stay strong and be firm. "And now you need this lawbreaker to give you some help."

"More like moral support."

"Because . . . ?"

"Can I tell you on the way?"

"Can I find Charmaine and let her know I'll be out for a bit and she's officially in charge?"

He stepped back and away from the counter so I could.

When it was all taken care of, I met Max out on the patio.

"Where are we off to?"

"Just the hardware store."

"Al's back at work?"

He nodded.

"And you need to ask him more questions."

This time, he shook his head. "More like a talk than a questioning. You want to walk?"

I did. Aside from the fact that Little's Hardware was close, it was a beautiful early fall day. Cloudless. Wide-open blue sky. Not too hot. Not too cold. As gorgeous as it had been the night before when Brynn and I paid that visit to Helltown.

"You cold?"

Leave it to Max not to miss out on the fact that I shivered.

"Just a shadow," I insisted.

He made a noise that made me think he actually believed me. "Who was that woman you talked to right before I walked into the shop?"

"You were watching?"

"Just waiting my turn to talk to you."

We crossed the street and strolled across the bridge over the canal. Below us, the water rolled by and I couldn't help but think about Sharona. I sighed. "It looks so pretty from here. So innocent."

Max didn't have to ask what I was thinking about. "Not the canal's fault. People commit murder. It's that person we're after."

"And speaking of that . . ." I told him about Dottie and what I thought it meant as far as Annalise, and he gave me a smile.

"Good work."

His compliment bolstered my ego and quickened my steps.

"Now you tell me something." I waited for him to tell

me to mind my own business and when he didn't, I ventured to ask, "What about that scrap of paper I found in Sharona's hand? I bet anything you've had it analyzed. What was it?"

"We had to call in a specialist. You know, so that bit of paper could be properly dried before we could get a good look at it. As far as anybody can tell, it's a scan of another document," he explained, "which is unfortunate. If it was an original, we might have a better idea of what it was a piece of. You know, like figuring out how old the paper might be by analyzing the ink and the fiber content. From what I could make out from the markings on that scrap you found, it could have been anything from a sliver of a picture to some kind of writing, but the experts believe it's a piece of a map."

"A map of Tinker's Creek?"

"That's anybody's guess. There's not much left of it. A line here. A line there. They might indicate roads."

"Why would a bride take a map to her wedding?"

"She wanted to find her way to true love?"

An answer that corny deserved a groan, so that's what Max got.

He didn't hold it against me. "Another question," he said. "Why was that map—if it is a map—so important to someone? It must have been, right? Because I think it was yanked out of Sharona's hand. That's why what you found was only a piece of it."

Still talking it over, we arrived at the hardware store.

"Hey, you two!" Al waved from behind the cash register, then hurried around the counter and folded me into a hug. "Can't thank you enough for all you did for me yesterday, Lizzie."

"Happy to help," I told him.

"But now . . ." Al's gaze shifted from me to Max. "This isn't a social call."

"It's not," Max told him. "We need to talk to you about—"

The phone on Al's front counter rang. He went over to answer it at the same time he held up one finger toward us, the universal sign for he'd be with us in one minute. "Yes, sure," he said into the receiver. "I know I have it. Why don't you stop by and—"

Al listened for a few seconds before he said, "All right, then. Hold on. I'll go and get it right now. I know exactly where it is."

He set down the phone and scurried by where we stood. "Be right back," he said quietly enough so the person on the other end of the phone couldn't hear. "It's Meghan. From the library. She ordered some replacement wheels for the book carts at the library and"—he leaned closer and whispered—"they were just delivered this morning. I put them in the storage room myself and figured I'd move them to my office with the other orders later. But of course, Meghan has to be one hundred and ten percent positive they're really here. She won't believe me until I'm holding those wheels in my hands."

"That's Meghan," I told him, because I knew it was true. Meghan Watkins was Prepared. For anything. She didn't like surprises. Not even on a trip to the hardware store.

"I'll be back in a jiffy," Al told us, and he hurried across the store and into a room marked Employees Only.

"So . . ." I skimmed a finger over the front counter. "What is it we're here to tell Al?"

Max chuckled. "You don't like surprises, either, do you?"

"It's not that," I insisted. "It's just—"

My explanation was interrupted by a crash from the storage room.

Max sprang right into action, and I wasn't far behind. When we got to the storeroom, we found Al on the floor, a pile of boxes on top of him.

"Don't move," Max told him, removing box after box. "We have to be sure you aren't hurt."

"Of course I'm not hurt," Al grumbled and pushed the last of the boxes away so he could sit up. "Good thing those are all small parts in those boxes, or I might have been."

"Just like I might have been hurt yesterday when that lead rod nearly conked me," I mumbled.

Al looked up at me from his seat on the floor.

Max set down the box he was holding, the better to prop his fists on his hips and give me a cop stare of epic proportions.

"What?" I asked both of them and neither in particular. "I was getting something from the office and some kind of lead rod rolled off the top of one of the boxes and—"

"I don't keep things like lead rods in my office." Al stood and brushed off the seat of his pants.

"Well, there it was. And it doesn't much matter," I insisted. "It missed me and slammed into your desk. I left you a note, Al."

"Haven't been in the office yet today," he explained. "Haven't had time."

I was standing next to Al and I didn't need to look at Max, I felt his gaze move from one of us to the other, sizing us up.

"Would it have hit you, Lizzie?" Max asked. "If you were a little taller? Say, as tall as Al?"

I knew how tall Al was, but I looked his way anyway, then shrugged in a very I-dunno sort of way. "That's what Phillip said. I was getting some kind of rubber mat he'd special ordered. He said if I was taller . . ." Rather than just stand there while I explained, I figured I might as well be helpful and bent to retrieve the box closest to my feet.

"Wait, wait!" Max's warning stopped me cold. "You!" He pointed my way. "Walk out of here the way you walked in. Carefully," he added and even though I didn't understand what he was up to or what he was getting at, I couldn't fail to recognize the ring of authority in his voice. Whatever idea had just popped into his head, he was taking it seriously. I did exactly as I was told. I walked back out into the store and stopped in the doorway.

"Now you, Al," Max said. "Very, very carefully." He even bent at the waist, the better to keep an eye on Al's feet when he moved. "Okay. Right there! Stop." Max held out a hand, then pointed down toward the floor.

And heck if I was going to miss whatever it was that was going on! I leaned into the storeroom, making sure to keep well away from where Max had Al standing as still as a statue.

"See it?" Max asked Al, but before Al could answer, I already saw what he was looking at.

Except for the way the light shone on it from this angle, it would have been invisible. Clear fishing line. Strung across the floor and over to the pile of boxes. The line went around the pile, back to the front, and—

My breath caught behind a tight ball of panic. "It was a booby trap! Designed to make the boxes come down on top of Al the moment he touched one of them."

The one nod Max gave told me he was thinking the same thing.

Al's shoulders drooped. His arms hung at his sides. "But how? Why?"

"For the same reason you would have gotten hit by that

piece of lead had you been the one to get Phillip's special order instead of Lizzie," Max said.

"You mean someone . . ." Al gulped. "Someone wanted that rod to hit me? The same person who brought these boxes down on top of me? No." He shook his head and kept on shaking it faster and faster, and because both Max and I knew we had to get Al out of there, that we had to sit him down and give him a minute to breathe, I gingerly stepped forward and took one arm and Max took the other.

"Step over it," Max said, pointing to the clear fishing line. "We don't want to move it any more than we have to. I'll give Josh a call and have him come over and take pictures and look over the scene. For now, Al . . ." He gently tugged Al out of the room. "Let's get you a bottle of water."

At the front of the store, I hung up the phone receiver without bothering to check to see if Meghan Watkins was still on the other end of it and deposited Al onto the high stool behind the counter. There was a mini-fridge in his office and, careful where I stepped and what I touched, I got him water, opened the bottle, and put it in his hands. He was so shocked, I had to tell him twice to take a sip.

He took gulp after gulp and finally came up for air when the entire bottle was empty. "This is just crazy. Why would anyone want to hurt me? How could anyone? It's not like I have any enemies or that anyone would gain anything from my death or—"

It sunk in then, both for me and for Al.

He gripped the front counter hard. "It was her, wasn't it? Svet—er, Sharona. The woman was crazy. She really did think I had money and she married me and . . ."

He didn't have to say the rest, we knew exactly what he was thinking.

"No, no. Wait a minute!" Al held out a hand. "If she

thought she'd inherit the store if I"—he ran his tongue over his lips before he said the word—"died. If she thought she'd inherit if I died, she'd be all wrong, wouldn't she? I thought I was marrying a woman named Svetlana Anatov and if I wasn't—"

"It's crazy," Max said, "but I've been wondering the same thing, and I checked with our legal folks at headquarters. When you get married, you marry the person, not the name. So if you marry someone who's using a false name—"

"You're still married." I made a face. "It doesn't make a difference."

Max pinned Al with a look. "If Sharona thought you had money and wanted to inherit, if she was really that ruthless, you can see how she might have tried to kill you and make it look like an accident."

I shivered thinking about it just as Max asked Al, "Was Ms. Schwartz ever here in the store?"

"I brought her here. Sure." Even though the water bottle was bone-dry, Al raised it to his lips. "I was so darned excited for her to see the place, I wanted her to get to know it, and I hoped she'd love it as much as I do and want to work here, too."

"But was she ever here alone?" Max asked.

Al thought about it. "I don't see how she could have been."

It was all too much, I couldn't blame him for not remembering. "Your keys were missing, Al," I pointed out. "That day at the falls. You said you always kept them in your jacket pocket and—"

"Yes!" As if he actually had the jacket on right then and there, Al patted down the front of his red golf shirt. "The keys, they weren't where they were supposed to be. Do you think that means that she took them and came over here and—"

He couldn't make himself say it.

I couldn't blame him.

Of course, Max didn't have the luxury of giving in to emotions or trying to be gentle with Al's feelings, not when it came to getting to the truth. He moved a step closer. "All this makes what we came over here today to talk about even harder."

"Harder than the woman I thought I loved trying to kill me?" Al's question pinged to the rafters of the old building.

"Yeah, see, we did some digging into Ms. Schwartz's background. The only person we could find who was ever close to her was an old business partner, but that woman died a few years ago. Al, Sharona doesn't have any next of kin. That leaves just you."

I knew what it meant, and it made my insides turns to ice.

It took Al a little longer to put the pieces together, but I knew exactly when it happened. That would be when his jaw went slack. "Are you telling me I'm responsible for burying the woman who wanted to kill me so she could inherit my hardware store?"

"I'm afraid so," Max told him. "Once the coroner releases the body—"

"No, no, no!" His cheeks red, his eyes bulging, Al bounded off the stool and raced out in the middle of the store. He held a fist up in the air. "You're not going to do this to me, you evil woman. You're not going to threaten my life and my livelihood and the people of this good town and then make me responsible for . . . for . . ." His shoulders heaved. His legs shook. "Oh!" Al's wail was like a voice from beyond the grave. "This is awful. What am I going to do? What am I going to do?"

Max closed in on him and put a hand on his shoulder. "For now, there's nothing you can do except close the store for the rest of the day and let the local police have a look around. The first thing we have to do is make sure you're safe."

"Yes. Fine." Al marched to the front of the store and threw the door open. "You two can go. I'll wait here for them. Tell them to knock loud. I'm going to my workroom in the basement. Maybe I can find some peace if I keep busy."

"It's probably not a good idea," Max said, but it was already too late. Al whirled around and disappeared through a door that led downstairs.

My heart ached for him. "Poor guy. How much can one person take? A dead wife? A woman who wasn't who he thought she was? And now this? Do you think she was really trying to kill him?"

"I think we need to find out." Max pulled out his phone and made the call to Josh, and because I knew it was best if I didn't touch anything, I stood at the front counter and waited.

Which meant I had the perfect angle to see the smoke when it started coming out from under the basement door.

"Max!"

My voice vibrated with urgency, and he ended his call instantly and came running, and a second later, he shoved the phone at me, told me to get outside and call the fire department, and headed for the basement door.

When he opened it, smoke poured into the store.

"Al!" Max called. "Al, are you all right? I'm coming down there. Say something so I know where to find you."

Al didn't say anything, but I did hear him cough. Max did, too, and, with his shirt pulled up over his mouth and nose, he disappeared into the billowing gray smoke.

I did as I was told, went outside and made the call and Josh pulled up in front of the store just as the fire department arrived. I told the cops and the firefighters what was going on, and kept well out of their way. "Al is down there," I told Josh and pointed back into the store and toward the basement door. "And so is Max."

"And they're both going to be fine." My cousin took my hand so he could lead me across the street, well out of the way of where the firefighters scrambled to do their jobs, then got busy stopping traffic and setting up a perimeter to keep our nosy neighbors away.

And me?

I paced the sidewalk across from the hardware store, watching as the windows smudged with smoke and the firefighters raced in and out with hoses. I'm pretty sure I never crossed my fingers for luck. This wasn't one of those situations where it seemed that luck was enough. Instead I prayed. Hard. For Al. For Max. For the brave firefighters and cops who handled the whole thing so professionally. And I cried. Oh boy, did I cry!

I cried some more when two firefighters came out of the store with Al propped between them.

And I cried harder when I waited for Max to emerge from the thick, nasty smoke.

And he didn't.

"It's good, cuz. It's all good." Josh stopped whatever he'd been doing long enough to fold me into a hug. "Max is the one who yelled to the firefighters to let them know where Al was. Good thing, because Al had passed out. They're giving him oxygen. He's going to be fine."

"And Max?"

How Josh had the nerve to smile, I don't even know.

"Max is a superhero, remember. Batted .303 his first year in the Bigs."

I sniffled. ".304," I corrected him just as Max had once corrected me.

Josh ruffled my hair. "You just wait. You'll see."

And I did. A second later, Max emerged from the curtain of smoke and my heart beat so hard, I was sure it was going to burst right out of my chest.

Perimeter or no perimeter, nosy neighbors or not, I raced across the street and grabbed him and held him close. The smell of smoke filled my nose. My clothes were instantly covered with soot. Tears stained my cheeks and I could only imagine the way they mixed with the ash from Max's clothes and made my face a gunky mess.

I didn't care.

I hung on to Max and refused to let go.

At least until he coughed.

"I'm good. I'm fine," he assured me and the paramedics who came to assist. "Maybe—" He coughed and gagged. "Maybe a little bit of oxygen?"

They took him over to a waiting ambulance and since I was holding his hand so tightly, I guess they figured there was no use telling me I should back off. When they sat Max down in the ambulance and hooked up the oxygen, I sat down next to him.

"I was so worried, Max!" I squeezed his hand. "Al came out and you didn't and—"

I stared at his shirt and at the little piece of something familiar stuck to it.

"Max!" I plucked at the object, then held it up for him to see. It was a tiny piece of wire, coated with green plastic.

# Chapter 15

*Wednesday*

I didn't like having to close the bookshop again.

When Love Under the Covers wasn't open, I missed my customers, our book discussion groups, working with Tasha Grimes to come up with dates for meetings of the local Writers of Romance chapter. I loved touching base with publishers' representatives who called the store and, of course, chatting with the occasional author (always a thrill) who stopped in to talk about their latest releases. There was a real sense of belonging and inclusion at my shop and my customers felt it, too. In fact, it was one of the biggest drawing cards. My store wasn't just a place to purchase reading material, it was the heart and soul of a wonderful community of readers and writers, and keeping it locked and dark for another morning left me feeling as gloomy as the weather that Wednesday.

Fat gray clouds.

Chilly winds that made it feel more like November than September.

And the mood.

The entire town of Tinker's Creek was in mourning, and let me just go on record as pointing out it wasn't for Sharona.

Sure, Al had lost his wife there in the park, but we'd all lost something, too. Maybe next time a stranger came to town, we wouldn't be as easy to trust, as quick to open our hearts, as naive as to think every story had a happily-ever-after ending.

And that was too bad.

Thinking about HEAs brought my mind back to the books at the shop—all those delicious books!—and how much I missed holding them in my hands and the buzz of excitement I always got fingering their covers and wondering what surprises waited for me in their pages.

I missed my routine. Pure and simple.

A routine like in the old days. One that did not include murder.

Or the funeral of a woman none of us knew. Frankly, if what Max and I discovered the day before really did prove Sharona was out to get Al, there was no way to muster up even the slightest bit of sympathy.

It was a funny way to feel, sitting there in a stiff-backed folding chair in the town hall, dressed in black slacks and an understated army green long-sleeved tunic top, waiting for the start of the quickly thrown together memorial service that had been planned and announced only the day before.

As it always does in Tinker's Creek, word had gotten around, and there were plenty of people packing the place. The hum of their conversations filled the air. What there wasn't, not out on the streets, not there in the town hall, was one scrap of emotion. Not anywhere. Not for Sharona.

And that was maybe the saddest part of the whole thing.

Uncomfortable, I shifted in my seat. Charmaine was running late that morning and insisted I leave before her so, in her inimitable words, I "didn't miss anything juicy." I'd saved the chair closest to the aisle for her and when Max slipped into the seat on the other side of me, I was ready for him.

"Did they check it out?" Like we were in some old spy movie, I spoke out of the corner of my mouth, sure to keep my voice down. Sharona Schwartz might not have had any friends in Tinker's Creek to mourn her, but Al Little had plenty, and just like they'd come out to help him celebrate his wedding, they had showed up on this gloomy day to remind him that he wasn't alone. I didn't want to risk anyone eavesdropping, so I scooted my chair closer to Max's.

Though he was dressed in his formal ranger uniform, scrubbed and shaved and looking official and officially delicious, I swear I could still catch a whiff of smoke on him. This, I couldn't risk thinking about or I'd lose it the way I'd lost it after I was back home the day before, certain he was going to be all right and so upset thinking that things might have turned out differently, I could only console myself with a long talk with Violet and most of a pint of coconut ice cream.

"That piece of wire," I reminded him. "Is it the same as—"

"Good thing you tucked that piece you found caught up in Sharona's veil in your purse at the wedding." He kept his voice down, too. "Yeah, it's a match. You know what this means."

I did.

"She was trying to kill him," I whispered.

"Good thing she wasn't very good at it. Instead of starting a fire there in the basement, all she managed to do with her cockamamie booby trap was generate a whole lot of smoke." He shook his head, amazed and disgusted all at the same time. "She'd scraped some coating off the wires down in the basement so when Al turned on the lights—"

"Kerflooey."

"Not exactly the technical explanation, but yeah, ker-flooey."

"She was late getting to the wedding. I told you that. How coldhearted could the woman have been?" I glanced to the front of the room, to the table that contained an urn and nothing else. She may have been ice-cold in life, but Sharona was red-hot when she left this world. "She stole Al's keys."

"And made sure to do what she wanted to do when she knew everyone in town would already be over at the park waiting for the wedding to start. Josh is going to talk to the limo driver today and I'm sure he'll help us with a timeline."

"It's sad."

"Awful."

"Baffling!" Yeah, like Max needed the reminder, and when it came out of me a little too loudly, I scraped my chair even closer to his. Sure, I knew every last person there at the hall was watching us. Absolutely, I knew these people would spread the news to the ones who weren't there. Yes, I was sure that pretty soon Tinker's Creek would be awash in Lizzie and Max rumors.

Ask me if I cared.

When I saw Max come out of that hardware store, a little worse for wear but largely unharmed, I couldn't have been happier.

And I didn't care who knew it.

Not even if one of those people was Max.

After I gave my arm a scratch, I leaned my head closer

to his. "Max, this just isn't adding up. Sharona wanted to kill Al, but someone killed Sharona instead. And it wasn't Al," I was sure to point out. "We both know that."

"We both think that. We both hope that. But we haven't proved it yet, not conclusively," he reminded me. "Until we do, I've got to keep an open mind."

As stealthily as I could, I cast a look around the room. "What about Dan Cameron?" I tipped my head toward where Dan and Galina sat, one empty chair between them. "She insists he didn't do it, and don't you think that's odd? They can't stand each other and yet she's defending him."

We didn't have time to get into the psychology. Just then, the door at the back of the room opened and shut and a cold gust of wind ushered Al into the hall. The voices around us stilled. A couple of people stood, their faces grim.

At least until the door slapped open again and Charmaine sauntered in.

Until just recently, there hadn't been all that many funerals in Tinker's Creek (thank goodness), so I suppose Charmaine can be excused for not having what some might consider proper attire. Today's outfit was navy pants, a neon purple top, and a string of yellow beads so bright they just about made my eyes hurt.

"Here, hon." She wound an arm through Al's and I heard her murmur, "There are a lot of things a man has to do alone, but this shouldn't be one of them."

She walked him to the front of the hall and deposited him in a seat in the front row, then came and sat down next to me, and the service started.

And the weird thing was, the memorial service reminded me a whole lot of the wedding. A few words from Cal Patrick. A reminder that communities celebrate one another's joys and support one another through every hardship. Not one word about Sharona. Nothing personal.

And then it was over.

A grim-faced representative from the local funeral home stepped forward and took the urn away. I'd heard that Al didn't want to keep the ashes. No big surprise there, right? He'd paid for a spot in the local cemetery and since he was a good and upstanding man, he'd ordered a headstone, too. After that, he said he was done with Sharona Schwartz.

And I, for one, couldn't blame him.

People stood and moved toward where Brynn had set up tables filled with pastries and coffee. Others gathered around Al, eager to extend their support. Max crab-stepped out of our row of chairs, his eyes on Galina.

"Going to have a talk with her," he told me, and at the same time I gave him the thumbs-up, I saw my opportunity to close in on Dan.

"What a week, huh?" Yeah, it probably wasn't the most sensitive way to greet the best friend of the bereaved, but, hey, there was no use beating around the bush. Like everyone else in Tinker's Creek, Dan knew the details.

The real question was, Did he know more?

"Hard to believe we were having such a good time at the wedding not all that long ago."

"Huh?" His attention had clearly been somewhere else. His gaze was on Galina where she talked to Max.

"She's having an affair, you know," Dan said suddenly.

"Galina?" The name squeaked out of me. But, then, surprise tends to knock me for a loop. "Why on earth would you say something like that?"

He grunted and turned his back on his wife. "Because I know, that's why. It's the way she acts. The way she talks.

Oh yes, I'm sure of it. Now all I have to do"—he scanned the room, glancing from Cal to shaggy-haired Mick from the diner to Ned Baker—"is figure out with who. Hmm . . ." His gaze drifted back to Max and Galina. "That ranger's her type. Hotshot baseball player. Must have some money from his days in the big leagues."

"Believe me, he's not the guy," I was quick to point out. "They're talking about the case." I brushed a finger along the back of the nearest chair. "What do you suppose she can tell him about what happened to Sharona?"

Dan grunted. "Nothing. How could she? Galina wasn't at the wedding, remember?"

"I remember she and Sharona got into it the night before."

"And, what, you think that means Galina killed her?" Dan's face twisted with disbelief. "That's crazy. And impossible. She was home."

"And you know that for a fact because you stopped home to change clothes in the middle of the wedding."

He flinched as if I'd jabbed him in the solar plexus. "Who told you that?" He didn't wait for me to answer. He didn't have to. His gaze shot to Galina. His top lip curled. His eyes glazed over with a combination of hatred and anger that made them look dark, dangerous.

"She's a horrible woman," he muttered.

"Why don't you divorce her?"

Dan winced and shook himself back to reality and, without saying another word, turned around and walked out the door.

A second later, Galina glided by. She didn't follow her husband. She went to the refreshment table, poured herself a cup of coffee, and sat down.

"So?" When Max stepped up to my side, I didn't take my eyes off Galina. "Find out anything useful?"

"She insists he didn't do it," Max told me. "Except . . ."

The single word sparked what almost felt like hope that we were finally getting somewhere. "Except?"

"That suit she says he wore to the wedding, then came home and changed out of? She says she was going to the dry cleaners yesterday so she went looking for it so she could take it along. She couldn't find it anywhere."

I left Charmaine at the town hall, chatting it up with everyone there, catching up on the latest news and, no doubt, trolling for gossip. I hightailed it back to Love Under the Covers, where I happily flipped the hand-lettered sign, which features hearts, cupids, and a couple in a torrid embrace, from Closed to Open and settled in to what felt like wonderful, book-filled normalcy.

For about thirty minutes.

That's when my phone rang.

"Love Under the—" I didn't have the chance or the inclination to finish the greeting. I mean, not with hearing the sobbing and the deep breaths coming from the other end of the phone.

"Lizzie!" Charmaine's voice was high-pitched, tight. "I stopped home to get—get that horoscope I was working on for Jean Hathaway, that nice new teacher at the elementary school and, Lizzie . . ." She pulled in a breath. "It's the back door! It's destroyed. Someone broke into my house!"

The way I remember it, I didn't bother telling her I'd be right there. There were a couple of longtime customers in the shop, and at the same time I scrambled for my purse, I asked them to please, please stick around and keep an eye on things (they gladly agreed) and raced out of the shop and ran toward home. I was at Charmaine's just a couple of minutes later and found her standing in the garden, tears rolling down her cheeks, wringing her hands.

Our burglar was bold and determined. He'd kicked the heck out of the door. It hung from one hinge, a mess of purple paint and splinters.

"You called the cops?" I asked her, but Charmaine didn't answer and that pretty much told me all I needed to know. I dialed the station, gave them the skinny, and put an arm around my aunt's shoulders.

"Josh is on duty today," I reminded her. "He's on his way over now."

I didn't expect Max to show up with my cousin, but as he explained, he'd been over at the station talking to Josh when the call came in and there was no way he was going to sit there and wait and not know what was happening at Charmaine's.

Josh and another younger cop named Dylan went inside and Max gave the garden a quick look-see. "Your house?" he asked me.

"My—" My breath caught in my throat. My heart bumped. I'd been so worried about Charmaine, I hadn't thought about my place on the other side of the garden. Or Violet!

I went right through Charmaine's herb garden, bits of chamomile clinging to my pant legs, the smell of lavender in my nose. I zipped around the fountain (it was being wonky again and I didn't stop to fix it), and raced to my door.

Locked.

And if the shaggy head and pink nose I could see looking back at me from the front window meant anything at all, Violet was just fine.

The tension drained out of me in a whoosh. My shoulders sagged. I leaned my forehead against my front door and calmed myself. Routine, remember. At times like these, routine was good for the soul. "Violet, I need to take Violet for a walk," I told myself.

I didn't even realize Max was right there at my side, not until he put a hand on my arm. "I'll tell you what, get her leash, and we'll ask Charmaine to take Violet for a walk. Right now, getting her away from here is probably the best thing we can do for her."

He was right, and Violet, of course, was game. The promise of an adventure at hand and purple leash hooked to purple collar, she trotted over to Charmaine and bumped my aunt's hand with her nose, extending the invitation.

Charmaine took the not-so-subtle hint and no sooner was she around the corner of the house and headed to Main Street than Max stepped through the mess at the back door and into the kitchen. Since he didn't say not to, I followed along just as Josh walked out of the dining room.

"Nothing down here," he told Max. "We're going to head upstairs and look around."

They did. Max went up after them. I brought up the rear and found Max looking into the first room at the top of the steps, the place Charmaine referred to as her studio. There was a large table in the center of the room, and though she hadn't mentioned it to me, Charmaine's latest obsession must have been oil on canvas. There were three canvases laid out on the table, all in various states of being painted, and tubes of paint everywhere, some opened, blobs of color bleeding out of them.

"Looks like the burglar was in here rummaging around," Max said.

I hated to disappoint him. "This room always looks this way. When Charmaine's into knitting, the place is wall-to-wall wool. When her latest obsession is scrapbooking, you have to wade through bits of paper as high as your knees.

No." I continued down the hallway to where I could hear Josh and Dylan in Charmaine's bedroom suite. "Trust me, Max, that's exactly the way Charmaine left that room."

Of course, that explains how I was in the bedroom before Max was.

How I was front and center when I watched Josh and Dylan check out the attached bathroom, and look under the bed, and peep behind the curtains.

It also explains why I had a ringside seat when Josh pulled open the closet door and a sound flowed out of it like the wail of a banshee.

It was dark in the closet and between that and the fact that Dylan moved in lickety-split to provide assistance, it was tough to get a really good look at what was happening.

No matter.

In that one brief second when the closet door swung open, I'd seen enough to know . . . well, maybe not what was what but definitely who was who.

It would have been impossible not to recognize those round, red glasses.

# Chapter 16

Annalise Kowalski dissolved into a puddle of mush the moment Josh and Dylan got a hold of her.

Not exactly the stuff doughty burglars are made of.

Propping her between them, they half led, half carried her downstairs, the sounds of her wailing growing duller by the moment. My ears were grateful.

There was nothing for Max and me to do but enjoy the blessed quiet and watch them go.

"Does this make any sense to you?" he wanted to know.

"Maybe." I thought about Annalise arguing with Sharona in front of Charmaine's house. I remembered Annalise showing up the day after the murder. "She doesn't know anything about trains," I reminded Max.

He was quick to catch on. "Which means something other than the train convention brought her to town."

"Something. Or someone."

We both knew who that someone was.

Eager to find out more, I hurried out of the bedroom to get downstairs before Josh and Dylan left because I was going to ask (and beg and plead if I had to) to go to the station with them while Annalise was being questioned. As it turned out, I didn't have to. Annalise was so distraught, her knees buckled the moment she was in the kitchen. Rather than have to pick her up off the floor, Josh and Dylan deposited her at the table and got her a glass of water and we gathered around, watching her fight for breath. Her wailing dissolved into blubbering, and once she was blubbered out, she sniffled, shuddered, whimpered. The lenses on those round-as-saucers glasses of hers were fogged. Her makeup was streaked with tears. Her shoulders heaved.

But, hey, just like Max, my cousin is a pretty smart guy, too. As soon as she took a deep breath, Josh saw his chance and jumped right in. Before the blubbering could start all over again.

"Do you want to explain what's going on, Ms. . . . ?"

"Kowalski." I supplied Josh with the name because of course, he hadn't met Annalise. "She's here with the train convention. But you don't care about trains, do you, Annalise? If you did, you'd be in Cleveland at that preservation society today with all the other train buffs. They're gone, and you knew everyone else in town would be at Sharona's memorial service. That gave you the perfect opportunity to—"

Josh signaled to me not to say anything else. I got it. He needed to hear the words from Annalise.

She winced. "I thought I had more time."

"Obviously." Big points for my cousin, he didn't make this sound like an accusation. He pulled out the chair across from Annalise and slipped into it, leaning forward, his elbows on the table. Even in the gray light of a gloomy day, the badge pinned to his dark blue shirt glinted. Just like the beaded curtain (pink, purple, green, and gold) that hung over the window above his mother's kitchen sink. "You planned to be long gone by the time the homeowner returned."

Her nod was barely perceptible. "That's what burglars do, right?"

Josh scraped his chair closer to the table. He was an average-sized, easygoing guy with light hair and wide shoulders and I knew for a fact he took his job and his duties to the people of Tinker's Creek seriously. I bet there was more than one troublemaker who'd come through town who was sorry he'd tangled with Officer Randall. Yet now, one-on-one with Annalise, he somehow managed to sound more like a friend than the arresting officer he was. "Want to explain what you're doing here?"

She picked at the nothing on the table in front of her and dared to slide a look toward Josh. "If I told you I was after valuables—"

"I'd say you chose the wrong house."

"But I couldn't have known that, could I?" Her story was as flimsy as they came, but she latched on to it with gusto and looked around the room at the framed menus from Charmaine's favorite restaurants and the autographed picture of Willie Nelson my aunt cherished, at an old china cupboard crammed with cookbooks (and a couple volumes on witchcraft), and a china teapot decorated with purple pansies and blowsy pink peonies.

"I was desperate for money." As if trying to convince herself, Annalise nodded. "You know, to feed my train habit. Yes, you see I go to train conventions all over the country and—"

"What kind of train runs through the park?" Josh asked

her, and when she didn't answer, he narrowed his gaze, leaned nearer. "How about we try this one. How many different locomotives does the railway in the park use? Nothing to say about that, Ms. Kowalski?"

She skimmed a hand over the table. "I'm just confused, that's all. I can tell you—"

"What's the horsepower on the locomotives? When were they built? How do they—"

"All right!" Her screech cut him off. "You're right. I admit it. I didn't come to this town because of the trains."

"You're in Tinker's Creek," I said, "because Sharona was here."

She darted me a look. "That doesn't mean I killed her."

"We didn't say you did," Max pointed out. "We did ask what you're doing here. Sharona shows up in town, you show up in town."

"You followed her." It was the most logical explanation, so I couldn't help but point it out. "Followed her from—"

"New Jersey." Annalise's shoulders wilted. Her spine collapsed. She took off her glasses and rubbed her eyes, and when she drew in a long, deep breath, it shuddered through her. "Sharona Schwartz was the most underhanded, despicable, awful woman on the face of the earth."

Those of us who knew Sharona had tried to kill Al weren't about to argue with this.

"See . . ." Annalise shifted in her seat. "Sharona and my mother were in business together."

"Back in New Jersey?" Max asked.

Annalise nodded. "My mother, she was Renee McCann. Mom and Sharona started the online dating business."

Now we were getting somewhere! I controlled a chortle of delight so I could put in a pithy "And . . . ?"

"And Sharona, well, like I said, she was sneaky, sketchy,

and unscrupulous. She and Mom worked side by side for years to make a go of things. Well, I should say Mom worked. Sharona, she just mostly enjoyed taking half the profits and bragging to everyone about how she was a business owner. She airbrushed all the women's pictures, you know. The women who were looking for husbands. And Sharona, she claimed she edited the women's online profiles, but what she really did was add lies to make the women seem more interesting. My mom, though, she worked like a dog. She handled all the details. All the nitty-gritty stuff like immigration papers and travel arrangements. Stuff Sharona didn't have the patience for. Mom ate and breathed that business. She wanted nothing more than to see it succeed."

"And did it?" Josh asked.

"Sure." When Annalise dabbed the sleeve of her black shirt under her red, raw nose, I took pity on her and got a paper towel from the roll near the sink. When I gave it to her, she dabbed some more. "There are so many desperate people! Women looking to break out of their go-nowhere lives in other countries, trying to escape family problems and poverty. They're eager for a new start, even if it means marrying a man they barely know."

"And the men?" Max asked.

"I guess they're desperate in their own way. Lonely, you know?" Annalise looked from Max to Josh to Dylan in a way that told me she thought they'd understand, that just like she had, they'd seen it time and again over the years. Lonesome men, eager to find companionship. "Mom understood that. So did Sharona at first."

"And later?" I wondered.

"Sharona didn't care about the people." Annalise blew her nose. I got her another paper towel. "My mom spent hours making sure she arranged just the right matches, that the couples were compatible. She was proud of her successes, kept pictures of the happy couples, sent birthday cards to their kids."

I handed the paper towel to Annalise. "Happy couples like Svetlana and Al."

"I guess," she said. "At least that's how it's supposed to work. It's what my mother believed in, to the very core of her being. But Sharona, she just wanted to make a quick buck. She didn't care who hooked up with who. She didn't care if the marriages worked out in the end. She wanted quick results and money in the bank. And for a few years, she got her way. The business went gangbusters."

"Until . . . ?" Josh waited for more.

Annalise's shoulders rose and fell. "It happened about six years ago. Don't ask me for details because to this day, I still don't understand how Sharona managed it. Some funny stuff with the books. At first Sharona convinced Mom it was all the fault of their accountant. Sharona said he was the one skimming the profits. But Mom was one smart cookie and it didn't take her long to figure out that Sharona was behind the whole thing. By that time, cooking the books was the least of Mom's problems."

Max inched forward. "Because?"

Annalise's bottom lip trembled. "That business meant the world to Mom. And then one day, she found out that Sharona had managed to have it transferred into her own name. Lock, stock, and barrel. Mom was out. And Sharona was the sole proprietor." She hung her head and a tear slipped down her cheek. "Mom fought Sharona with all the energy she had, and all the money, too. But in the end, the stress was too much. Mom had a heart attack and died."

"And you didn't keep up the fight?"

Max didn't mean the question as an accusation, but apparently Annalise had heard it one too many times. Her chin came up. Her eyes sparked. Her voice pinged against the sparkly chandelier over the table. "Don't you think I tried? Just like Mom did. I had to. For her."

"So that's why you followed Sharona," I said. "You were looking for revenge?"

Annalise's sallow complexion turned a particularly unflattering shade of green. "You mean like I came all this way to kill her? I might have done that," she admitted, "back when it all first happened and I watched it eat away at my mom's health. But after all these years?" She looked from Dylan to Josh to Max, hoping to make them understand. "It doesn't make any sense, does it? No, what I did was try to talk to Sharona, try to get her to come clean. She always dodged me and my questions. She didn't return my calls. So I started following her."

She looked down at the table, not at the cops in the room. "And then one day when I followed Sharona, she was having coffee with some woman, and I heard Sharona say she was coming to a place called Tinker's Creek, Ohio."

"Did she tell this friend why?" Max wanted to know.

"I didn't care. I listened, got the details. My plan was just to show up where Sharona would have fewer places to run and hide. Then maybe she couldn't dodge me. I mean, really, Tinker's Creek? There couldn't be all that much going on, could there? Only I found out there was."

"The train lovers."

She nodded when I said it. "The only way I was possibly going to get a hotel room anywhere nearby was to join the convention, so that's what I did."

"It puts you in the right place," Max pointed out. "At the right time."

"Yeah," Annalise admitted. "But I didn't kill her. Why would I? When I talked to her the other night . . ." She looked my way. "When you walked around from the back of the house and saw us out on the sidewalk . . . well, Sharona was plenty surprised to see me, that's for sure. You saw how she treated me."

"All the more reason for you to be angry with her," I pointed out.

"Except the next day, she tracked me down. She called me and told me she'd been thinking about it. She said she was done with the online bride business. That it was a hassle and she was sick of it. That she didn't need it anymore."

"Did she say why?" Max asked her.

"Well, as crazy as it sounds, she said she was about to inherit a fortune."

Since Max and I were standing side by side, it was easy for us to exchange looks. I let him take the lead.

"Did she say where this fortune was coming from?" he wanted to know.

"I didn't ask," Annalise told him. "I didn't care. All I know is she said she'd have the papers drawn up transferring ownership of the business to me. She told me to stop by and pick them up."

"Sunday." I nodded. "That's why you were hanging around outside the house."

"Which I wouldn't have done," she pointed out, "if I knew she was dead, right?" When she looked at Josh, her eyes were pleading. "Right?"

"Or maybe that's what you want us to believe," Josh suggested. "That you knew Sharona was dead and you came here anyway on Sunday, playing dumb. Hoping to throw us off the scent."

"No!" Annalise slapped a hand to the table. "All I

wanted was those papers. I didn't care about anything else. Truth be told, I don't even care about the stupid bride business. I did all this for my mom. Just so I could get the business back, so I know Mom could rest in peace. And when I found out Sharona was dead, well, she said she'd have the papers and I figured . . ." Her gaze skimmed to the mess that used to be Charmaine's back door.

Josh's did, too. "You were pretty determined to get in here."

"Well, yeah. Because I knew Sharona stayed here, so I figured this was where the papers were. With nobody here, I thought I could look around and find them."

"Did you?" Josh asked.

She really didn't need to answer. The way her shoulders drooped told us everything we needed to know. "She probably lied about the papers, just like she lied about everything else."

It was a plausible story, all right, and I, for one, was willing to believe it. But, then, like Annalise, I was convinced Sharona was underhanded, despicable, and awful.

Max didn't have the luxury of letting opinions and emotions get in the way of his investigation. He edged closer to the table.

"Where were you on Saturday afternoon?" he asked Annalise.

She looked up at him. Gulped. "You mean, during the wedding? When . . . when Sharona was killed? I was in the park. I swear! I was with the train nerds. They actually spent the better part of two hours staring at railroad tracks, talking about things like fishplates and fasteners and sleepers. Whatever those are. Gads." She threw back her head and groaned. "They are the most boring people on the face of the planet!"

"And can any of those boring people attest to the fact that you were with them?" Max wanted to know.

Annalise thought it through. "It's not like I had a whole lot to say to any of them."

"But they could tell us you were there?"

Her shrug said it all.

"Then how about we try this." Max braced his hands against the table and leaned toward Annalise. "Did you know when she came here that Sharona was going to be impersonating Svetlana Anatov?"

"No. I mean, how could I?"

"And you don't know where the real Svetlana Anatov is?"

Annalise didn't have to think about it. "I don't know anything about the woman. Like I said, Mom was pushed out of the business years ago. Whatever Sharona's been up to since then . . . well, I don't know a thing about it. I can't tell you anything about Bride of Your Dreams."

I had been to an odd memorial service, in on the discovery of a break-in at Charmaine's, piled on with facts (or were they stories?) from Annalise. Was it any wonder I was confused?

As if it actually might help me get the facts straight, I tugged at a curl of my dark hair.

"But Bride of Your Dreams, that's the business you were desperate to get back. The one your mother put so much of her heart and soul into," I said. "Why did you just say—"

"Sorry. It's been . . ." Annalise pulled in a stuttering breath. "I've never been arrested before. I'm a little upset and it's hard for me to get the story straight. Sharona changed the name of the business. After she stole it out from under my mom. Bride of Your Dreams is what she called it. Back when Sharona and Mom were partners in the business, it was called Cupid's Choice."

# Chapter 17

*Wednesday*

After Annalise dropped that bombshell, I was plenty anxious to dig deeper. Bride of Your Dreams was once Cupid's Choice? The company Dan Cameron used to arrange his marriage with his not-so-dearly-beloved Galina?

Oh yes, this was as juicy a tidbit as can be, and I was itching to find out more about it. That, though, would have to wait.

Love Under the Covers, remember.

I'd left customers in charge and I couldn't ask Charmaine to go work at the shop, not after what had happened at her house. I had responsibilities, and it was time for me to set aside my Nancy Drew dreams. At least for now.

I went back to the shop, showed my appreciation to the two wonderful customers who had taken over for me by loading them down with free books, and waited.

There is the Tinker's Creek grapevine, after all. And

though it can sometimes be less than factual, and sometimes be more than a little dramatic, it is always speedy.

I knew it would take no time at all for word of Annalise's arrest to make its way around town.

"Did you hear?" Glory Rhinehold was talking even before the door of Love Under the Covers closed behind her. She scurried up to the front counter, and her silvery bob, usually so neat, was a mess around her head. Like she'd been running her fingers through it. "Well, of course you've heard. She's your aunt. She would have called you even before she called me. I'm frantic with worry. Poor Char!"

"You're headed over there?" I really didn't need to ask. Glory had a vintage wicker basket slung over one arm and I saw a bottle of wine inside along with a box of crackers, three different kinds of cheese, and a Whitman's Sampler. She and Charmaine had some serious commiserating to do. "Al's going over to fix the back door," I told Glory. "Charmaine is supposed to wait at my place with Violet. Make sure she stays there, will you? She doesn't need to see the mess and be reminded of what happened."

"Like she could forget." Glory clicked her tongue. "It's an outrage. A violation." She lifted the wine and the cheese and right before she bustled back to the door, I got a glimpse of clothing folded at the bottom of the basket. "Brought my jammies. I'm going to insist on staying at Char's tonight."

"Good plan. And if you need more wine, feel free to help yourself from the rack in my dining room."

"You got it, kiddo." She opened the door and stepped out just as Dottie from the train convention walked in.

"Told you I couldn't get a read on that one." Dottie's jaw was set, her dark eyes blazed. "A person like that can give our group a bad name."

"Everyone knows the train society had nothing to do with the burglary."

She eyed me up and down. "Why'd she do it?"

I pretended not to know.

"And what's going to happen to her now?"

"Last I heard, she's spending the night in jail. She'll go before a judge tomorrow and—"

"I hope they throw the book at her!" Dottie pounded the front counter with her fist. "How dare she latch on to us as an excuse to come into town and break into peoples' homes! Shameless." And with that, she spun around and marched out of the shop.

After all that, it took me a bit to catch my breath and once I did, I made coffee, took care of a few more sales and a lot more gossip about the woman who was already being called the Tinker's Creek Creeper by half the town, and because I realized I hadn't had time to eat anything after the memorial service and it was long past lunchtime, I went into the office and raided Charmaine's stash of Snickers bars. Just one. I swear. It tasted like heaven.

I'd just swallowed the last of it when Max walked into the shop.

I guess I didn't realize just how much I'd gotten caught up in the Annalise/Bride of Your Dreams/Cupid's Choice drama. At least not until I blurted out, "Did you nail them to the wall?"

He set his laptop down on the counter. "I'm guessing you're talking about Dan and Galina Cameron."

"Who must have lied about knowing Sharona, right? She's the one who arranged their marriage!"

"Or Dan and Galina had nothing to do with Sharona because Renee McCann took care of all the details of their marriage."

I hated when he was the voice of logic and shot my theories so full of holes, all the enthusiasm I'd had for them drained like air from a punctured balloon.

Stinging from the correction at the same time I had to admit he just might be right, I did my best to keep things professional and reined in my (maybe unfounded) enthusiasm. "All right, so maybe Dan and Galina didn't know Sharona. But they provided information anyway, I bet. What did you find out from them?"

"Nothing. Haven't talked to them yet. And before you can go off and tell me I'm wasting valuable investigating time . . ." He eyed me because, let's face it, that's exactly what I was going to tell him. "They're not going anywhere. And I wanted to do a little more background work before I"—he cleared his throat—"as you so succinctly put it, nailed them to the wall."

"So what are we going to look into?"

"I'm"—he put a whole lot of emphasis on that one little word—"going to look into the day of the wedding. You're going to help me."

"How?"

Like a magician pulling a rabbit from a hat, he produced a USB flash drive from his pocket. "Finally got the wedding video."

It was funny how fast bookshop owner disappeared and Nancy Drew showed up again.

I scooted closer to the counter, anxiously waiting for him to open his laptop.

He didn't, but instead said, "You know Charmaine hired the president of Tinker's Creek High School's video production club to record the wedding, right?"

I remembered Charmaine's frantic search for just the right videographer and how, in the end, she wasn't left with much of a choice. "It was kind of last minute," I told Max. "And professionals are hard to find around here."

He waggled the USB drive at me. "I'm thinking Bryan Hinds is probably about as far from a professional as we're likely to find. Hoping you might tell me I'm wrong and I've got nothing to worry about."

I couldn't, so I consoled him with, "Bryan's a good kid. I'm sure he tried his best. He's got a good heart."

"And from the little bit I watched of the video before I came over here, I'd say he has a shaky hand, too. I think he was mainlining Red Bull that day."

"Nervous. First big client. There was talk bandied about of Al paying two hundred dollars for his services, and Bryan was a little overwhelmed. With that kind of money on the line, he wanted to make sure he got everything just right."

"Well, let's hope we got Al's money's worth."

Since Max was still standing there—just standing there—I gave the USB drive another look. I shifted my gaze to the still-closed computer. Okay, so subtle I was not, but I was itching to find out what was on the recording. "How's this going to work? Like when we watched those security tapes after Brody was killed? You needed me to identify the perps?"

"The way I remember it, you didn't so much identify perps as you tried to deflect suspicion off Charmaine."

I was hoping he'd forgotten all about that, and to cover, I crossed my arms over my chest. "Only because she didn't do it."

"And this time, I don't need you to tell me who's who. I pretty much know everybody in town. But I thought if you watched, you could fill in any gaps. Like who's doing what, what might have happened before, what happened after, if you might have seen anything going on that Bryan missed. You know, your take on what people were saying and doing, how you remember things."

"Ready anytime you are," I told him, and breathed a sigh of relief when he finally opened the computer, popped in the drive, and started up the video.

"That's the ceiling of the park pavilion," I told Max, pointing to the screen and the (not very artistic) shot of the wooden rafters and the balloons and streamers hanging from them. "Bryan made a recording of the pavilion ceiling?"

"He assures me he's going to edit the whole thing and make it into what he called a stunning work of art. I reminded him that since Sharona is dead and was lying to Al all along, it's highly unlikely that Al's ever going to watch the footage, so artistic merit doesn't much matter. Bryan was crushed."

"When you're planning a stunning work of art . . ."

"Yeah."

The camera panned down and we got a sweeping and kind of jumpy view of the entire pavilion. Everything was decorated and the guests were starting to arrive. The camera bounced from one to another and after a minute, my stomach bounced, too. I was glad when I saw something I could focus on.

"Dan Cameron," I pointed, even though Max knew exactly who we were looking at. "He was up at the front of the pavilion, waiting with Al. And there's Cal Patrick and look, Otis Cameron, too. He's Dan's grandfather. First time I ever met him. Not exactly Mr. Friendly."

"I zipped through this part of the recording before I came over here. The first half hour is mostly just like this and not what I'm interested in. Sharona arrives, Cal performs the marriage ceremony. The whole thing is over in a heartbeat." As if he was having trouble wrapping his head around it, he wrinkled his nose. "Seems kind of perfunctory, don't you think? Kind of heartless. I mean, shouldn't there be more to a wedding ceremony than that?"

It was a surprising comment from a guy, and I should know. After all, I was an expert when it came to romance novels and I knew that most guys (and therefore most romance heroes) didn't have that kind of understanding of the poignant emotions that bubbled beneath the surface of a wedding. At least not at the start of a book, anyway. Curious, I couldn't help but ask, "What makes you say that?"

"Well, I was just thinking, that's all. When I get married, I want my wedding to be more personal, more genuine." He pulled a face. "Even though my mother will be quietly sobbing somewhere in the corner."

The thought of it made me smile. "She doesn't want to lose her little boy?"

"She doesn't think any woman is good enough for me."

"Maybe she's right."

He stepped just a hairsbreadth closer. "I don't think so. I'm pretty sure there's someone out there who's just right."

I scratched my left arm just as he asked, "How about you?"

"How about me?" My gulp was neither confident nor attractive. "Being the right person?"

Max laughed and relief—and embarrassment—flooded through me. He wasn't talking about what I thought he was talking about.

Good for me. Because I didn't have to deal with the vibration of excitement I felt humming between us.

Bad for me. Because now I looked like a total dork.

Big points for him, rather than pointing it out, he asked, "How about you? What's your mother going to be doing at your wedding?"

"Oh, I'm sure she had it all planned out once upon a time. Mom's like that. Likes all her ducks in a row. These days, I think she's pretty much given up on the mother-of-the-bride dream," I confessed.

"You've never been close?"

"To getting married? Nope. How about you?"

He had to think about it, but not for long. "Not close. I've never been that serious about anyone. Not that there haven't been plenty of young ladies out there who aren't interested." He threw his shoulders back and lifted his chin and I found myself thinking that even if he was kidding, he didn't have to convince me. He was gorgeous. He was once a successful professional athlete. He was now following his dream and living a life most people think of as macho and exciting. And as if all that wasn't enough, he happened to be a darned nice guy, too.

I guess if I wasn't so busy thinking about that, I wouldn't have been caught at a disadvantage when he leaned just a bit closer. "I've never been that serious about any woman. Not yet, anyway."

Yeah, gulping was pitiful. Not to mention tiresome. Like I could help it?

His eyes were pools of cocoa deliciousness. His aftershave reminded me of the heady aroma that rises off the greenery in the park after a summer rain. His smile was edged with just a bit of mischief, just a little warmth, and a whole lot of sexy delectability.

Thank goodness for Justin Bieber (whoever would have thought I'd say that?) or I might have been a goner. When "Yummy" rocked through the park, the pavilion, and vibrated the computer speakers, it knocked me back to reality.

Max not so much. "Music?" he asked.

"The DJ, Declanx, he was in charge of the—"

"Not this music. Your music. What kind of music are you going to have at your wedding?"

It was like one of those awful, corny questions a guy might ask at a speed dating event, and just like what had happened to me when I tried that road to nowhere a time or two, I found myself completely tongue-tied. "Not something I've ever . . . I mean, I don't exactly stay up nights thinking . . . I mean, what I mean is I haven't thought about it."

"I don't believe you." He raised his arms, gesturing all around. "You're a romantic! And romantics always think about music."

Yeah, when their heads weren't spinning and their hearts weren't pounding and their blood wasn't making funny whooshing sounds in their ears so loud it even drowned out good ol' Justin.

"Nat King Cole?" I squeaked.

"Nice." He nodded his approval. "And not bad for a song or two. Just to change things up a bit before the real music starts."

It was hard not to be intrigued. Believe me, I tried. And when he flicked off Bryan's video and logged onto the Internet and a second later, Love Under the Covers was filled with the sounds of twangy country music, I can't say I was all that surprised.

Max pointed to the screen, where four rows of people—all wearing jeans, boots, and cowboy hats—stepped and hopped and turned to the infectious beat, perfectly coordinated and looking like they were having the time of their lives. "Cowboy boogie! You know how to do it, right?"

I shouldn't have had to point out the obvious. "I'm from Chicago."

"They don't dance in Chicago?"

"Not the cowboy boogie."

"So you don't—" He hit the mute button on the computer, the better to ask, "Are you telling me you don't know how to do the cowboy boogie?"

He was so darned serious, I waited for him to serve me with another ticket: failure to cowboy boogie. I got the feeling my transgression was right up there with the federal law I broke when I got too close to Brandywine Falls.

Lucky me, no ticket, no fine. Instead, Max touched the keyboard and a new video popped up, this one of a guy in a cowboy hat and a woman in jeans and a midriff top. Before I could even imagine what he might have in mind, Max grabbed my hand.

Gulping didn't cut it.

Panic was my only option.

Cutting and running might have been right up at the top of the list, too, only the way he held on tight, I knew Max wasn't about to let me off so easily.

"Now watch." He started the video. "And just do what they do."

Do? What they do? When heat was flooding my hand and shooting up my arm and I was one hundred percent certain my cheeks were on fire?

"Get moving!" Max gave my hand a tug and spoke along with the guy demonstrating the steps. "To the right. Slide. Step behind. Slide. Then a hitch step. You know, bend your leg and kick it up a little."

He managed all this seamlessly. But, then, professional athlete and all that.

Me? Not so much.

Max wasn't one to give up. "Now the other way, to the left," he said. "Slide, step behind. Slide, hitch."

I did as I was told, nowhere near athletic or seamless. Especially that last little hopping hitch step. When Max did it, he looked like he was putting an especially playful emphasis on the beat. I had a terrible feeling I looked more like how a tuba in an oompah band sounded. Clunky and chunky. Not a pretty combination.

Like the cowboy on the screen, Max did not give up the faith. "Now forward," he said. "Step, hitch, step, hitch. Now back, back, back."

Since he was hanging on to me I had no choice but to move the way he was moving. "One more hitch. Now boogie!"

Boogie?

"Put that leg down." He looked at where my leg still dangled in the air, thanks to that last hitch step. "Step down and move those hips, girl! Shimmy and shake 'em."

He sure did, rocking his hips to the beat, and as much as I tried my best to concentrate on how I was supposed to be moving the same way, too, that just about did me in. Except then we started back at the beginning.

"Come on." He gave my hand a tug. "To the right!" Max said, and obviously enjoying himself, he fell back into the steps of the dance.

I will admit, it took me not one walk-through or even two, but by the time we started over for the third time, I got the hang of it.

"To the right. Slide, step behind. Slide, step behind." Like the beginning bumbler I was, I mumbled the instructions, but darned if I didn't start moving to the beat.

Max threw back his head and, like the true Texan he was, yeehawed. "There you go! Again!"

The next time through, we were Ginger Rogers and Fred Astaire with a cowboy flair, flawless and so fearless that when the song ended and Max reeled me in, then spun me around, I was so busy laughing, I didn't have time to be uneasy.

Together we applauded and side by side, we leaned back against the front counter, fighting to catch our breaths.

"You catch on quick."

"You're a good teacher."

Still breathing hard, he pivoted to stand in front of me. "Anytime you want to dance, give me a call."

And, oh, how I wanted to say something clever! Something like, "Practice makes perfect," but the words wouldn't come.

I managed "Yes." Which wasn't exactly scintillating, but made Max smile.

Lucky for me, I was saved from having to say anything else and risk ruining the moment, because the customer who came into the store pretty much took care of that. Erotica. Oh yeah, just what I didn't want to think about, but I helped her find the book she was looking for, took care of the sale, and by the time I was done, Max had the wedding video queued.

Magic moment over.

It was time to get back to work.

"I fast-forwarded through all the boring stuff," he said. "The party has really started now."

"There's Al." We watched our favorite hardware store owner make the rounds of the pavilion, chatting with friends and neighbors, shaking hands, looking appropriately lovestruck when he glanced at his bride.

"And there's Dan Cameron," Max commented. "He's wearing that suit Galina says she can't find now. Is it what he was wearing after you found Sharona in the canal?"

I groaned. "I wish I could say. The last thing I was thinking about was Dan's fashion choices."

"No worries." Max gave my shoulder a pat. "What about Otis? He's still sitting where he was sitting during the ceremony. See?"

I wasn't sure how much background Max knew. "He's blind. I know that doesn't completely rule him out as a suspect, but I'm thinking it's unlikely. And see . . ." This time I didn't bother pointing, I tapped the screen with one finger. "There's Sharona stepping out of the pavilion and there's Al following her."

"So he could have been going to—"

"No. No. Watch." I remembered the moment well and focused his attention on the fluttering fuchsia dress. "That's me when I went outside for a little peace and quiet. That's when I found the two of them arguing. That means we know Al didn't go off and kill Sharona then. They both came back inside before I did."

"Did they?" Max watched the next scene. "Yeah, there's Sharona grabbing a drink. There's Al coming back in. Poor guy looks like he just got kicked in the gut."

It was painful to watch.

But it proved what I'd been saying all along. "Al didn't do it. He's right there. In the middle of the party."

"For now," Max admitted, and we kept on watching.

When another flutter of fuchsia brightened the screen, he pretended to be shocked. "You said you didn't dance, and there you are in the arms of Phillip Wilmington."

"Not exactly in the arms," I was quick to point out. "And it sure wasn't the cowboy boogie. We danced a couple of times, then he went his way and I went mine. Except . . ." Bryan had apparently decided to up the ante and try a few artistic shots. The screen showed a close-up of the cake, my bouquet and Sharona's framing it. But in the background . . .

I squinted at the screen. "There!" Yeah, Max saw what

I saw, but I pointed anyway and maybe even jumped up and down. "There's Sharona. Look, she's taking a piece of paper out of her purse and looking it over. Could it be what I found in her hand? And now, she's walking out of the pavilion."

Just so he didn't miss a thing, Max tilted the screen to a better angle. "And look at that," he said, and whistled below his breath. "There's Phillip going right after her."

# Chapter 18

I figure I owe you."

What Max said didn't really explain why he showed up at the shop just as I was closing up that Thursday, so I locked the door and waited for more. "You were a good sport. About the cowboy boogie, I mean."

"It was fun." I tucked the bookstore key in my purse and started out across the patio. "You don't owe me for that. Unless—" I stopped cold and turned to Max, and a tingle of excitement shot up my spine. "Are you talking about the investigation? You want me in on something?"

"All we're going to do is talk."

He didn't need to say any more. I thought about what we'd seen on the video the day before. "Phillip Wilmington?"

One corner of Max's mouth pulled tight. "Out of town. Some kind of geology symposium in Columbus."

"He could be using the symposium as an excuse. You

know, like he's buying time because he's really fleeing the country."

"There really is a symposium. He really is registered. He checked into his hotel room in Columbus last night."

I reminded myself never to forget that Max did his homework. "Then it's Dan Cameron and Galina you're going to see," I decided. "I thought for sure you would have talked to them already."

"Seems like everyone is somewhere today that isn't Tinker's Creek. Dan and Galina went up to Cleveland," he explained. "When I talked to him this morning, he said they'd be back in time for dinner, so I'm taking him at his word and going over there now."

"And I can help?" Just thinking he trusted me that much with the details of the case made me nearly do a cowboy boogie hitch right then and there.

"You can listen while we talk," he made clear. "You can offer an opinion once we leave. It's my case."

"Yeah, but we're like partners now, right?" Just so he didn't think I imagined one session of cowboy boogie was some kind of lasting commitment, I was quick to add, "You know, investigating partners."

"More like . . ." He gave up with a sigh. It had rained early that morning and since then, the temperature had dropped considerably. Max's breath clouded in front of him, gray and wispy like the pockets of fog that stacked up against the brick wall of the bookshop patio. "All right, you might as well know it right up front because you're bound to find out, and then you'll just get annoyed. When I called Dan and told him I needed to talk to him, he asked me to bring you along."

My enthusiasm melted. "What you're telling me is that we're not investigating together."

"We are. It's just that—"

"You don't really want me to go along."

"I would, but—"

"But you don't. And Dan does. Why?"

"He told me he trusts you. He said if he needed anyone to back up anything he says about the wedding, you're the perfect one to do it because you were there, right at the center of things."

"And you'd still rather I didn't come along."

"It's not your job."

"I'm good at it."

"Just because you helped solve one murder—"

"Doesn't mean I can't do it again."

"You're not a professional, and it could be dangerous."

"It's not. It won't be. We already caught the Tinker's Creek Creeper, right? And that wouldn't have happened, not if I didn't point you in the right direction."

Yeah, this was stretching the truth. Just a tad. And Max knew it.

He raised his eyebrows and looked down at me. "We found her in your aunt's closet."

"Yeah, but—"

He groaned. "You could start a fight in an empty house! Here's the thing, you can come along with me right here and now. But only if you keep quiet and let me do the talking."

I didn't have a lot of choice but to agree. Max drove his patrol car, and just a few minutes later, we pulled into the Cameron driveway just as the door of their garage was going down.

"Good timing," I told Max. "Looks like they're home."

He unhooked his seat belt and got out of the car. "Then let's get to work."

As I'd promised, I kept my mouth shut when Galina grunted her hellos at the front door, when she walked us back to the sunroom where only a few days before we'd found Al, alone and miserable and contemplating the way his happily ever after had fallen apart so suddenly and so horribly. That day, the weather had been glorious and the landscape outside sparkled. Now, it was hushed with fog, colorless. The red wine Dan was just pouring stood out against the monochromatic scene. It reminded me of the color of blood. Or that band of raw skin around Sharona's neck when I found her.

Dan handed one glass of wine to Galina, who'd followed us into the room, kept a glass for himself, and tipped the bottle toward us.

Max put up a hand. "Working."

I dared to violate my keep-quiet promise long enough to say, "Sure, would love some." After all, there had to be some compensation for being the silent partner.

We settled ourselves side by side on the couch, me and Max. Dan took the seat across from us and, glass of wine in hand, Galina disappeared. I heard her rummaging around in the kitchen.

Max didn't waste any time. No sooner had I swallowed my first sip of a very nice pinot noir than he said, "You knew exactly who Sharona Schwartz was."

If he was surprised the cat was out of the bag, Dan didn't show it. He took a sip of wine, rolled it around his mouth, swallowed. He set his glass on the table in front of him before he said, "What makes you think so?"

"Because she arranged your marriage, for one thing." His elbows on his knees, Max leaned forward. "You knew who she was the moment you walked into that dinner the night before the wedding."

"And Sharona knew who you were, too!" The memory popped into my head and really, I couldn't have stopped the words from coming out if I tried. Not even when Max shot me a look. "That's why she dropped her drink just as she and Al were about to toast. She was floored. She never expected to see you here, and she knew her cover was blown."

"Why wasn't it?" Max asked. He wasn't one to let any grass grow under his feet. "You knew from the start the bride wasn't Svetlana Anatov, and you never told anyone. Not even Al. Why is that, Mr. Cameron?"

"Hold on there!" Dan sat back. He was wearing dark pants, a white shirt, and an orange tie with tiny fall leaves on it in shades of red, green, and gold. He loosened the knot on his tie. "First of all, if I did know the woman—"

"If?" A simple enough question, yet Max's look was so intent, his voice was edged with so much steel, Dan squirmed in his seat.

"All right. Yes." He lifted his glass and slugged back a drink. "I knew her. Right from the start. Not someone I'd ever planned to see again, that's for sure. When Sharona arranged our marriage, we met for coffee a time or two. It was standard operating procedure. You know, so the Cupid's Choice people could get to know the prospective groom and so we could talk about the kind of women we were looking for. I was working on a project in New York and living there for a few months. I'd bet a dime to a donut Sharona had never even heard of Tinker's Creek then, so you can only imagine how surprised I was to find her in Charmaine's garden."

"You didn't let on."

"No. Well . . ." Dan set down his glass, picked it up again, took another drink. "When you're dealing with a woman as ruthless as Sharona Schwartz, I've learned it's better to sit back and observe for a while, to figure out what she's up to and what's really going on."

"So that's what you were going to do? Sit back and see what was going to happen?"

"I saw how excited Al was. How happy he was. And yeah, call me a softy, but I didn't have the heart to let him down. Besides, I figured he knew. Who Sharona really was. I mean, nothing else makes any sense, does it? I was willing to just wait and see if Al came clean. To see what would happen. Galina, not so much. You'll remember . . ." He looked my way. "The two of them got into it before dinner was ever served."

"Moscow mules everywhere," I said, because, after all, I'd been invited along specifically to corroborate the facts, and this was one of them. "Obviously, Galina and Sharona weren't arguing about family in Russia, not like you originally told me. Sharona didn't have any people in Russia. And let me guess, they weren't having words about you flirting with Sharona, either, were they, Dan?"

He'd just taken another sip of wine and he choked, pounded his chest, coughed. Automatically, he shot a laser look in the direction of the kitchen. "Is that what she told you? That I could possibly—"

"That you were having affairs. Just like you told me Galina was having an affair." Another fact checked. I nodded. "Seems they must have been fighting about something else altogether."

Dan set down his glass, the better to scrub a finger along his jaw. He sat quietly for a minute before he finally said, "There were two women who ran Cupid's Choice. Sharona and some other lady."

"Renee McCann." Max supplied the name.

Dan grunted his agreement. "That other one, that Renee,

she was the one I started working with, and she didn't seem all that bad. Conscientious. When she took some vacation time, that's when I met with Sharona. But then . . ." He grumbled a curse. "My grandfather got involved. Of course he did. Otis can't keep his nose out of anything. Ever. After that, the whole thing went off the rails."

Max leaned back. In any other situation, it would have seemed like a casual move, but I knew better. I think Dan did, too. He saw the glint of interest in Max's eyes, the way he set his hands on his thighs, like he was loose, relaxed—and ready to spring into action at any moment. "Because . . . ?"

"Because when my grandfather found out that I was looking for a bride and who I was dealing with, he called the Cupid's Choice office and instead of talking to Renee, he talked to Sharona. The two of them deserved each other!" He snorted. "He's a power-hungry so-and-so who wants to control every aspect of my life. She was a money-grubbing dragon who used people, then chewed them up and spit them out. Together . . . well, let's just say that there's never been a more ruthless or nasty pair. The two of them put their heads together, and Otis, he made Sharona an offer she couldn't refuse. He paid her big bucks to find me a bride and bigger bucks to find an attorney to draw up a contract that said no matter what, there was no way I could ever divorce the bride they found for me."

It was positively Dickensian, so of course I was obliged to let slip, "But that's just loony. What kind of hold could Otis possibly have over you to talk you into anything so crazy?"

I knew the answer even before Dan opened his mouth and when he did, he confirmed what I was thinking.

"Money." The way he wrapped his tongue around the

word, I couldn't tell if he idolized the concept or was disgusted by it. "If I didn't go along with the marriage and abide by every word of the contract that was drawn up, I'd be cut out of his will and cut off from receiving any income from the company he founded and I worked for. And before you criticize"—his gaze raked us—"it's a whole lot of money."

"It must be," Max admitted, "if you're willing to be miserable in order to have it."

"It's mine by right, though, isn't it?" Dan popped out of his chair and did a turn around the sunroom, his hands stuffed in his pants pockets, his steps banging against the slate pavers on the floor. "My father worked for Otis as long as he could stand it. Without his drive and his ingenuity, Otis never would have amassed what he has now. This was my way of getting what's rightfully mine."

"It seems like an awfully steep price to pay," I dared to comment.

Whether he knew it or not, Dan's shrug was more eloquent than any protest could have been. "We have our own lives, Galina and I, our own interests. I told you, Lizzie, she's having an affair and, well, if someone else can make her happy, more power to both of them. She's such a shrew, I feel sorry for the poor guy."

"And that poor guy is . . . ?" Max waited for more.

Dan barked out a laugh. "Thought it might be you, Ranger."

Max managed a smile that didn't fool me. I saw the way his teeth were clenched behind it.

"Could be anyone," Dan admitted. "Sometimes I'm curious. Sometimes I just don't care."

"And because of the deal Sharona and your grandfather struck," Max said, "you're stuck together. Seems to me that's the sort of thing that would cause you to hate Sharona."

"Motive?" I was surprised when Dan smiled. "Of course I hated her. I hated what she'd done and how she made money on other peoples' misery. But you know what?" He slipped back into his chair. "I hate my grandfather more. Every single minute of every single day, I hate that nasty old man. So you see, if I was going to kill someone, it would be Otis. Oh yes, it definitely would be Otis."

His words were as sharp as a knife, and my stomach bunched.

Max, though, took the whole thing in, as calm as if they were discussing nothing but the miserable weather. "Why did you leave the wedding?" he asked Dan.

"Who says I did? Oh." Dan shot a look in the direction of the kitchen.

"She told me you changed clothes," I said. "And that the suit you wore to the wedding is now missing."

"The little—" The last word was lost under Dan's growl of anger, and I was just as glad. He was out of his seat in an instant, out of the room right after that, and I tensed and worried about what might happen in the kitchen.

Turned out I didn't need to. Rather than listening to a heated exchange between Dan and Galina, we heard his footsteps pound across the kitchen floor, up the winding staircase in the foyer. Just as quickly as he left, he was back, a navy blue suit in a plastic dry cleaning bag slung over one arm.

"There." Dan dropped the suit in our laps. "There's the suit I wore to the wedding. Galina couldn't find it because I'd already taken it to the dry cleaners. You know Syd at the dry cleaners, Lizzie. You know he has drop-off hours on Sunday morning. Go ahead, ask him. He'll tell you the suit was there when he got to the shop on Monday morning. I picked it up this afternoon."

What with all the moisture in the air, the dry cleaning bag clung to us and Max plucked it away and deposited the suit on the table between us and where Dan sat. "Why?"

Dan huffed his impatience. "Because I want to wear it, of course. And because Syd's had it since first thing Monday morning and that gave him plenty of time to get it cleaned, and—"

The irritation melted from his voice. "Oh, you're not asking why I picked it up. You want to know why I came home, changed, and took the suit to the dry cleaners in the first place."

"That," Max pointed out, "would be helpful."

Dan rubbed his hands together. "It was stupid," he said. "And it had nothing to do with what happened to Sharona."

Max pinned him with a look. "I'll be the judge of that."

"It's just . . ." After a quick look toward the kitchen, Dan scooted forward in his seat and lowered his voice. "I gave way to temptation. At the wedding."

My mouth dropped open. "But you swore you're not having an affair!"

He shot me a look. "Not a woman. A cigarette."

Not exactly the monumental confession either Max or I was expecting. He tipped his head, urging Dan to explain.

"Otis," he said. Which was obviously not much of an explanation, so he added, "It's another one of his conditions. The man is totally unreasonable, and totally against the use of any kind of nicotine products. Back in high school, before I knew just how ruthless he could be, I swore to him I'd never smoke. And I can't tell you how many times since then he's reminded me of that promise. Oh yeah, he's dangled it like a juicy worm on a hook. If he finds out I indulge now and then, he says he's going to cut me off."

"And yet you took the chance," Max said.

Dan nodded. "Like I said, the temptation was too much. I smoke when I'm nowhere near Tinker's Creek. I know better than to take the chance. But what with watching Al marry Sharona and wondering what she was up to, and worrying about him and about what was going to happen . . . well, someone outside lit up, and I couldn't resist. I walked out of the pavilion and bummed a cigarette."

"And then you went home to change because . . ." Max waited for more of the explanation.

"Because Otis was there, of course. And because Otis is blind. That man has a sniffer like you wouldn't believe. After I realized what I'd done, I knew I had to change. He would have caught on to me in an instant. I came home."

"Just like Galina told me," I reminded Max.

"I changed my suit."

"Just like Galina said," I commented.

"And I went back to the wedding."

"And we know that because you were there on the tow-path when I got fished out of the canal," I said.

"The next day, I panicked. I mean about the smell of cigarette smoke on my suit. Not that Galina would report me to Otis. She knows if she did and Otis was as good as his word and cut off our income, she'd be up a creek, too. I just . . . I don't know. I guess I've spent so many years bow-ing to Otis's will, I was convinced he was somehow going to show up and find out my secret. I couldn't let that happen."

"Well, then that answers my questions." Max stood, and I finished my wine and got up, too.

"I'll show you out," Dan offered, but Max held up a hand.

"I'd like to talk to Galina first."

"Sure." Dan waved a hand, pointing us in the right direction. "Whatever she tells you, just don't forget, she lies like a rug."

"She wasn't lying about him coming back home during the wedding," I told Max once we left the sunroom.

He didn't comment. But then we found Galina in the great room, watching some mindless reality show on a TV bigger than my carriage house, and Max cut right to the chase.

"You argued with Sharona about arranging a marriage you couldn't get out of," he said.

She was so busy watching two women on screen trying on party dresses, I wasn't sure she heard.

That is, until Max marched over, grabbed the remote from the table near Galina, and turned the TV off.

"You were angry at Sharona. She arranged a marriage you couldn't get out of."

She'd already finished her glass of wine and she threw one arm across the back of the leather sofa. "This I should be angry about? You are very wrong."

"Then what did you fight about that night at Charmaine's?" I asked.

"She is the one who started it." Galina's top lip curled. "That Sharona. Terrible woman! She is the one who told me I was so lucky. I have married into money, she said. I am a—a digger of some kind."

"Gold digger." I supplied the words.

"Yes, this is what she said. She said I am just like all the other women from my country who she has arranged marriages for. That we only care how much money we can . . . groom?"

"Grub," I said. "And money wasn't what you were looking for?"

Galina laughed. "Of course it was! It was an extra, a bonus. But I would have come here anyway to marry Dan, even if there was no money. Just to start a new life. Maybe . . ." She studied her empty wineglass. "Maybe we would be happier if we had no money. But you see . . ." When she looked our way again, she smiled. "I had no reason to kill Sharona. She did right by me. I am sitting pretty, yes?"

"Even though your husband thinks you're having an affair?"

She snorted and stood. "Dan is miserable. So he makes everyone around him miserable. He makes up stories, yes? He holds in his anger and when he sees Sharona, he is very, very angry."

"Angry enough to kill her?" Max asked.

She shot him a look. "I told you, he did not, but I am thinking. About the suit."

"The one he picked up from the dry cleaners today."

"He told you this?"

"He told me he'd been smoking, and he didn't want Otis to find out about it."

Galina made a little noise under her breath. "This is what he says, yes? But you know the truth?" She came to stand near us and she didn't speak until she darted a look over our shoulders to make sure Dan was nowhere near. "Dan, he has never been a smoker. Never in his life."

"Thank you for the information, ma'am." Max nodded, and together, we left the house.

"Well"—I buckled my seat belt—"where did that get us?"

"More questions," Max admitted, and he wasn't happy about it. He wheeled out of the driveway. "Was Dan telling the truth? Or did he come home and change because he got soaked when he tossed Sharona into the canal?"

# Chapter 19

*Thursday evening*

Truth be told, I was hoping we'd leave the Cameron house and head right to Nick's for pizza. It was late, and I was running on a glass of red wine. Oh, how I craved a slice adorned with sausage and banana peppers!

That, of course, is the reason I sat up and paid extra attention when Max drove only so far down the driveway, then made a sharp left turn. I knew what he was thinking and where he was going, and it wasn't to dinner.

That explains why I grumbled.

From his seat behind the wheel, he slid me a look. "We're right here. There's no use going all the way back to town and coming out here another day."

"Yeah, but—"

"You're the one who wanted to be in on the investigation."

I did, so I kept my mouth shut, thanked my lucky stars he hadn't taken me home and dropped me off before he came back to the Cameron compound, and watched as the scene outside the car window changed little by little.

As I know I've mentioned, Dan and Galina's house was neat and chichi, the landscaping was pristine. I wouldn't go so far as to say the house was welcoming. After all, Dan and Galina lived there. But it was certainly as elegant as any house in a trendy decorating magazine. No heart. No warmth. No personality. But it sure had style!

Now, as we twisted and turned along a very long drive that led deeper into the property, it seemed as if the trees, tame and contained on Dan's lot, were a little more wild. Before I knew it, they hugged the pavement on either side of us and their branches met overhead, blocking out what little daylight was left. The grass here wasn't neatly cut. It clumped between the tree trunks and once or twice— thanks to the gathering darkness, the drifting fog, and my overactive imagination—I thought there were people with crazy hairdos crouched there in the woods, their eyes watching our every move.

This, I did not bother to mention to Max. He is, after all, a cop and thus, a man of logic, and besides, I didn't want him to think I was loony.

It wasn't my imagination, though, when we rounded a turn and got a gander of the house up ahead. I blurted out, "Oh, my."

Max slowed the car and gave the hulking mansion a careful look. "*The Munsters*?" he asked. "Or *The Addams Family*?"

It looked like Max enjoyed streaming old TV shows just like I did, and I thought back to bingeing the crazy monster shows at the same time I tallied up the architecture of the house in front of us. "Steps up to the front porch," I said. "And a lancet window above that. See?" I pointed through the gloom. "Tall, narrow, pointed arch at the top. Could the whole place be any more Gothic? The way I remember it, the TV Addams family lived in a place that was a little more Italianate. You know, a square and neat-looking house, like a Renaissance villa. This is *Munsters.* Definitely *Munsters.*"

Max hummed a couple bars of the theme song. Which gave me a new appreciation for his knowledge of the arts. "Let's hope Herman doesn't meet us at the door."

There was only one way to find out.

We parked and made our way through the fog that swirled around our feet to those steps (yes, they were creaky) to Otis Cameron's front porch. Max rang the bell.

Unlike at the Munster house, it did not play Chopin's Funeral March.

We waited, and a minute later, a light flicked on behind the heavy red draperies that covered the front windows.

The door was opened by the man I'd seen with Otis at the wedding. Fortyish, khakis, white golf shirt, Crocs. He had short-cropped dark hair and wide shoulders. He introduced himself as Charles, and Charles's expression? It wasn't as welcoming as it was simply tolerant.

At least until Max explained who he was and why he was there.

Charles stepped back so we could walk into the house.

Yeah. *Munsters.* Definitely.

Those heavy curtains, the color of blood.

A marble floor.

Oil portraits of the long dead lining the walls.

A chandelier that looked as old as the house and flickered off and on just as we walked in, throwing scattered shadows against the walls.

"Mr. Cameron doesn't like change." As if he were reading my mind and thinking what I was thinking—that the place looked like it had been built when Victoria was queen and had been suspended in amber since—Charles led us down a hallway paneled in dark wood that gleamed with the reflection of the light that glinted from silver sconces long since past needing to be polished. "When you're blind," he explained, "it's easier to maneuver around the house when you know exactly where everything is. Please don't touch anything."

He stopped at a closed door and rapped it lightly with his knuckles.

"Mr. Cameron?" Charles opened the door just enough to peek inside. "You have visitors. A Ranger Alverez from the park and a Ms. . . . ?" He'd never gotten my name or figured out that I was about as far from official as it was possible to get, so it was just as well that we heard Otis bark out from inside.

"I'm having my dinner. Why are you bothering me?"

"If you'd like"—Max raised his voice—"we can wait right here until you're done."

Otis grumbled a word and Charles got the message. He opened the door wider and waved us inside.

I can't say I was surprised by the dining room. More dark wood paneling. A sideboard with two serving dishes on it. A silver coffeepot. A dining room table big enough to seat twelve but with only one place set at the head of it and one person sitting there.

Otis was wrapped in a red smoking jacket, and just as I stepped into the room, he rubbed the last of a piece of bread around the beef stew gravy on his plate.

"I know you." He pointed my way with the sopping bit of bread. "You were at the wedding."

I walked across an Oriental rug in rich shades of blue and green. "You have an incredible memory, Mr. Cameron."

"Don't be ridiculous." He popped the bread down and chewed with his mouth open. "My memory has nothing to do with it. It's your smell. Shampoo. Green tea and honey. You were the maid of honor at that ridiculous wedding. Charles here"—he knew exactly where his aide was standing and looked in that direction—"he told me you were as cute as a button in that pink dress of yours that day. Were you?"

"Pink's not my color," I admitted.

When Otis laughed, the sound reminded me of a chain grinding over metal. "It's refreshing to meet an honest woman, and now you know Charles thinks you're good-looking. What do you think of that?"

I, too, looked Charles's way and saw a blush race up his neck and into his ears.

"Charles is being kind."

"And you're interrupting my dinner." His hands on his knees, Otis turned Max's way. "What is it you think I can do for you, Ranger? Or maybe there's something you can do for me. You've already talked to my good-for-nothing grandson. I know that for a fact. Did he admit he was smoking at the wedding? I say yes. Charles here swears he never saw a thing. But then," Otis huffed, "Charles is a terrible liar."

Max was smoother than a chocolate malt over at Frosty Cones when he answered, "We're not here to talk about your grandson. We're here to ask you about Sharona Schwartz."

"Yeah." Otis scrubbed a napkin across his chin. "Figured you would be eventually."

Charles put a piece of apple pie on a china plate in front of Otis, and he finished half of it before he added, "You're going to ask if I knew that woman."

"Did you?"

He wolfed down the rest of the pie and tossed the napkin at the table. It missed by a mile and, his footsteps muffled by his Crocs, Charles stepped forward and plucked it from the floor. "I sure didn't see her at the wedding, did I?"

Max didn't rise to the bait. Or give Otis the satisfaction of getting annoyed by the irritation that colored every one of the old man's words. "I didn't ask if you saw her, I asked if you knew her."

Considering this, Otis cocked his head. "Why isn't that other one talking? The cute one? Why don't you have anything to say?"

"Let's just say I'm observing," I pointed out.

At which Otis croaked out another laugh. "Something else I can't do. At least not with my eyes. No." He turned just enough in his seat so that his face was illuminated by the light of the chandelier over the table. It was not an attractive face. For a scrawny man, he had large features. His nose was doughy. His cheeks sagged. His ears were too big, and I wondered if he knew that when Charles shaved him (because after all, Charles was his caregiver and must have provided those kinds of services for his employer), he'd missed a spot on Otis's left jawline. The patchy bristles of gray reminded me of those clumps of grass along the driveway, wild and uncut.

"I didn't see the Schwartz woman at the wedding," Otis barked, "but naturally, I heard her talking. And, yes, phony accent or no phony accent, I recognized her voice. Svetlana Whatever? Not a chance. I knew exactly who she really was."

"But you didn't say anything," I pointed out. "Not to anyone."

He waved a dismissive hand. "Why should I? Figured

she was up to something and figured it was none of my business. Or maybe . . ." When he grinned, the light sparked off his dentures. "Maybe that Schwartz woman and Al, maybe they were into some kind of fantasy game. You know? Her pretending to be some mysterious woman from another country. Him acting like she was taking him in when he knew all along what was going on." He wiggled sparse, bristling eyebrows.

"But," I pointed out, "if that wasn't what was going on, if Al didn't know, you must have known he might get hurt by whatever Sharona was up to. Like everyone else in town, you've known Al all his life. You know he's a decent guy. He didn't deserve to be treated so badly."

Otis's top lip curled. "Well, I didn't know he was going to be treated badly, did I?"

"You knew Sharona wasn't the most honest person on the face of the earth," Max said.

As if he had to think about it, Otis pursed his lips. "You think so? Why? Because she helped me put together that happy little match between Dan and Galina? She got me what I wanted: an ironclad way to make sure my grandson doesn't fritter away his life. And just so you know, getting what I want is the only thing that matters to me. And what I want now"—he scraped his chair back—"is to go to my library like I do every evening after dinner. And then I'm going to have a cigar and a glass of sherry. And I'm going to be left alone."

"A cigar?" Oh, how I wish Otis could see. Then he couldn't miss the dodgy look I gave him. "When you've made Dan promise he'll never use tobacco?"

Otis croaked a laugh and pointed a finger at me. "I told you. I knew you talked to him about his smoking. That proves it, doesn't it?" As thrilled as if he'd won the lottery, he slapped a hand to the table. "That proves that no-good grandson of mine is smoking behind my back."

"It proves you're a hypocrite," I said. "You won't let Dan smoke, but—"

"Do as I say, not as I do," Otis growled. "What I do in my house is my business and my business only. And what I want to do right now is to be left alone. There's nothing more I can tell you. Unless"—his face cracked with what was almost a smile—"you think my grandson killed the Schwartz woman, don't you?"

"We're just beginning our inquiries," Max said. "We don't know anything definitive yet."

"Well, if he did"—Otis slashed a hand through the air—"he's out of the will for sure."

"But he's your family." Yeah, I knew it would get me nowhere to debate with Otis. Like he said, his house, his rules, and really, it was totally none of my business. Still, the thought rankled. "Why are you looking for excuses to cut him out of your will?"

"More for me, then, isn't there?" Otis hauled himself out of his chair, and instantly Charles offered his arm and the two of them moved toward the door.

"And what are you going to do with it all?" I asked.

He stopped directly in front of me, and if I didn't know Otis was blind, I would have said he was sizing me up. And finding me sorely lacking. "Maybe I'll leave it all to Charles here."

I wonder if he realized Charles rolled his eyes.

"Or maybe I'll give it to a charity. Or burn it in the backyard one of these chilly nights. I only know that for now—"

"For now," Max put in, "as long as your grandson abides by the terms of his marriage contract—"

"And never smokes," Otis shot back.

"And never smokes," Max echoed.

"And never drinks," Otis spit out.

I didn't dare look at Max or I knew—somehow—Otis would find out about the pinot noir.

"Bah!" Otis waved a hand and went to the door. "If he killed her, he had reason to kill her," he said, and chuckled. "He blames her for all his troubles with Galina. You'd think, though"—he grinned—"if he wanted to kill someone, it would be me."

Max waited for just the right moment. Just before Otis and Charles stepped into the hallway, he asked, "And if you killed her?"

Otis whirled to face us. "I didn't have a reason, did I? Schwartz and I, we did our deal and we haven't talked to each other since. If you're really still looking for suspects, there's always Galina, of course. Foolin' around, you know."

"With . . . ?" Max asked.

"Who cares. Woman should know she has it good. Dan and Galina . . ." He shook his head and kept on going down the hallway. "They ought to just learn to get along."

A minute later, we heard a door close and just after that, Charles returned to the dining room.

"He was with me at the wedding," he said as if he knew what Max was going to ask. "The entire time. There's no way he could have . . ." He couldn't make himself say the words, so he shook his shoulders and darted me a look. "And as far as me saying you were cute—"

"Hey!" I gave him a smile. "Cute isn't a bad thing."

He walked us to the foyer and just like when we walked in, I imagined the eyes of all those people in the old portraits were watching us.

A woman with frizzled hair in a gray gown, her expression as grim as her clothing.

A man standing with a spaniel at his side, a rifle over his shoulder.

Three men seated around a wooden table, a map in front of them, pointing, talking. The light that fell on their faces came from the candles in holders on the wall, and the man in the center, lean and hard, had to be a Cameron. He had the same mean look in his eyes as Otis did.

The man to his left had bulging forearms. His fingers were as thick as sausages. The man to the right had a long gray beard and the firelight gleamed in his dark eyes.

"Relatives?" I asked Charles.

He looked over the painting as if he'd seen it so many times, it was just another detail in a house jam-packed with history. "I suppose. Otis wouldn't have the painting otherwise. He sees himself as the culmination of all these people. And he figures that's the only reason they were ever alive. Just so their lives could lead to his."

It was not a comfortable thought, and I wasn't able to shake it until we were outside on the rickety front porch. I pulled in a long breath of cold, damp air and watched Max do the same.

"Pizza?" he asked.

He didn't need me to answer.

I usually do takeaway from Nick's Pizza and Pasta Emporium, a mainstay of the Tinker's Creek culinary scene. But, then, I usually had something to do at home, like catching up on my reading or taking care of Violet. I called Charmaine on our way back into town, and she not only promised to walk and feed Violet but to take her home for what she called "a girl's night." Violet, I knew, would be thrilled, and having the dog in the house would make Charmaine feel a little safer. It was a win-win all around.

Nick's was hopping, but we scored a table by the window, ordered, and sat back. The wonderful aromas of pizza sauce and cheese beat the smell of musty Munster house any day!

I squeezed lemon into my ice water and sipped. "It's all crazy making, isn't it?" I asked Max.

"You got that right." He'd ordered a glass of milk—I mean, really, who drinks milk with pizza?—and he took a gulp. "I never did think Otis did it."

"It wouldn't seem he was capable, but since Charles says he was with Otis through the whole wedding—"

"Charles, who thinks you're cute."

Was that the tiniest spark of jealousy I heard in Max's voice?

Because I liked to think so, I grinned. "What's wrong with cute?"

"Not a thing. If you're a bunny rabbit. Or a toddler. Or a bug's ear. You, however, are a grown woman, and you'd think ol' Charles would have noticed that, in addition to being cute, you're also capable and intelligent."

I had to brush aside the compliments. Before they swirled through my head and made me say or do something crazy. "I was cute in my pink dress. You missed it. By the time you saw me—"

"You were sopping wet, smelled like stagnant water, and looked like what the cat dragged in."

"That bad?"

"Not cute."

I couldn't argue, so instead I said, "Charles didn't do it, either. He had no motive. And besides, Otis is so shrewd, he would have known if Charles slipped away during the wedding."

"And I don't think Annalise is our perp," Max said. "She wanted those papers from Sharona that transferred the business to her. She wouldn't have risked killing Sharona before she got them. And we know she didn't get them because she wouldn't have risked breaking into your aunt's house if she already had what she wanted."

He was right. I sipped and thought some more and got back to the same ol', same ol' nowhere place I'd been for nearly a week. I was better off thinking about something else. Too bad that something else wasn't any cheerier than our discussion about murder.

"And what about the real Svetlana?" I asked as I'd asked so many times before. "Every time I think about her, I get more worried."

"The FBI is checking," Max said. "So far, nothing. We might have to face the fact that she could be dead."

"Or out there. Alone." I glanced out the front window and the fog that gathered in the nooks and crannies of Tinker's Creek, and I shivered. "That maybe would be even worse. If she doesn't speak much English, if she doesn't have any money or any identification, who knows what kind of trouble she could be in."

He reached a hand across the table and gave my hand a squeeze. "All we can do is keep looking."

"For the real Svetlana and for the killer."

"And for dinner." When the waitress brought our pizza to the table, Max breathed in deep, smiled, and dished it up. He handed me the first slice. "We'll figure it out," he assured me, and I liked to think he was right.

The big question was, when?

* * *

W‌hen?

It's not like I'm an expert or anything.

I mean, it was only my second murder investigation and there had been plenty of bumps in the road.

But when, it turned out, was exactly at three forty-seven the next morning.

That's when I sat up in bed, suddenly wide-awake and seeing what I should have seen hours earlier.

# Chapter 20

Of course I called Max. I mean, not right then and there at three forty-seven in the morning because I figured he probably wouldn't have appreciated that. I waited until six thirty. He didn't answer.

My next call was to Charmaine to ask her to please, please open the shop that day.

And the third call?

That was to Al, of course, who swore after all I'd done for him over the past week, he didn't mind going to the (now booby-trap-free) hardware store early. No matter what I wanted there.

What I wanted was a good look at the portrait that hung behind the cash register and after I got it and confirmed what I suspected, I jumped in my car and went back to the Cameron compound.

It was early, and the sun was having a hard time breaking through the veil of fog that still wreathed Otis's house.

The light was anemic. It snaked around the upstairs porch with its witch-hat roof and crawled between the shrubs near the front porch. It outlined the branches of trees and made them look like skeleton fingers.

I climbed the creaky steps and rang the bell, and when Charles opened the door, he was still dressed in green-and-white-striped pajamas, his trusty Crocs on his feet.

"He's not up yet," he said instead of greeting me.

"I don't really need to talk to him. I mean, not yet, anyway. I just wondered . . ." I leaned forward a tad, enough to peek into the foyer. "I saw a painting. Last night. If I could just take another look?"

He had to think about it and, believe me, I didn't hold this against Charles. He would have had an easier job if the Munsters really did live there and he had to deal with Eddie's pet dragon, Spot.

"I'll be quick," I promised. "And quiet."

That was enough to convince Charles. And, who knows, maybe being cute helped, too. He ushered me inside and I scooted right to the painting of the three men seated around a table, looking at a map. I took a few quick pictures of it with my phone before I said, "That's got to be a Cameron, right?" I pointed toward the mean-eyed man in the center of the group. "And this one, the one with the flowing beard—"

"That's Junius Little and you know it, or you wouldn't have come back here."

In answer to my question, I heard Otis's voice behind me and cursed my luck. I should have known he wouldn't miss a trick. Or a stranger in the house.

"The real question, young lady, is why do you care?"

I don't know why I bothered, but I pasted on a smile before I turned to him. He was wearing the same red satin smoking jacket he'd had on the night before, his feet poked into gray slippers, his hair a grizzled nimbus around his head. "I didn't mean to disturb you," I told him.

"Then you shouldn't have come. And Charles . . ." When he looked the way of his caregiver, Otis narrowed his eyes and bared his teeth. "Charles shouldn't have let you in."

"I just wanted to see the painting again," I said.

"Because . . . ?"

"Because this is your ancestor, isn't it? One of the men in the portrait." A thought struck and feeling suddenly like an idiot, I made a face. "Have you ever seen it?"

"You think I've been blind all my life?" Otis spat out. "Macular degeneration. Age related. Just wait. Live long enough and all your body parts start to go. You'll see. Yeah, I've seen that painting. A thousand times. Back in the day."

"Then you'll remember that you bear a strong resemblance to the man in the center of it."

Otis barked a laugh. "Good-looking, is he?"

"He had your eyes," I said, neatly avoiding his question. "Or I guess I should say, you have his."

"Ezekiel Cameron. My great-great-great-grandfather."

"He knew Junius Little."

Otis scratched a finger along his doughy nose. "Not surprising. In those days, there weren't many settlers in these parts. The men who worked the canal must have all known one another."

"But maybe it was more than that?" I suggested. "I mean, when you have your portrait painted with someone, that must have been a really big deal. They must have known each other well."

"Does it matter?"

"I don't know," I had to admit. "That's what I'm trying to figure out."

"By bothering me."

"Like I said, I didn't mean to."

One corner of his mouth lifted and for a second, I thought he might actually smile.

"Who's the other man," I asked in that one moment when I had the upper hand. "The man with the big muscles and the thick fingers?"

Otis snorted. "They all worked on the canal together. Ezekiel, Junius, Lemuel. Hard work. Sure to break down a man. Either put him in his grave or in the poorhouse."

I looked over the painting again. Though the men were not elegantly dressed, their clothes looked warm and comfortable, their boots were sturdy. "They look prosperous enough."

He grunted. "Hopeful more than prosperous. They were partners. In business together."

"Junius Little owned the hardware store then?"

"From what I've read in the family history, when this picture was painted, they were all still working on the canal. That's when they decided to get together and run their side business. Junius started the hardware store a few years after this portrait was painted. My ancestor . . ." He looked at the exact spot where the picture hung. "He worked on the canal for years, then went on to work for the railroad when it came through. Put down roots here, the two of them, helped settle the area."

"And Lemuel?"

"Went back east. Couldn't take the life. The way I heard the story, couldn't get along with Junius or Ezekiel or anyone else, either. Imagine anyone not being able to get along with one of my kin!"

"What happened to him?"

"Who cares." Otis waved a dismissive hand. "These days, we'd call Lemuel Schwartz a loser."

My heart stopped cold, then whacked back to life so hard, I flinched. My blood shot through my veins like fire. My brain kicked into high gear, then my more sensible self told me I was being too fanciful, too suspicious.

I told it to shut up and went with my gut.

"Schwartz? Why didn't you . . . how could you . . . Why didn't you tell anyone?" I stammered.

"Lots of people are named Schwartz. It doesn't mean anything."

"But it could. It might. The name of our murder victim is the same as the name of the man your great-great-great-grandfather was once in business with. Don't you get it? Haven't you heard the rumor like everyone else in town has? Sharona came here to marry Al because she thought Al had money. Lots of money. What if she thought that money went back to the business her ancestor owned with Al's? If she thought the business was still viable, or she thought that somewhere down the line, it had made them piles of money—"

"It didn't," Otis assured me. "Because if it did, I'd know it, wouldn't I? Some of that money would be mine."

"And you don't have any of it."

"Bah." He turned and started to shuffle down the hallway, then spun around again. "I've got old diaries. I've seen old papers. No one ever made one, single solitary penny off that partnership. Lemuel, he claimed they did, even took Ezekiel and Junius to court over it. But he could never prove a thing. No, it was a go-nowhere idea from the start, and Lemuel, he just wouldn't accept the fact. That's why he went crawling back to New Jersey. Too proud to admit he was wrong. Now, Charles!" Otis turned and barked out the name. "Where's my morning coffee?"

"Coming right up." Charles hopped to and skittered past me and I knew I'd been dismissed.

Except I wasn't quite ready to give up.

"Just tell me one more thing," I said, following Otis as far as the dining room doorway. "What were they up to? It looks like they have a map in the portrait. Were they land speculators? Farmers? What kind of business did they start together?"

As if I were so insignificant, he'd already forgotten I was there, Otis paused and turned, his mouth screwed up with confusion. "What's that? Oh, the business. You mean Ezekiel, Junius, and Lemuel's business. Makes perfect sense they'd be looking at a map. Those three, they staked a claim to a gold mine."

Yes, yes, of course I called Max again. As soon as I got back to my car. His phone went right to voice mail and when I called the ranger office thinking I might have a better chance of catching him there, I found out he was in Cleveland for an all-day conference.

Didn't it figure?

I called his cell a second time, left a message, telling him I finally felt I was onto something significant, and did the only other thing I could think to do.

I went in search of information, and of the one person I knew might be able to help. After all, if anyone could tell me about gold mines, it would be Phillip Wilmington.

I didn't know Phillip well, but in Tinker's Creek, where the hills are always alive with the sound of gossip, I'd heard enough about him to know he'd recently built a home on the outskirts of town on property once owned by the Gordon family. The Gordons had a daughter the same age as me. During the summers I visited Charmaine, we used to hang out. I knew exactly where I was going.

I found the newly built log cabin with a huge stone chimney, a roomy front porch, and a view of the park with no problem.

Trouble was, Phillip wasn't home.

I didn't have his phone number so I wrote a note, *Please call when you have a chance.* I'd just tucked it in his front door when his pickup truck rolled up the driveway.

He got out, carrying two grocery bags.

"Lizzie!" He waved and closed in on me. "You're out and about early."

"Sorry to bother you." I waited for him on the porch, and when he unlocked the door and motioned me inside, I stepped into a wide-open great room with a huge fireplace, hardwood floor, and leather furniture.

It was a guy's sort of place, rugged and outdoorsy. There was a shelf full of books nearby and, of course, I had to take a look. Science. Rocks. Fossils. None of it a surprise.

"Coffee?" Phillip asked.

I'd been so anxious to talk to Al and then Otis, I hadn't had any before I left the house. I followed Phillip into the kitchen and I was glad to see he was something of a coffee snob. None of those easy-to-use but not always tasty coffee pods for Phillip. His machine was state-of-the-art, and he ground his own beans. Once he added water and started making the magic happen, he leaned back against the rustic wood cabinets and crossed his arms over his chest. "What can I do for you?" he asked.

"You can tell me about gold mines in Ohio."

Was that a flash of surprise I saw on Phillip's face?

Or was there something more to the there-and-gone expression? The same something that caused him to push away from the counter to busy himself emptying those grocery bags he'd brought inside? The ones that didn't seem important until just that moment.

He stowed a bag of Oreos in the cupboard along with a jar of honey. "You thinking of getting into prospecting?"

"You're telling me I wouldn't have to go out west for that?"

He closed the cupboard and went through the other bag, putting away orange juice, half-and-half, a pound of butter. "You'd have a better chance of finding gold in other places, that's for sure."

"But it's possible to find it around here?"

Before he gave me his full attention, he smooshed together the blue plastic grocery store bags and deposited them next to the fridge in a container marked Recycle. "Why are you asking?"

"Just thinking about possibilities. Is it? Possible?"

By this time, the coffee had finished brewing and he poured two mugs of it, asked if I wanted cream or sugar, then led me out of the kitchen and back to the great room. Sipping his coffee, he scanned the bookshelves, found what he was looking for, and pulled out an oversized slim volume. He took it over to a desk near the window, sat down with it, and flipped open the book.

"Look." He flattened the pages of the book so I could take a better look. "Here's a map of Ohio, and it shows all the places where, over the years, gold has been found."

I whistled low under my breath. "Who knew Ohio was some hotbed of riches."

Phillip chuckled. "I didn't say it was a hotbed. And I didn't say there were riches. I just said gold had been found in these places." He looked my way to make sure I got the message. "Not a lot of it. And not very frequently. But there's always been some. Because . . . see here." He flipped some pages and pointed to another map, then morphed easily into professor mode.

"Gold in Ohio comes from deposits that took shape in association with silica-rich igneous rocks and those rocks were never formed here. They were formed in Canada and carried here by glaciers during the Ice Age." To demonstrate, he swept his hand top to bottom of page, from where Canada was shown all the way down to Ohio. "We call them glacial erratics. What with weathering and erosion, the gold that's in them is washed into streams and it has been found throughout the glaciated two-thirds of Ohio. And before you get any ideas about riches beyond your wildest dreams, all the gold that has been recovered is in the form of tiny flakes, maybe only a millimeter or so in diameter. Anything bigger is practically unheard of. And every commercial mine that has ever been established here has been a flat-out financial failure."

"Like the one Otis told me about."

"Otis? Cameron?" Phillip sat back. "Why would you two be talking about anything, much less gold mining?"

"Long story," I told him. Which really wasn't much of an explanation. "I just wondered if gold mining around here was actually possible."

"Certainly. There are plenty of streams, and there's the river, of course. Prospectors could pan there. Once in a while, I bump into a hobbyist out prospecting on weekends. More power to them. In my expert opinion, they're never going to find enough gold to pay for their panning supplies."

"Then a real mine—"

This, he had to think about. But it didn't take him long. "I've explored any number of caves nearby and I suppose any of those might have been a mine. Back in the day. But . . ." I imagine that over the years, his students had seen him look the way he looked at me, his eyebrows raised just the slightest bit, his mouth pulled tight, not so much with skepticism as with forbearance. "It's a great fantasy, Lizzie." He pushed back his chair and stood. "But if you're looking to get rich quick—"

"If there were mines in the area, historically, I mean, would anyone know?"

"I've never heard of any. Farther west. A little farther south. But not around here."

"But if someone thought there was—"

"If someone did, my guess is the first person they would have come to talk to about it was me. And, believe me, no one's mentioned gold mines to me. Not until today, that is."

There was nothing more I could say and I finished my (very good) coffee and headed back to town. By the time I got to Love Under the Covers, Charmaine had the shop open and the two customers who'd arrived early left with bags full of books (hoorah!) and were happy and satisfied.

The store empty and Charmaine fussing with a display of new bath salts, I went to my office to sit and considered what I knew.

It wasn't nearly as long of a list as what I didn't know.

Lemuel Schwartz left town more than one hundred years before, claiming he'd been scammed out of his share of a mine that his partners insisted was a total bust. But if Sharona thought it wasn't . . .

"It makes sense," I mumbled, then realized Charmaine had walked into the office so I pretended I was talking to her rather than to myself. "If Sharona thought there was a gold mine—"

"Did she?" Her eyes alight, Charmaine dropped into the guest chair next to my desk. "That's so exciting. Do you think she was here on a treasure hunt?"

"I think she was here because she thought the mine might still be here, and that if it was, that Al still owned it."

She nodded. "The fortune she thought Al had."

"You got that right." Because I hated sitting there with my brain whirling and going nowhere, I got online and, just for the heck of it, looked into gold prospecting in Ohio. There were a couple of websites that talked about history and pretty much told me all the things I'd already learned from Phillip. There were a couple more that listed places for prospecting and what they called family-friendly week-ends panning for gold and sharing stories by the campfire. There were more sites devoted to selling prospecting equipment.

I glanced over the pages.

"Aha!" If my exclamation didn't make Charmaine pay attention, the way I pointed at the computer screen sure did. She sat up and leaned closer for a better look.

"You can test to see if a rock is really gold by holding a magnet to it." I tapped the picture of just such a magnet there on the screen. "It says here, gold isn't magnetic. So if the rock reacts to the magnet—"

"It's not gold."

Seeing that magnet sparked an idea, and I quickly looked through more of the equipment site.

"Just what I thought!" Yeah, another outburst from me. Maybe by now Charmaine was getting used to me jabbering. She didn't bat an eyelash.

"Unglazed tile," I told her. "They say if you scratch the tile with a rock and it leaves a black streak, there's no way it's gold. If it leaves a gold streak, it is. And look." I pointed again. "They even sell small pieces of glass you can take along on your prospecting trips." I read the description beneath the photo. "If the rock scratches the glass, it's definitely not gold."

She'd been following along until right then and there. Now, Charmaine looked at me as if I was spouting gibberish.

I definitely was not.

"Magnet," I said. "Piece of glass. Unglazed tile." I waited for the pieces to fall into place for her, and I knew when they did because Charmaine's eyes popped open. She sat up like a shot and slapped the arms of her chair.

"That's what Sharona had in her makeup case!"

I nodded. "And that pretty much proves it, don't you think? She was here in town looking for gold, looking for the mine. She had that stuff with her so that if she found any rocks she thought might be gold, she could do a quick test on them and see if she was headed in the right direction. And you know what, I bet anything I know where she was looking for the mine, too. Helltown. That explains why she dog-eared the page in the chamber of commerce booklet over at Al's store, and why that plant from the park was stuck in Arlo's license plate."

"And don't forget the scratch on my passenger door." Charmaine's top lip curled. When it came to Arlo she took scratches very seriously. "Oh, that Sharona, she was a clever one, all right," Charmaine mumbled. "And fiendish."

I had no doubt the fiendish comment was referring to poor Arlo so I didn't let her dwell.

"I bet prospecting can get expensive," I said. "Just look at all this equipment." I looked over the pages, but my mind was on other things than gold pans and sluices. "What if that scrap of paper in her hand was a map that showed her where in Helltown the gold mine is?" I asked Charmaine and myself.

"Oh!" She clapped a hand to the front of her orange shirt. "You mean she was looking for the mine—"

"And someone knew she was looking for the mine."

"And that same someone—"

"Wanted to make sure he found the mine before Sharona did. That's why he killed her."

"He." Charmaine's voice dripped drama. "Or she."

"Or she," I had to concede. "Except Phillip's pretty convinced nobody around here knows or cares about gold mining or prospecting or—"

As if they'd been snipped with scissors, my words cut off. But, then, I was busy staring at the computer screen and at the rubber mats displayed there. Green. Maybe ten inches wide. They were grooved. Some of those grooves went straight across, others were V-shaped.

"Son of a gun!" I slapped my desk with so much force, Charmaine jumped.

"Sluice box matting," I said and pointed. "That's what Phillip picked up from the hardware store the day I worked it for Al. Mighty fishy, don't you think? For a man who says no one around here searches for gold?"

# Chapter 21

*Friday evening*

I was anxious to tell Max all about this, of course, but that had to wait.

The train convention was winding down and members of the society were spending their last days in Tinker's Creek. Fortunately, they were also out spending their money. Love Under the Covers was packed, and Charmaine and I ran for the rest of the day. When closing time rolled around, I was exhausted. Charmaine headed to Glory's because Glory insisted Charmaine still needed babying, what with the break-in and all, and wanted to treat her to her world- (okay, Tinker's Creek's) famous lasagna. I headed home and promised myself I'd give Max a call. Right after I walked Violet, got back, fed Violet, and put my feet up for a few minutes.

I never had the chance. At least not for the feet-up part.

Walk Violet.

Check.

Come home.

Check.

Feed Violet.

Absolutely. She wouldn't have been happy if I didn't.

But just when I finished, I happened to look out the window and saw something odd.

At that point, I couldn't say if it was a person or an animal. I only knew there was something in the garden. It was low to the ground. Only natural if it was an animal. But if it was a person, that person was crouching, and a crouching person, I think I can say with some authority, is surely up to no good.

My phone tucked in my pocket just in case, I put a finger to my lips to let Violet know she had to be quiet, then slipped out of my door and silently closed it behind me. I peered through the gathering darkness, my breaths suspended.

Yup, that shape was still there. Right between the marigolds and the herb garden, bent low and moving ever so slowly and carefully toward Charmaine's back door.

Yeah, the one that had just recently been kicked in and smashed to smithereens.

"Oh no!" I cried out and darted forward, yelling for all I was worth. "You stay away from Charmaine's house! One break-in is enough for anybody."

In an instant, that person was on his (or her, as Charmaine would have pointed out) feet. He darted in and out of the shadows, ducked behind the massive rose of Sharon bushes that were the pride of Mrs. Castille next door, and disappeared around to the front of the house and the street beyond.

At least that's what I thought.

I mean, it was only natural, right? Sneaky person is discovered. Sneaky person takes off. I had every reason to believe sneaky person was long gone and I had the luxury of stopping next to the fountain—it was plop, plop, plop-ping again—pulling out my phone, and calling the local cops.

The fact that I was in the midst of asking the boys in blue to stop by explains why I didn't realize sneaky person had circled back.

By the time I heard the footsteps behind me, it was al-ready too late. I whirled around just as something smacked me on the head. Supernovas burst behind my eyes and every last bit of air in my lungs escaped in a yelp of sur-prise. The shadows blurred and blended, their edges sharp, then as soft as a watercolor, mixing and mingling until they flowed together to form one, impenetrable pitch-black smudge.

That's when I went down like a rock.

The last thing I remembered was the fountain plop, plop, plopping water over the edges of its bowl and trickling down on me.

D on't move."
     Yeah, I knew it was good advice, but when I came to and found my cousin Josh looking down at me, I shot him a sour look and tried to sit up.

"Do you ever listen?" He pressed my shoulders back to the pavement. "The paramedics are on their way. We've got to be sure you don't have a head injury or that your neck isn't broken or something."

I had a headache, that was for sure, and before I could lie about it and convince Josh I was all right, I groaned.

"See." He sat back on his heels and gave me the kind of

look he had so often shot my way when we were teenagers and he'd offered advice that I hadn't followed—usually to my detriment. "Just relax."

"But somebody—"

"Yeah, you said when you called. Somebody was out here in the garden." I was sure he'd already checked, but, his eyes narrowed, he looked around anyway, studying every shadow.

"There was no one here when we got here, that's for sure. No one but you and that water bottle that got dropped over there." The plastic bottle caught the light. "I'm pretty sure that's what you got hit with. Full, they can really pack a wallop. Don't worry," he added quickly because, hey, Josh and I went back a long way and he knew I was going to ask. "We're going to bag it and dust it for prints. As for our perp . . ." He sucked in his bottom lip the way he always did when he was disgusted.

"No one was lurking around out front when we arrived. I've got Dylan cruising up and down the streets, checking for anyone who looks out of place or like they're trying to put distance between here and wherever. We'll find him."

"But what did he want?" I didn't have time to consider it before I hit the pavement, but I thought about it now. "Annalise broke in because she wanted those papers Sharona promised her. There's no other reason for anyone else to want to get into your mom's house."

Josh's shoulders rose and fell. Like most cops, he was levelheaded and analytical. He hated not having the answer. "We'll find out," he promised.

I squirmed. It was all well and good lying there and waiting for the paramedics to come and check me out, but with the way the fountain was splashing, it wasn't the most comfortable of spots. "Getting wet," I told Josh.

"Sorry." He slipped off his jacket and covered me with it.

As much as I appreciated his assistance, I had to tell him, "Not working too well."

"Well, here come the paramedics." He got up and moved out of the way so they could take over.

A couple minutes later and only after I swore that I was fine, that nothing was broken, and that I'd get checked out by my doc first thing Monday morning, they finally let me sit up.

I was soaked and I shivered.

"Let's get you home." Josh offered me a hand. "You need some dry clothes."

I wasn't about to argue. With his arm around my shoulders, I got to my feet and honestly, except for the pounding in my head, I didn't feel bad at all. But let's face it, I'd had something of a shock. I'd been attacked. My stomach swooped. My knees were rubbery. They buckled.

Hanging on to Josh for dear life with one hand, I threw out the other one to steady myself and smacked into the fountain.

It swayed.

It shimmied.

It rocked.

And then that fountain, which had stood at the center of Charmaine's garden for as long as I could remember, did the weirdest thing.

It toppled right over.

Fortunately, it fell in the other direction, but we both jumped back, anyway, and I gasped.

For the record, that had nothing to do with the fountain crashing down or with the water that splattered everywhere.

And everything to do with the fact that when the fountain fell, I saw why it had been acting up ever since Sharona came to Tinker's Creek.

* * *

An hour later, my soggy clothes exchanged for warm and comfy lounge pants and a long-sleeved T-shirt, Max was on one end of my couch and I was on the other, wrapped in a blanket because I couldn't keep the chill away. It occurred to me that this wasn't the first time I'd found myself in the same predicament since that fateful day I found Sharona floating facedown and as dead as a doornail. Me and the canal. Me and the water bottle. Me and the fountain. These days, things weren't going well between me and water.

"I'm glad you called." Max slid over and put an arm around my shoulders.

"I'm glad you were finally back from that meeting so you could get here." I leaned into him, enjoying the warmth and the strong, steady beat of his heart. "No word on Phillip Wilmington?"

"His house is locked up tight and there's no sign of his truck. Josh is going to keep an eye out."

"Do you think—?"

He answered even before I finished asking. "Can't say if he was the one who attacked you or not. I do think it's odd that he just so happens to be ordering gold prospecting equipment when Sharona comes to town to look for a gold mine."

Yeah, this had occurred to me as more than a little weird, too.

"Except . . ." Since my brain was still a little cloudy I took my time and made sure I had my thoughts straight before I put them in words. "Phillip ordered that stuff from Al, right?"

"Yup."

"And he picked it up on Monday."

"Yup again. That's the day you worked the hardware store."

"I know a thing or two about how long it's taking to process and deliver orders these days. My guess is Phillip must have ordered the sluice mat before Sharona ever got here."

Max thought this over and while he did, I asked him, "Could they have been in on it together? Like he knew Sharona was coming and he had other prospecting gear ready and he ordered the mat to use, too, and he was just waiting for her?"

"I plan on asking him," he assured me, "once we track him down. For now . . ."

As if we'd choreographed the move, both our heads turned and we looked at the package Josh had brought into the house and set on my coffee table.

"Sharona couldn't take the chance of anybody finding whatever's in that packet," I said. "She had to hide it someplace no one would think to look. She put it under the fountain."

One corner of Max's mouth pulled tight. "I think we can bet on it."

"For her to be that careful with it, it's got to have something valuable inside." A thought hit, and I sat up. "The map, the one she had the scan of? Could we be that lucky?"

"There's only one way to find out." He slipped on a pair of latex gloves, and he had laid out a pile of evidence bags on the couch next to him so he grabbed one of those, too. The bundle we'd found stashed under the fountain was wrapped in waterproof paper and sealed with packing tape, and he carefully cut through it, stashed the strips of tape in the first evidence bag, then looked through the papers that had been so meticulously wrapped and so cleverly hidden.

"Nothing in here looks like legal papers transferring ownership of Bride of Your Dreams to Annalise," he said.

I clicked my tongue. "No surprise there. Of course Sharona lied. Too bad. The promise of owning a business would give Annalise something to look forward to when she gets out of jail."

Max extracted a paper from the pile. He took a photo of it, then slid it into an evidence bag.

Now that the paper was secured, I leaned forward for a better look.

The ink was faded, the lines drawn over the page twisted this way and that. I recognized a crooked shape at the center of the page, and the narrow, straighter track sketched out at its side.

"The river! And there's the canal towpath. It's the original map!" I practically whooped with joy.

He didn't want to blunt my excitement, but he shook his head. "My guess is it's another scan." Max rubbed a hand over his chin. "Sharona wouldn't risk having the original with her. I'll bet anything we'll find it at her house back in New Jersey. But original or not, she had to make sure no one else would find the map. She kept one copy with her. You found the piece of that one in her hand. She hid the other one. I'll give her that much, she was clever."

"And fiendish." When I realized I'd said it out loud, I blushed and told him, "At least that's what Charmaine says."

"For once, I don't think she's being overly dramatic. Sharona had big plans, and since that included Al meeting an untimely end, I'd say fiendish just about fits. Maybe the rest of these papers will tell us more." Max started through the same rigamarole with the rest of what was in the package, stowing it page by page into individual bags. "More scans," he said. "And if I'm not mistaken . . ." He'd laid the pages out in a neat line on the coffee table, and when he leaned over for a better look, I did, too.

These pages hadn't fared much better than the map. The ink was faded, but instead of lines and shapes, the pages were covered with cramped handwriting.

"Lemuel Schwartz's diary," I said. "I'd bet anything! He was convinced Junius Little and Ezekiel Cameron cheated him out of his share of the gold mine. He even tried to sue them. If that's the story Sharona heard—"

"If she'd read the diary over the years and—"

"She knew the three men had staked their gold mine claim at Tinker's Creek."

"And then when Al signed up with Bride of Your Dreams—"

"And she recognized the name. Not just the town name, but Al's name. Little."

"It's why she planned the whole thing!" Certain we were on the right track, Max plunked back against the couch cushions. "That explains everything."

"Except why she was convinced there was money. Al says he never knew anything about the mine. And Otis said there was never money made from it anyway."

"But I bet that's not what the diary says," Max said. Eager to find out more, he picked up the first diary page and slid across the couch so he could hold it under the light of the nearest lamp. I followed along, leaning over his shoulder to try and catch a glimpse.

"It says"—he squinted—"something about un . . ." He grumbled his frustration.

"I bet it's *unscrupulous*," I said and when I looked closer, my suspicion was confirmed. "And here"—I pointed—"I can see the name *Little*. Lemuel is talking about the mine. He must be."

Max grabbed another page, and together we studied it.

"More of the same," he pointed out. "At least what I can see of it. Here's the word *mine* again, I can read that clearly. Then something about *swindling*. Good ol' Lemuel didn't pull any punches."

"Could he have been right?" I wondered. "Phillip told me there has never been enough gold found anywhere in Ohio to amount to anything. And Al swears his family never had money. But what if there was gold in the mine?"

Max's shrug spoke volumes. "Maybe Lemuel actually believed he'd been cheated out of a fortune. Or maybe he wrote all this just to try to convince other people. You said the case went to court. Maybe he wrote this out as a sort of narrative for his attorney. You know, the story of how Ezekiel and Junius done him wrong. If that's the case, it's no wonder Sharona thought she was onto something when Al's wedding plans fell into her lap."

"It's all so crazy." I scraped my hands through my hair before I sat forward and propped my elbows on my knees. Whatever the paramedics had given me for my headache, it had worked a miracle, but I cradled my head in my hands anyway and fingered the bandage on my forehead. I hadn't been brave enough yet to look at the injury, but I knew my forehead was swollen, and from what the paramedics told me, I was going to have one heck of a bruise by morning. "I hope this nonsense about a mine didn't cost the real Svetlana her life."

Max patted my knee. "We're going to find her."

"And are we going to find this fantasy gold mine, too?" I wondered.

"Sharona sure thought she was. She even took the map to the wedding with her. She must have thought the mine was nearby. That's why she slipped out, just to have a quick look around. And . . ." When Max slapped his own forehead, it made my forehead hurt and I winced. "You're the one who told me," he said. "How Sharona agreed to have the wedding in the park. She said—"

"That Al loved the great outdoors and she'd do anything for Al. All she was really doing was giving herself a few minutes to look around to try to get the lie of the land, mapwise. That park pavilion isn't all that far from Helltown, where she'd been just a couple of days before and she was hoping for another quick look." Disgusted, I crossed my arms over my chest. "Sharona didn't care a thing about Al. You know, I think Charmaine is right. Sharona was fiendish."

I guess it was the word *fiendish* that made me remember my own recent adventure in Helltown. "You know, Max, Helltown is where I just so happened to run into Phillip Wilmington recently."

Max slid me a look. "You've been to Helltown?"

I sat up straight and tall. It was the best way to prove that talk of Helltown didn't scare me. "Lots of times when I was a kid," I told Max. "And I've been back, sure. It's not any big deal."

"You're not even afraid of the mutants?"

He was teasing. He absolutely deserved the poke in the ribs I gave him.

"Then how about the snake?" He wiggled his fingers in a spooky sort of way.

"No mutants, no snake," I assured him at the same time I reminded myself that there had been something out there in the tall grass, something besides Phillip. I shook away the thought. "Phillip said he was out taking in the last of the fine weather."

"But he could have been looking for something else."

"Because now . . ." I scrambled through the pile of evidence bags on the table and found the one that contained the map. I waved it at Max. "We've got one scan," I said. "And we've got a piece of another scan that looks like it comes from the same map. But that means someone else has the rest of that map, the rest of what he tore from Sharona's hand when he strangled her."

He nodded, not so much like I was right and he was happy to acknowledge it, but more like he was making a promise to himself, and swearing he'd get justice for Sharona's murder.

"Find the map," he said, "and we find the killer."

Just when I was finally starting to warm up, his words sent an icy chill through me. I tugged the blanket around me just as Max hopped off the couch.

"You've got stuff to make hot cocoa, right?" he asked and he headed toward the kitchen.

Fine by me. With Max gone, I pulled the evidence bag with the map in it closer and flattened it with one hand so there wasn't too much of a reflection in the photo I snapped of it with my phone.

By the time Max was back, two mugs of cocoa in hand, that map was right back where it started from.

And headache or no headache, I had plans for the next day.

# Chapter 22

*Saturday morning*

I bet there are people out there who think places like bookshops are inanimate objects.

I get it. Sort of. I mean, brick and mortar, right? Floorboards and light fixtures, shelving units, computers, desks, and books. And books, I suspect those same people would say, are nothing more than paper and ink.

But see, that's not how readers think.

And above all else, I am a reader. As much as I know in my head that Love Under the Covers is a place of business— a real, solid place in a real, solid world—I also know the shop has a way of calling to me. Way down deep in my soul where the love of reading spreads roots that run deep, I am sure Love Under the Covers and I share a heartbeat.

Which is a long and slightly poetic way (sorry, I've been hanging around with Charmaine too much!) of explaining why I felt pretty lousy stopping in the store that Saturday morning only long enough to let Charmaine know she was in charge. I wanted to dust shelves and unpack orders and goggle over new covers.

I had things I had to do first.

Charmaine did not come right out and ask what was up, though she did skim a look over my jeans, my hiking boots, the hoodie I wore under a lightweight jacket. I'd ditched the bandage on my forehead and she tsked about the bruise, a purple and red mess that went from hairline to just about the top of my left eye. There was no way she couldn't notice that Violet was with me, either. But, then, my doggy friend had left a trail of white fur from the front door to the office.

"Going somewhere?" Charmaine asked.

"Testing out a theory," I confided.

"And if Max shows up looking for you?"

I was pretty sure he wouldn't. Between the mysterious person who had slugged me in the garden, the pages of Lemuel's diary, and the poorly drawn but intriguing map, I had a feeling Max's hands were full.

I hoped the wink I gave Charmaine was conspiratorial. She loved that sort of thing. "Tell him I'll be back," I said and, yeah, I guess I liked a little drama, too, because I added the proper Arnold Schwarzenegger accent to those last three words.

Before she could question me further and I was tempted to reveal the plans I knew were best kept secret and would annoy Max if he learned of them, Violet and I hurried out of the shop.

From downtown Tinker's Creek to the shores of the Cuyahoga River isn't far, and after we parked the car, my furry buddy and I found ourselves back where I'd been so many times before.

"Helltown." I whispered the name at the same time I took a few steps down the path that would lead to where

Brynn and I had encountered Phillip just a few nights before. In the light of an early fall morning, Helltown looked nothing like the figments of the bad dreams I'd had all during my growing-up years. The light around me was crisp and clean. The birds tittered their fall songs. Flowers nodded on long, sturdy branches, yellow sunflowers and delicate white asters. If I listened really hard, I could hear the rush of the river and the sounds of laughter and splashing as a flotilla of kayakers paddled by.

Of course, old habits die hard. So do old terrors.

Sunshine or no sunshine, I darted a look all around and listened extra carefully, too. I mean, there was the python to worry about. And that shape Brynn and I had seen skulking through the high grass the night we were here?

I was glad I had Violet for moral support. Not to mention the uncanny accuracy of her super sniffer. She romped in the tall grass on the side of the path, whiffing and swerving on the trail of each delicious scent. And if one of those smells happened to lead to a mutant? I was sure Violet would let me know in plenty of time.

While she took care of the recon, I got down to business. On my phone, I brought up the picture I'd taken of the old map, and I enlarged it and gave it a long look.

"River over that way," I told Violet and pointed over my shoulder. "So this shape on the map might show those rocky outcroppings up ahead." Of course things had changed plenty in the years since the original map had been drawn, but keeping in mind that the river was still the river and that it and the canal alongside it pretty much still ran the same course, I turned and headed for the water's edge. If the map was right—and if I was reading it correctly—it looked like there were a series of circles along the riverbank.

Caves?

I hoped so, because to me, who knew nothing about prospecting, little about gold, and zero about nineteenth-century maps, caves just might be where to find mines.

Like I said, though, things change. If the markings on the map indicated caves, those caves were long gone. Or maybe they were never there in the first place.

Fifteen minutes of poking and prodding along the riverbank got us nowhere.

Another fifteen minutes, and I was discouraged. Not to mention sweaty. Violet's tongue hung out of one corner of her mouth.

"I get it," I told her. "I'm feeling the same way," and I pulled off my jacket, tied it around my waist, and plunked down on a nearby boulder so I could grab her water dish from the backpack I had slung over one shoulder, fill it from my water bottle, and watch her dive in. Dappled sunlight played hide-and-seek over her, adding touches of gold to her luxurious white fur. Leaves rustled in a whispering breeze and the longer hairs on her pointed ears wafted back and forth. Voices carried, a man and a woman.

I'd been so lost in thought watching Violet, it took a moment for the significance of what I heard to sink in.

"Shhh!" I advised Violet, and since she had just been about to stretch out for forty winks, she didn't argue.

I sat up like a shot and while I was at it slid off the rock and took Violet with me, and we ducked into a dense cluster of trees. My head tipped and my eyes carefully scanning the rocky river shoreline on one side of me and the bushes and trees that were the beginnings of forest on the other, I waited.

"Go this way, I'll go to the other one."

What with the sound of the gurgling water, the creaking of swaying branches, and the call of birdsong all around me, I couldn't tell who was speaking or, for that matter, exactly where the sound was coming from. I only knew that a few seconds later, a figure pushed out of the undergrowth up ahead and stepped out onto the riverbank.

Phillip Wilmington!

As much as I wanted to race out of my hiding place and confront him, I put a hand on Violet's head to remind her and myself that we had to stay quiet and stay put. Phillip was dressed for rock hunting. Or prospecting. Jeans, sweatshirt, sturdy boots. He had his satchel slung over his shoulder.

He had something else, too.

There was a paper in his hands, and even from where we stood I could tell one corner of it was missing.

Yeah, like someone had yanked it out of the hand of a way overdressed bride right before he strangled her and dumped her in the canal.

I kept my place and kept an eye on him, too, watching to see what he'd do and waiting for whoever he'd been talking to.

No one else showed up and Phillip didn't seem to mind. One more look at that map and he nodded, confirming something to himself, then turned and went to the spot where the riverbank rose to a rocky slope. Maybe in the winter when things weren't as lush, it would be easy to see what was what and what was where, but with bushes sprouting all around and vines twining here and there, around and between and over boulders, I had to wonder what Phillip hoped to find.

The minute I saw him part a curtain of vines and saw the dark, empty space behind them, I knew.

"The mine!" I mouthed the words and pointed just in case Violet missed the significance.

Together we waited until Phillip turned on a high-powered camping lamp, held it at arm's length to peer into the cave, then followed its light inside.

"That's got to be it!" I told Violet. "The mine. We'll see what he does when he comes out."

Only he didn't.

Violet and I waited for ten minutes.

We waited for twenty.

"I guess it's only natural for a guy who's all into rocks to get involved in looking around a cave," I told Violet, and I would have been perfectly willing to believe it, too, if I didn't hear a *boof* from inside the cave. The sound of a heavy object striking. It was followed by a sharp intake of breath, an anguished moan. A thud.

Sure, I had to call for help. But first, I had to see what was going on, and make sure someone wasn't seriously injured.

With that in mind, I hurried to the entrance of the cave and tied Violet's leash to the nearest tree so my hands were free. I grabbed the flashlight I'd brought along and parted the vine curtain that had hidden the mine for more than a hundred years. The entrance to the cave had been reinforced with rocks and, once upon a time, with timbers. They had pretty much rotted away and now a piece here, a piece there poked from between the teetering rocks, like the fingers of a skeleton fighting to claw its way out of the darkness.

None of it looked too sturdy, that was for sure, but when another groan echoed from somewhere in the darkness I knew I didn't have the luxury of being a chicken. I stepped into the darkness.

"Phillip?" My voice was small. It pinged into the darkness up ahead. I skewed the light around. Here at the entrance to the cave, the passage was narrow. The rock walls on either side of me didn't leave a whole lot of room for maneuvering. I followed the path up a slight rise.

That's when I saw the glow of Phillip's lamp.

It was on its side on the ground right between a giant boulder and Phillip. He was on the ground, too, lying in the center of a small chamber with a rounded rock ceiling. He wasn't moaning anymore. In fact, he wasn't even moving.

Yeah, I know. I get it. Here I was in a dark cave with a man who had murdered a woman on the day of her wedding just so he could get his hands on an old map. Running toward Phillip probably wasn't the smartest thing to do. But as it turned out, running the other way wouldn't have been the best idea, either, because just as I got to Phillip and knelt at his side to check for a pulse, I heard a rumble and roar. Then somewhere behind me and back toward the entrance, the roof caved in.

The thunderous noise that followed knocked me to the floor. Dust swirled around me, blinding me, choking me. I squeezed my eyes shut, ducked my head, and covered it with both arms, but not before I watched in horror as a couple soccer ball–sized rocks rocketed out of nowhere and rolled our way. When they came to a stop just inches from where Phillip still lay motionless, I sobbed with relief.

The racket ended as quickly as it began and, as awful as it had been, it wasn't nearly as frightening as the eerie silence that took its place. It wrapped around me like a living thing, disrupted only by the staccato plink when smaller stones dropped from the ceiling.

Too afraid to look, too afraid not to, I lifted my head, then ducked again when a stone smacked down beside me, way too close for comfort. I waited for a dozen heartbeats before I dared to move.

Phillip's lantern had been smashed, but lucky for me, though I'd dropped my flashlight, it was still working. I grabbed it and held on tight. Cave-in, bad. Cave-in and pitch-dark . . . If I thought about it I would have a full-blown case of the screaming meemies to add to my woes.

And I already had enough to worry about.

Phillip, for one thing.

I scooted over, my back to that giant boulder, the better to see what I was doing when I grabbed my water bottle out of my backpack and poured water into my hand.

"Phillip?" I splashed water on his face and brushed his lips with my wet fingers to get rid of the dirt that coated them, and when he groaned, I almost whooped with delight. I would have if not for the dirt that clung to me, the dust that clutched at my throat, the furious beat of my heart reminding me that we were in a cave—and that something told me when I made my way back to the entrance, I wasn't going to like what I saw.

"Phillip, I'm going to call for help." I somehow managed to say this with all the gumption of an intrepid explorer who was sure what had just happened was nothing more than a tiny inconvenience and we'd be right as rain in just a few moments.

This, however, was not how I felt.

Especially when I tapped my phone and realize I had no cell service.

"No worries," I told Phillip. As if with his eyes closed and his breaths coming in shallow gasps, he could see the dodgy looks I gave my phone. "I'll just . . ." Just what, I really couldn't say, but somehow, I knew my role in the investigation of Sharona's murder had just changed from super snooper to head cheerleader. Bracing myself against that big rock, I pushed myself to my feet, ignored the tear in my jeans and the wet splotch of blood on the exposed skin under it, and carefully stepped through the detritus of the cave-in. "I'll just go to the cave entrance," I told Phillip with all the cheerleader rah-rah I could muster. "I'll make a call and someone will be here lickety-split."

That in itself says a whole lot about how I wasn't thinking clearly and how I was stressed to the max.

I mean, who ever really says *lickety-split*?

Setting the thought aside, I picked my way back toward the cave entrance.

So far so good. A rock here, a rock there. Some bigger ones I needed to climb over to get down the short path that led outside. Down the gentle slope.

That's when I saw that except for a few holes that let the outside light in like pinpricks, the cave entrance was completely blocked.

"Oh." The tiny word whooshed out of me, small and pathetic, and hardly suitable to the occasion. My stomach bunched. My heart squeezed. And every inch of me that was already coated in dust was suddenly and completely smothered by panic, too.

Then I heard the barking.

My head came up, my heart thudded with relief. The rock wall in front of me suddenly looked as if it had been painted by a watercolor artist. But then tears streamed out of my eyes. They mixed with the dirt on my cheeks and turned into muddy sludge and I scraped it away at the same time I hurried closer to the impenetrable rock wall.

"Violet!" When she responded with another bark, I smiled through my tears. "Violet, you're okay? You're not hurt?"

The enthusiastic woof I got in response told me she was fine.

I closed in on the rock wall and bent to press an eye to a small hole between the rocks.

A pink and black nose blocked the daylight.

"Oh, Violet!" I wiggled one finger through the tiny opening and she gave me a lick. "What are we going to do, sweetie? I've got an injured guy in here and you out there and—"

I heard the scramble of her paws on the rocks.

"You be careful," I advised, but honestly, I don't think Violet was listening. She scratched at the rocks again. She pawed at the opening. A few minutes later, with me standing back and Violet working furiously, what had been a hole the size of a shot glass was as big as a saucer. Fresh air rushed in. It caressed my face and filled my lungs.

Violet grinned at me through the opening.

"Good girl!" I ruffled the top of her head. That is, right after I stuck my phone out of that opening and finally got a cell signal.


Is he going to be all right?"

Phillip was on a stretcher being carefully maneuvered through the cave by two firefighters. With my bleeding knee bandaged, my pulse and other vitals checked, and (most of) the gunk wiped from my face, it was the first chance I had to talk to Max. He was standing over on my left, and he flattened himself against the rock wall so the paramedics could get by. I joined him there just as his mouth curled down at the corners. "It wasn't Phillip I was worried about."

"I told you when I called, I'm fine."

"You had no business being here in the first place."

"All I was doing was walking Violet in the park." Yeah, a little white lie, but, then, this hardly struck me as the moment to be brutally honest. "That's when I saw Phillip with the map. That was the map, wasn't it? What he had in his hands?"

When Max rubbed a finger under his nose, he left a smudge of dirt. "That's what you say you saw, but he didn't have anything with him. Not when we got here."

"Then it's still got to be here someplace." I whirled to start the search.

Since Max grabbed my arm, I never had the chance. I wondered how I'd never noticed that his eyes flashed fire when he was angry, that his face—all planes and angles and deliciousness—hardened like the stones around us when he was furious.

I caved (ouch, bad choice of words!) and confessed, "As soon as I saw Phillip, I was going to call you. Honest. Then I heard a terrible sound. Like he was in trouble and—"

"So instead of doing the smart thing, you came in here to see what was happening."

It wasn't like I could deny it.

"Dang, woman!" Since Max was so tall, he'd taken off his Smokey Bear hat when he came into the cave rather than have it scrape the ceiling, and he slapped it against his leg and stalked down the pathway toward the front entrance, now cleared thanks to the able hands and muscled bodies of an army of police, fire, and volunteer rescuers. "It's a good thing I'm not leaving the park anytime soon. Somebody's got to stick around here and make sure you don't do something so plum crazy you get yourself killed."

"I know." I hung my head. "And you know I wouldn't have done it unless—" Just as quickly, my head came up again. I scrambled to catch up with Max. "What do you mean, you're sticking around?"

He didn't turn to me. Against the muted evening light that flowed from outside through the newly opened entrance, he looked like a silhouette cut from black paper.

"Just what I said," he grumbled. "I'm staying."

"Here?"

"Not here in the cave."

If he bothered to turn around, he would have seen the sour look I gave him. "I know that. I meant, you're staying? Here? In the park? In Tinker's Creek?"

He grumbled.

"Well, obviously you're not happy about it," I grouched back. "You'd rather be stationed anywhere else."

"Totally my choice." Max stepped outside. "Just shows you what a damn fool I am."

I knew better than to pursue the conversation. I mean, there were too many people around, and too many people listening are never a good idea at a time like this. Instead, I considered all that had happened and all I just learned, and hobbled out of the cave, my knee smarting and my ears still ringing. All that was forgotten as soon as I saw Josh standing near the river, Violet at his side.

"You're a hero!" Sore knee or not, I knelt so I could give Violet the hug she deserved. "You're the best dog ever. And you didn't get hurt!" I buried my face in her fur. "Oh, Violet, I'm so glad you didn't get hurt."

"Not like Phillip." When Josh spoke, I looked up to where he watched the stretcher getting carried farther down the path. Here, there was no room for an ambulance, but I had no doubt that's where they were headed. Through the trees, I saw its flashing lights. "Must have hit his head on something, huh?"

I thought back to the scene. The mouth of the cave. The path inside. The chamber where I'd found Phillip.

"It's not a big spot," I told Josh. "Still, I had plenty of room to stand, and except for his hat, Max didn't have any problem." It hit me then. Like one of those stones that had rained down from the ceiling of the cave. I hauled myself to my feet and hurried toward the ambulance, calling back to Josh, "There was nothing Phillip could have hit his head on."

Winded, I made it to the waiting ambulance just as Max stepped away from it.

"There was nothing Phillip could have hit his head on," I told him, my words bumping over my staggered breaths. "You need to find out exactly what happened in that cave."

He looked from me to Phillip, all bundled up and ready to head off to the hospital and I honestly thought Max was going to brush me off. Until I saw him raise one hand, a signal to the paramedics to wait just one minute.

He hopped into the ambulance and because he didn't tell me not to, I followed right along. Max stood on Phillip's right. I took a spot on the left.

"Mr. Wilmington?"

Phillip's eyes fluttered open.

"You're on your way to the hospital, sir, but before you go, we need to ask what happened in that cave."

Phillip shook his head. He shut his eyes.

It was my turn to try. "Phillip." I took his hand and gave his fingers a squeeze. "It's me. Lizzie. I was there with you and—"

"Yes." Phillip ran his tongue over his lips. "Lizzie, you saved me. Too bad you didn't stop me from going into that cave. Then I wouldn't have proved what a darned fool I could be."

"Because . . . ?" Max asked.

"Gotta go!" A paramedic jumped into the ambulance and shooed us off. "You can talk to him later. At the hospital."

"Sure," Max told him, "but—"

"But . . ." Phillip's voice was no more than a whisper. "That cave. I didn't notice the marking on the map until I was already inside. Until it was too late. You see, there's another way in."

# Chapter 23

I'm not sure which of us made it back to the cave first, me or Max. I do know he wasn't enough of a gentleman to step aside so I could go in ahead of him. But, then, he's like that when he's working. And hot on the trail of the perp. The real perp.

"He didn't do it, did he? Phillip, I mean." When I walked out of that cave, I swore I'd never walk into it—or any other cave—ever again. And yet there I was, scurrying along behind Max down the dusty corridor, up that little slope, refusing to be left behind now that we were so close to finding out not only what happened to Phillip but what had happened to Sharona, too.

I could feel it in my bones.

When we got to the chamber where Phillip and I rode out the cave-in, Max propped his fists on his hips and looked all around. "You're right. I should have seen it sooner. There's nothing here he could have bumped his head on. And he sure didn't clunk himself on the head."

I paced the cave. "And he said there's another way in. And the other way in—"

Max found it there behind that big boulder, a tunnel at ground level, maybe three feet high and just as far across. He radioed the information to his fellow rangers outside, got down on his hands and knees, and crawled inside.

He knew I was right behind him. Of course he knew. A guy as smart as Max doesn't miss a trick. But he didn't tell me to stop or go back.

And in the great scheme of things, I decided to take that as a good sign.

When he crawled out of that tunnel and into another chamber very similar to the one in which I'd found Phillip, I stayed hidden in the shadows of the tunnel.

That meant Galina didn't see me when she trained her .38 on Max.

I flicked off my flashlight and slunk farther into the darkness.

"You will stand there." When she nudged the gun to the side to demonstrate, the light of her lantern glinted off the steel. "You will keep quiet and you will wait right here until I am long gone."

Max is no dummy. He looked all around—but not at the tunnel where I was still crouched. "Another cave. A different outside entrance. And this one—"

Galina's sharp laugh cut him off. "You would think a man as smart as Phillip would know this, yes? This is the real mine. Not the place I sent him."

"So you knocked him out and left him for dead." Max's voice was soft and even. They were talking facts, nothing more, his steady words seemed to say. Life and death did not hang balanced here in the tiny mine. "You know you wasted your time, don't you?"

She tipped her head. "What you are talking about?"

"The mine." Max was one cool cucumber. A gun pointed right at him, and he never flinched. "Sharona had the story all wrong. There never was any gold."

"But . . ." I saw the gun in her hand waver and held my breath. "Yes, there is gold, there must be gold. Phillip, he has been looking for gold near here for a very long time."

"And when you got wind of Sharona having a map . . ." I'm not sure how he did it, but he packed his voice with admiration. "How did you manage it? Why would she tell you the secret?"

"Stupid woman. She brings the map to her wedding, no? Stupid, stupid woman."

"You didn't know." Max considered this. "Even though you were supposed to be home, you showed up at the park during the wedding. You were hoping for the perfect opportunity. You planned to kill her all along and then you swore Dan was innocent, just to make him look more guilty. You wanted him to go to jail."

She snorted. "It was one way to finally get rid of him, yes? If only it would work! Then I could have taken care of both the people who made me so unhappy. Dan does not care about me. He only cares about his grandfather's money. Sharona is the one who arranged my marriage to Dan. I hate her for this. I see her at that dinner party and I decide. Yes, she must die. She deserved to die."

"But you got something extra for your efforts. That map. And you knew exactly who to show it to. Phillip, the only guy around here who would know what was what when it came to rocks and mines."

If I had more room to move and no big bruise, I would

have slapped my forehead. I should have seen it all along! Dan told me Galina was having an affair. Otis said the same thing. And I'd had the truth staring me right in the face at Brandywine Falls.

The glove dropped on the boardwalk.

Phillip knew it belonged to Galina and really, how many guys would actually notice something like that if they only had a passing acquaintance with a woman?

The thought barely had time to sink in when I heard Max say, "Bad news, Galina. Phillip's on his way to the hospital. He's going to live. And he's going to tell us exactly what happened, how you lured him into the other mine, how you knocked him out. And, just to be sure he wasn't going anywhere or telling anyone the truth, you somehow managed that cave-in, too."

"By the time he tells them what happened, I will be gone." She backstepped toward a path that led into the darkness. "I could not leave before now. Someone would see me. But those workers, they are leaving now. I can tell. It is quiet. They won't be a problem. You will not be, either, Ranger."

Her fingers twitched and there was no way I was going to wait to see what was going to happen next. I shot forward, leaped out of that tunnel, and I guess all those years of watching baseball paid off.

When I threw my flashlight, it hit her shoulder like a Hall of Fame fastball.

Galina lost her footing just as Max lunged at her. She slid to the side and her head met the rock wall of the mine with an ugly thump that caused her eyes to roll back in her head.

It was only strike one.

But she was definitely out.

# Chapter 24

L izzie, I need you."

I hadn't gotten much sleep since Saturday. I mean, what with dreaming about rocks crashing down on me and ruthless murderers and how being trapped in a cave is just about the worst nightmare ever.

I can be excused for being a little out of focus. For letting my mind wander.

Besides, I was shelving books in the erotica room. It was only natural I let my fantasies run away with me.

Only natural I imagined I heard Max croon those words.

*Lizzie, I need you.*

"Uh, Lizzie?"

That wasn't my imagination! I looked up from my work and found Max leaning against the doorway. "Are you asleep on your feet?"

"I'm . . ." I set down the stack of books I'd been holding. "Just a little off-kilter. What with all the excitement."

He understood. He nodded. "Exactly why I haven't had a chance to stop by and see how you're doing. Talk about reams of paperwork! Today, though . . ." He pulled in a long breath and pushed away from the doorway. "Today is different. We've got more important things to worry about than murder charges. Lizzie"—he held out a hand to me—"I need you."

Who was I to refuse the request of a handsome ranger? I put my hand in his. Well, after I gave my arm a scratch. "You want to tell me what's going on?"

"Romance," he said, and he led me to the front register. "We need romance by the bucketful, and the way I see it, you're the best one to provide it."

Maybe I *was* asleep. I shook my head, hoping to wake up from this crazy dream. When I was done, Max was still there standing beside the front counter. His eyes glowed in a way that told me he was expecting something. Now if only I could figure out what. By this time, Charmaine had gotten wind that something was up and she came out of the office, wiping bagel crumbs off the front of her yellow shirt at the same time she shot me a look and mouthed the words "What's up?"

I shrugged and struggled to make sense of the situation. "Romance novels?" I asked Max.

He made a face. "No time for reading. We need something splashy."

"Roses?" Charmaine suggested.

He gave her a smile. "Perfect. You can get them? Now?"

Unlike me, Charmaine doesn't need excuses or explanations. Already tingling with anticipation—even though she had no idea what it was all about—she scurried off to accomplish the mission.

Which left me with Max.

And about a million questions he didn't give me a

chance to ask before he turned his cocoa gaze on me. "Get crackin'. We don't have a whole lot of time. You got a basket or something? Something we can fill with candles?" He set three of them on the front counter. "And some of these bath salts." He took a whiff of one marked Nighttime Seduction and nodded his approval. "And . . ." He checked out the other displays there at the front of the shop, from the decks of cards that featured classic Gothic romance covers to tins of teas with names like Bridgerton's Best and Outlander Oolong. "Chocolates? How about some chocolates?"

We'd run out the week before and, things being what they were, I hadn't had a chance to reorder. I opted for the next best plan. "Charmaine's been spoiling me rotten," I told him. "She brought in brownies this morning."

"Perfect."

He waited for me to fetch the brownies along with a gift basket I had back in the office. "We gotta hurry," he said, checking the time on his phone. "We don't want to be late."

Because I knew he wasn't going to answer, I didn't bother to ask what was going on again. Instead, I worked quickly and efficiently, bunching tissue paper at the bottom of the basket, arranging the candles and the bath salts as artistically as I could, nestling the brownies in the center of it all and hoping they didn't end up smelling too much like Nighttime Seduction.

"Good enough?" I asked him.

"Perfect."

"For . . . ?"

Instead of answering, he grabbed the basket with one hand and me with the other and we marched to the door.

He strode down Main Street and I walked fast to keep up with him, and we arrived at Little's Hardware just as Al stepped out the front door. He looked just as confused as I was feeling.

"What's up?" I asked Al.

"Got me." He ran a hand over his white golf shirt. "Max called and told me to get out here and, hey, who am I to argue? He said stand outside and wait."

"And you're not going to have to wait long." Max set the gift basket at Al's feet just as Charmaine puffed over, her cheeks red.

"No roses at the Sparkle Market." She thrust a bouquet of white carnations and orange mums at Max, who immediately handed them over to Al, who juggled them from hand to hand.

After that, there was no time for questions. A black sedan rounded the corner. It stopped in front of the hardware store, the back door popped open, and a woman stepped out of the back seat.

She had honey-colored hair, a long slim nose, smooth skin, and lively eyes and when she looked at Al, she smiled broadly.

Watching him smile back, my heart bumped by ribs. "It's Svetlana. The real Svetlana!"

"Yes, ma'am." Max stepped back, his weight against one foot, and together with Charmaine we watched Al present the flowers. Svetlana choked back tears.

"I am finally here," she said, and pressed a kiss to Al's cheek.

"And I . . ." His smile was so broad, I thought he'd burst, "I couldn't be any happier."

Her smile was coy. "I make stop on way," she said. "For Milky Way."

"My favorite. You remembered!" Al positively glowed.

"And I still have a stash of your favorites over at the house," he said. "Honey roasted peanuts."

"Yes!" She jumped up and down with excitement.

Honey roasted peanuts and Milky Way bars. It was the highest-calorie happy ending ever.

Charmaine out-and-out blubbered.

Okay, all right, so I'm a softy. I did a little sniffling and crying, too.

"Max, how did you—?"

"Long story. And we wouldn't have had a happy ending without the help of law enforcement all over the country, including these two FBI agents who drove Svetlana here." He waved to the man and woman sitting in the front seat of the sedan. "See, when Svetlana arrived from Moscow, Sharona told her she'd hold on to her identity papers for safekeeping. Then she sent Svetlana on to meet her new husband." His mouth thinned with annoyance. "She put this poor girl here who hardly speaks any English and who barely had enough money to buy herself a couple burgers along the way on a Greyhound to New Mexico. Svetlana's been trying to figure out where she was and how she could get back ever since."

"She's not dead." The words gushed out of me on the end of a sigh of relief. "And, Max . . ." I grabbed his arm with both hands even as I watched Al and Svetlana smile into each other's eyes. "You made it happen."

"No." He slipped an arm around my shoulders and I don't think I imagined it, Charmaine started crying even harder. "We made it happen. All of us. Everyone here in Tinker's Creek."

I smiled through my tears. "This is exactly what we've all been waiting for. A real happily ever after."

# Chapter 25

*Tuesday evening*

In my family, Charmaine got the drama gene. And the center-of-attention gene. And the watch-me-now-folks-because-I'm-going-to-do-something-unbelievable gene, too.

And really, that had always been fine with me. With an aunt like Charmaine, I never had to worry. Since everyone was always busy watching her, I could happily stay in the background and read.

Which explains why when I got out of my car in front of the neat bungalows where the park rangers lived, I was just a tad nervous.

Let's face it, when it comes to exploring abandoned mines, catching murderers, finding justice, and revealing the truth, I can be pretty daring.

But in my private life?

For a second, my nerve wavered, and the nagging little voice inside me I'd been listening to all my life told me I was about to make a fool of myself.

I told it to shut up and knocked on Max's door and when he opened it, I was ready for him.

"Howdy," I said.

I caught him in the middle of dinner. He popped the last bite of a ham sandwich into his mouth and swallowed it down before he grinned.

"Why, Miss Lizzie Hale, if you ain't a sight!" He glanced over my jeans, my boots, the ten-gallon hat I'd bought just that afternoon from the local feed and seed shop. Pink, as I may have mentioned, is not my color, but it was the only hat on the shelf that fit over my curly hair and it certainly made a statement.

And an impression, too, if the smile on Max's face meant anything.

"You want to tell me what's going on?" he asked.

"Do you ever tell me when you're up to something?" I pushed past him and into his apartment. It was small and neat, a couch near the window, a chair and lamp across from it, a coffee table in between. I saw a kitchen beyond. I set the laptop I was carrying on his coffee table, the better to kick aside the rug in the middle of the hardwood floor.

He pointed a finger at me. "You're up to something."

"Very astute, officer." I opened the laptop, clicked to the page I'd bookmarked, and turned up the volume. Twangy country blared from the speakers.

I slapped my hand in Max's.

"Come on," I said, "it's time to cowboy boogie."

## ACKNOWLEDGMENTS

Every book is a team effort. There's the author, of course, the editorial staff (thank you, Sareer Khader and Tom Colgan), my wonderful agent (Gail Fortune), and all the cheerleaders who are always there for me—my brainstorming group (Stephanie Cole, Serena Miller, and Emilie Richards) as well as a host of friends and relatives who lend an ear when necessary and send up a cheer to help me celebrate goals met and books published.

As always, my family plays a big part in my success. Thanks to David, my own personal romance hero, and to Anne and Sam, David and Tara. And, of course, to Eliot the Airedale, who mostly leaves me alone when I'm trying to work.

In case you're wondering, there really is a place called Helltown in the Cuyahoga Valley National Park and yes, there are stories about the giant python and the mutants that haunt the place, too. If you're ever feeling brave enough, visit. Who knows what mysteries you might uncover!

Ready to find
your next great read?

Let us help.

**Visit prh.com/nextread**

Penguin
Random
House